Acclaim for Beth Wiseman

Her Brother's Keeper

"Wiseman has created a series in which the readers have a chance to peel back all the layers of the Amish secrets."
—*RT Book Reviews*, 4 1/2 stars and July 2015 Top Pick!

"Wiseman's new launch is edgier, taking on the tough issues of mental illness and suicide. Amish fiction fans seeking something a bit more thought-provoking and challenging than the usual fare will find this series debut a solid choice."
—*Library Journal*

Hearts in Harmony

"Beth Wiseman has penned a poignant story of friendship, faith, and love that is sure to touch readers' hearts."
—Kathleen Fuller, author of The Middlefield Family novels

"Beth Wiseman's *Hearts in Harmony* is a lyrical hymn. Mary and Levi are heartwarming, lovable characters who instantly feel like dear friends. Once readers open this book, they won't put it down until they've reached the last page."
—Amy Clipston, bestselling author of *A Seat by the Hearth*

Amish Celebrations

"Wiseman's (*Amish Secrets*) collection of timeless stories of love and loss among the Plain People will delight fans of the author's heartfelt story lines and flowing prose."
—*Library Journal*

Home All Along

"Beth Wiseman's novel will find a permanent home in every reader's heart as she spins comfort and prose into a stellar read of grace."
—Kelly Long, author of the Patch of Heaven series

Love Bears All Things

"Suggest to those seeking a more truthful, less saccharine portrayal of the trials of human life and the transformative growth and redemption that may occur as a result."
—*Library Journal*

The Promise

"The story of Mallory in *The Promise* uncovers the harsh reality American women can experience when they follow their hearts into a very different culture. Her story sheds light on how Islamic society is totally different from the Christian marriage covenant between one man and one woman. This novel is based on actual events, and Beth reached out to me during that time. It was heartbreaking to watch those real-life events unfolding. I salute the author's courage, persistence, and final triumph in writing a revealing and inspiring story."
—Nonie Darwish, author of *The Devil We Don't Know, Cruel and Usual Punishment*, and *Now They Call Me Infidel*

"*The Promise* is an only too realistic depiction of an American young woman motivated by the best humanitarian impulses and naïve trust facing instead betrayal, kidnapping, and life-threatening danger in Pakistan's lawless Pashtun tribal regions. But the story offers as well a reminder just as realistic that love and sacrifice are never wasted and that the hope of a loving heavenly Father is never absent in the most hopeless of situations."
—Jeanette Windle, author of *Veiled Freedom* (2010 ECPA Christian Book Award/Christy Award finalist), *Freedom's Stand* (2012 ECPA Christian Book Award/Carol Award finalist), and *Congo Dawn* (2013 Golden Scroll Novel of the Year)

The House that Love Built

"This sweet story with a hint of mystery is touching and emotional. Humor sprinkled throughout balances the occasional seriousness. The development of the love story is paced perfectly so that the reader gets a real sense of the characters."

—*Romantic Times*, 4-star review

"[*The House that Love Built*] is a warm, sweet tale of faith renewed and families restored."

—BookPage

Need You Now

"Wiseman, best known for her series of Amish novels, branches out into a wider world in this story of family, dependence, faith, and small-town Texas, offering a character for every reader to relate to . . . With an enjoyable cast of outside characters, *Need You Now* breaks the molds of small-town stereotypes. With issues ranging from special education and teen cutting to what makes a marriage strong, this is a compelling and worthy read."

—Booklist

"Wiseman gets to the heart of marriage and family interests in a way that will resonate with readers, with an intricately written plot featuring elements that seem to be ripped from current headlines. God provides hope for Wiseman's characters even in the most desperate situations."

—*Romantic Times*, 4-star review

"You may think you are familiar with Beth's wonderful story-telling gift but this is something new! This is a story that will stay with you for a long, long time. It's a story of hope when life seems hopeless. It's a story of how God can redeem the seemingly unredeemable. It's a message the Church, the world needs to hear."

—Sheila Walsh, author of *God Loves Broken People*

"Beth Wiseman tackles these difficult subjects with courage and grace. She reminds us that true healing can only come by being vulnerable and honest before our God who loves us more than anything."

—Deborah Bedford, bestselling author of *His Other Wife*, *A Rose by the Door*, and *The Penny* (coauthored with Joyce Meyer)

THE LAND OF CANAAN NOVELS

"Wiseman's voice is consistently compassionate and her words flow smoothly."

—*Publishers Weekly* review of *Seek Me with All Your Heart*

"Wiseman's third Land of Canaan novel overflows with romance, broken promises, a modern knight in shining armor, and hope at the end of the rainbow."

—*Romantic Times*

"In *Seek Me with All Your Heart*, Beth Wiseman offers readers a heartwarming story filled with complex characters and deep emotion. I instantly loved Emily, and eagerly turned each page, anxious to learn more about her past—and what future the Lord had in store for her."

—Shelley Shepard Gray, bestselling author of the Seasons of Sugarcreek series

"Wiseman has done it again! Beautifully compelling, *Seek Me with All Your Heart* is a heartwarming story of faith, family, and renewal. Her characters and descriptions are captivating, bringing the story to life with the turn of every page."

—Amy Clipston, bestselling author of *A Gift of Grace*

THE DAUGHTERS OF THE PROMISE NOVELS

"Well-defined characters and story make for an enjoyable read."
—*Romantic Times* review of *Plain Pursuit*

"A touching, heartwarming story. Wiseman does a particularly great job of dealing with shunning, a controversial Amish practice that seems cruel and unnecessary to outsiders . . . If you're a fan of Amish fiction, don't miss *Plain Pursuit!*"
—Kathleen Fuller, author of The Middlefield Family novels

HER Brother's KEEPER

Also by Beth Wiseman

The Amish Journey Novels
Hearts in Harmony
Listening to Love (available
September 2019)

Plain Promise
Plain Paradise
Plain Proposal
Plain Peace

The Amish Secrets Novels
Her Brother's Keeper
Love Bears All Things
Home All Along

The Land of Canaan Novels
Seek Me with All Your Heart
The Wonder of Your Love
His Love Endures Forever

**The Daughters of the
Promise Novels**
Plain Perfect
Plain Pursuit

Other Novels
Need You Now
The House that Love Built
The Promise

Stories
A Choice to Forgive included in *An Amish Christmas*
A Change of Heart included in *An Amish Gathering*
Healing Hearts included in *An Amish Love*
A Perfect Plan included in *An Amish Wedding*
A Recipe for Hope included in *An Amish Kitchen*
Always Beautiful included in *An Amish Miracle*
Rooted in Love included in *An Amish Garden*
When Christmas Comes Again included in *An Amish Second Christmas*
In His Father's Arms included in *An Amish Cradle*
A Love for Irma Rose included in *An Amish Year*
Patchwork Perfect included in *An Amish Year*
A Cup Half Full included in *An Amish Home*
The Cedar Chest included in *An Amish Heirloom*
The Gift of Sisters included in *Amish Celebrations*
A New Beginning included in *Amish Celebrations*
A Christmas Miracle included in *Amish Celebrations*
When Love Returns included in *An Amish Homecoming*
A Reunion of Hearts included in *An Amish Reunion*

HER
Brother's
KEEPER

AN
AMISH SECRETS
NOVEL

BETH
WISEMAN

ZONDERVAN®

ZONDERVAN

Her Brother's Keeper

Copyright © 2015 by Elizabeth Wiseman Mackey

This title is also available as an e-book.

Requests for information should be addressed to:
Zondervan, *3900 Sparks Dr. SE, Grand Rapids, Michigan 49546*

ISBN: 978-0-310-35462-8 (repack)
ISBN: 978-1-4016-8600-0 (e-book)

Library of Congress Cataloging-in-Publication Data
Wiseman, Beth, 1962-
Her brother's keeper / Beth Wiseman.
pages; cm—(An Amish secrets novel; book 1)
ISBN 978-1-4016-8596-6 (softcover)
1. Amish—Fiction. I. Title.
PS3623.I83H47 2015
813'.6—dc23
2015002002

The book *Pennsylvania German Dictionary: English to Pennsylvania Dutch* by C. Richard Beam is
referenced in this novel.

Scripture quotations are from the King James Version of the Bible.

Printed in the United States of America

19 20 21 22 23 24 / LSC / 6 5 4 3 2 1

To Karen and Tommy Brasher

Pennsylvania Dutch Glossary

aamen—amen

ab im kopp—off in the head; crazy

ach—oh

aenti—aunt

baremlich—terrible

boppli—baby or babies

bruder—brother

daadi haus—grandparents' house, usually a smaller
   dwelling on the same property

daed—dad

danki—thank you

die Botschaft—The Message

Englisch—a non-Amish person

fraa—wife

gut—good

haus—house

kaffi—coffee

kapp—prayer covering or cap

kinner—children

maedel—girl

mamm—mom

mammi—grandmother

mei—my

meidung—shunning

mudder—mother

nee—no

Ordnung—the written and unwritten rules of the Amish; the understood behavior by which the Amish are expected to live, passed down from generation to generation. Most Amish know the rules by heart.

Pennsylvania Deitsch—the language most commonly used by the Amish. Although commonly known as Pennsylvania Dutch, the language is actually a form of German (Deutsch).

rumschpringe—running-around period when a teenager turns sixteen years old

sohn—son

wie bischt—How are you?

ya—yes

yummasetti—a traditional Pennsylvania Dutch casserole

HER
Brother's
KEEPER

Dear Ethan,

My therapist said that I should write you letters in an effort to process my grief. I don't know if it will help or not, but I'm willing to give this a try since I can't seem to move forward without knowing what happened to you. My heart is shattered.

I've sent letters to Hannah, and while your fiancée did write me back, her notes were brief and offered no explanation. None of my phone calls were answered or returned either. Since I'm not getting any answers, I've decided to spend some time in Lancaster County, to live among the Amish, as one of them. Yes, it's deceitful, but I have to know the truth. From what I've read about the Amish, they aren't very trusting and aren't fond of outsiders. Maybe this is why, after you became a member of their group, you detached yourself from the people who love you. Either way, I'm not above playing dress-up and telling a few lies to find out what happened to my only brother.

Even as I write this, ten months later, my grief overtakes me. Ethan, I miss you every single day. I don't know if the Plain People in Pennsylvania lured you into their world, twisted your thoughts, or what, but the Ethan I know is a survivor, a fighter. We had both been through so much, and yet . . . we lived to tell about it. We survived. What happened, Ethan?

Rest in peace, my beloved brother. I, on the other hand, won't rest until I know the truth.

Char

$\mathcal{C}$ harlotte watched the taxi until it was out of sight, then she left her luggage on the sidewalk and made her way up the steps leading to the porch of the farm-house. Two side-by-side front doors stood open, and through the screens, the aroma of freshly baked cook-ies wafted outside. She took a deep breath. Based on her research, the Amish people knew how to cook, so that would be a perk while she was here.

She smoothed the wrinkles from her plain blue dress, put her sunglasses in the pocket of her black apron, and tucked a few loose strands of blond hair beneath the prayer covering she was wearing. Shaking her head, she eyed the black loafers and black socks that rose to just above her ankles, knowing she wouldn't win any fashion awards in this getup. She jumped when she heard foot-steps, then took a step back when a woman about her mother's age pushed the screen open and said, "You must be Mary." The Amish woman put her hands on full hips, smiled broadly, and extended her hand.

Charlotte nodded, acknowledging the name she'd chosen to use while she was here—Mary Troyer. "Lena?"

"*Ya, ya.* I'm Lena King." She looked past Charlotte, raised a hand to her forehead, and peered. "*Ach, mei.* A lot of suitcases, *ya?*"

Charlotte glanced over her shoulder at the three suitcases. "Yes, I guess so." She fought to mask the tremble in her voice, reminding herself to use the little bit of Pennsylvania Dutch she'd learned. "*Ya. Ya.* A month is a long time." She doubted she would stay anywhere near that long, but that's what Lena had insisted on via the letters they'd exchanged, so Charlotte had packed accordingly, just in case.

Lena scurried past her and quickly latched on to two of the suitcases. "Let's get these inside and get you settled. We are just so thrilled to find out that we have cousins down in Texas." She grunted a little as she carried the luggage. Charlotte grabbed the third one and followed her. "We'd heard rumor that there were Amish folks in Beeville, Texas, but to find our kin there . . . well, just so *gut* to know, even if it is cousins several times removed."

Charlotte recalled finding the small group of Amish people who had migrated to Texas from Tennessee. She'd built her secret identity based on information she'd gathered by spending time with them, and they'd directed her to a resale shop where she'd purchased her Amish clothes. They'd been nice enough, if not a bit suspicious about all of Charlotte's questions.

Lena set the suitcases on the landing below the staircase, so Charlotte did the same with hers.

"Jacob can haul these upstairs when he gets home." Lena smiled again. Charlotte knew Lena was referring to her sixteen-year-old son. "You must be hungry from your travels. Come, come." She motioned for Charlotte to follow, and once in the kitchen, Lena pulled out a chair at the head of the table. Before them lay enough food to feed an army.

"I didn't know what you liked, so I made chicken salad, tuna salad, and egg salad." She pointed to three more bowls on Charlotte's right. "That's barbequed meatballs, cheddar meat loaf, and my special chicken casserole." She pressed her palms together and then pointed to the middle of the table. "That's bread I made this morning, and to the left is apple butter. Chowchow is in the other bowl." She spun around, rattled off something in her native language, then returned with a glass she set in front of Charlotte. This was going to be an area of concern, her inability to understand or speak much of the dialect, which she'd read was an offshoot of German. She offered up the best smile she could, hoping to fake her way through the conversation.

"Everything looks very . . . *gut.*" She'd learned a handful of words most commonly used by the women in Beeville. She'd camped out at a nearby hotel and visited the farmers' market daily for a couple of weeks in an effort to gain information. The women sold canned goods and homemade crafts. Charlotte always bought several jars of jams and jellies as unspoken payment for their help. She figured she had enough jellies for the next several years, but it had been worth it for the valuable information.

"I hoped that everyone could be here to welcome you, but it just didn't work out." Lena sighed as she sat down to Charlotte's left. "After dinner, you should rest. Tomorrow, Hannah and I are adding to the flower beds. We like to spruce things up with Tiger Eyes every August. They only bloom for about eleven weeks, but they are always a nice addition when some of our perennials finish blooming."

Charlotte stiffened at the mention of Lena's daughter, Hannah, but cleared her throat with a slight cough. "Hannah's a couple of years younger than me, right? Twenty-three or twenty-four?"

Lena nodded. "*Ya*. She's twenty-four."

That seemed old to still be living at home.

"Hannah had wanted to be here, but Widow Hostetler called and needed someone to cart her to the doctor. She doesn't drive her buggy anymore." Lena chuckled. "And we are all safer on the streets because of that."

Charlotte bowed her head when Lena did. The Amish prayed silently before every meal, so Charlotte sat quietly with her eyes closed and waited.

"Did you say Widow Hostetler *called*?" Charlotte had seen the women in Beeville using cell phones, but she wanted clarification that she'd be able to use her phone while she was here. It was Charlotte's understanding that some Amish districts allowed the use of cell phones, while others did not.

"*Ya*, our bishop allows portable telephone calls for emergencies." She winked at Charlotte. "Funny how many emergencies pop up." Lena frowned. "Oh, *nee*. Are you against the use of mobile telephones? Or does your district allow it?"

Charlotte swallowed a bite of bread, the tastiest she'd ever had. "Yeah." She paused, kicking herself again. "*Ya*. We are allowed phones." Lena handed Charlotte the bowl of chicken salad and Charlotte spooned a small amount onto her plate. Then she got two meatballs and a small scoop of chicken casserole.

"I hope you'll eat more than that." Lena sat taller, her eyes wide. "That's not enough to feed a bird."

To Charlotte, it looked like a ton, so she was a bit taken aback and not sure how to respond. "I-I've had a stomach bug recently." One more lie to add to the collection.

Lena clicked her tongue a couple of times. "We've had something going around here too. Hannah took sick last week."

Charlotte tensed again, knowing she would have to stop reacting every time Hannah's name was mentioned, but she couldn't shake the idea that maybe Ethan's fiancée had something to do with his death. Or at the least, knew why her brother had killed himself.

"Save room for dessert," Lena said as she motioned toward a chocolate pie at the far end of the table.

Charlotte fought a yawn before she nodded. She wasn't sure how she'd eat one more bite, and for a brief moment, guilt nipped at her for enjoying the food so much. She forced the thought aside and decided her lies were justified.

Lena excused herself to the bathroom, so Charlotte took a good look around at the modest surroundings. The table was in the middle of a large kitchen, and as she ran her hand along the table's edge, she took note of the fine craftsmanship. Eight oak chairs were around the table. On the counters were canisters, paper towels, a pitcher of tea, and a platter of cookies. Nothing decorative.

Charlotte took her napkin and dabbed at the sweat beads on her forehead. In Texas it would be unheard of not to have air conditioning. She doubted it got as warm here, but she was already dreading her time here without it. At least she didn't have to worry about her makeup running down her face since her role as a well-bred Amish woman didn't include cosmetics. She glanced at the back of her hands and recalled having the nail tech remove her gel fingernails and file them short.

She piled more butter on the homemade bread and let it melt in her mouth. She rarely ate bread at home, but it didn't taste like this. She closed her eyes and sighed, letting the warm, buttery taste settle onto her palate. If she kept eating like this, she would be huge by the time she went home. Opening her eyes, she saw Lena come through the living room and stop at the window.

"*Ach, gut,*" Lena said as she made her way back to the kitchen. "That's Hannah pulling in now. She's been eager for you to get here, to have someone close to her age to pal around with."

"And I've been looking forward to coming," Charlotte said, finding comfort in her truthful response. Running around with Hannah might shed some light on what happened to Ethan, but Charlotte bit her tongue and fought the tremble in her bottom lip as Hannah walked into the kitchen. She was just as beautiful as Ethan had said. On the outside, anyway.

∽

Hannah wasn't in the mood to make small talk. She never was on the days she strayed off the beaten path. After she'd dropped off Widow Hostetler, she'd gone to her special place, the spot where she'd buried her memories of Ethan. He'd died almost a year ago, and she was sure she'd never find that kind of love again. But she was determined to be polite to this cousin they'd recently found. It seemed important to her mother to have discovered relatives all the way in Texas, but a month's visit was a bit long.

"This is Mary," her mother said as she put a hand on Mary's shoulder. "It's her first time to Pennsylvania, so after we work in the garden tomorrow, maybe you can show her around."

"*Ya.* Of course." Hannah eased into a chair next to Mary and across from where her mother took a seat. She bowed her head and offered thanks before she reached for a slice of bread. "Welcome, Mary. We've been looking forward to your visit." She smiled at her cousin, but hoped she wouldn't be the only one entertaining Mary for a month. She was certain that was her mother's plan, for Mary to help Hannah find her way back into the world of the living.

"Tell us, Mary . . . what do you do best?" *Mamm* always asked this question, assuming everyone had a special talent. "Hannah is our seamstress. She sews much better than I do. Jacob tends the fields with his father, but he also takes care of the animals since he has a special knack for that. And *mei* husband is a masterful carpenter." *Mamm*'s eyes twinkled as she placed a palm on the table. "He made this table and chairs and most of our other furniture."

"And *Mamm* is probably the best cook in our district," Hannah added. "She comes up with her own recipes and shares them with the other women." Her mother waved a hand and shook her head. "She also has a green thumb."

"I believe the Lord blesses each of us with a special gift. What is your special gift, Mary?" Hannah's mother laid her fork across her plate and tipped her head to one side.

"Uh, well . . ." Mary glanced back and forth at Hannah and her mother. "Uh . . . I'm not sure. I guess I dabble here and there. I used to paint, but I haven't in a long time."

"Paint?" Hannah halted her fork in midair. "Paint what? Walls? Fences?"

"No. *Nee*. I-I used to paint pictures . . . landscapes." Mary's cheeks took on a pinkish tint.

Hannah nodded. "*Ach*, and you sold these paintings?" There was a man in their community who painted pictures of Amish homes. Word was that he sold them to the *Englisch* for a lot of money. Hannah had heard her mother say she didn't approve of this, but Hannah didn't think it was much different from the ways that others in their community made an income. Handmade quilts and Amish furniture brought in a lot of money.

Mary shifted her weight in the chair, her cheeks still rosy. "Um. No. It was just for fun." She shrugged. "A hobby."

For fun? Hannah managed a smile as she wondered what Mary could contribute while she was here, how she could ease their workload for a month. But Mary was a guest, so Hannah shouldn't expect too much. Maybe such hobbies were encouraged in Mary's district. "You have a nice accent. Very southern."

"Yeah. *Ya*. People from Texas get that a lot. We have a drawl. And some of us say *y'all* a lot."

Even the Amish folks? Mary fidgeted with her fork and shifted her weight in the chair again. Hannah had

11

an urge to straighten Mary's *kapp*, but her cousin was already blushing, so she didn't want to embarrass her further. It was strange that Mary had the strings from her prayer covering tied under her chin. She'd never seen anyone tie theirs before. "Where are *Daed* and Jacob?"

"They went to the lumberyard this morning and said they would eat in town." *Mamm* turned to Mary. "Most days, *mei* husband and *sohn* eat lunch with us."

Mary nodded as she scooted her chair back and stood up when Hannah and her mother did. "I think I'll take a nap, if that's okay. It was a long flight."

Hannah glanced at her mother. Even guests would offer to help with cleanup after a meal. But traditions and rules varied from state to state, even district to district.

"I told Mary she should rest," *Mamm* quickly said as she dried her hands on the dish towel. "Why don't you go help her get settled while I clean the kitchen? I told her Jacob could haul her suitcases upstairs later."

Hannah would have rather done cleanup, but she nodded and walked with Mary to the stairs and picked up the third suitcase after Mary latched on to two. Apparently their cousin didn't want to wait on Jacob. "Lots of luggage."

Mary looked over her shoulder and smiled. "I probably overpacked."

I'll say. When they got to the top of the stairs, Mary stepped aside so Hannah could walk ahead of her down the hallway. "My room is the first one on the left. Jacob's is on the right." She paused at the third door. "This is your room. We share the bathroom at the end of the hall. *Mamm* and *Daed*'s room is downstairs; they have their own bathroom. The mudroom on the first floor is set up as our sewing room."

Hannah set the suitcase down, walked to the window, and rolled up the green shade, then lifted the window. "I bet our weather seems very pleasant to you. I've heard it's miserably hot in Texas—and humid."

"It is. Thank God for air conditioning." Mary chuckled, but stopped when she caught Hannah's expression.

"You have indoor cooling?"

"No, no, no." Mary shook her head. "I meant . . . you know . . . like in the malls. In public places. Hair salons. Places—places like that."

"Things must be very different where you are from." Hannah had never been in a hair salon, and they avoided the malls. Everything they needed could be purchased nearby at the fabric store or the market.

Mary walked to the window. "There's a guy out by the barn."

Hannah joined her cousin at the window, noticing Mary's scrutinizing gaze. "Everyone is excited when they lay eyes on Isaac Miller for the first time." She allowed her cousin a few more moments to take in Isaac's well-proportioned, muscular body and wavy, dark hair peeking from beneath his straw hat. If her cousin looked hard enough, she might get a glimpse of Isaac's kind eyes, as blue as a robin's egg. "Twenty-seven years old and never married."

"He's gorgeous." Mary's eyes were fixed on Isaac. Luckily she didn't notice Hannah's scowl. *Gorgeous* seemed a strange word to describe a man. "Why hasn't anyone snagged such a hunk?"

Hannah narrowed her eyebrows. She wasn't sure she liked this Texas slang. "Many have tried but Isaac shies away. Maybe he just hasn't found the right girl. Plus, his father is ill."

"Hmm . . ." Mary kept her eyes on him. "What's he doing out there?"

Hannah leaned closer to the window, squinting against the sun's glare at the tall, dark-haired man she'd grown up with. "He comes by once a week and leaves *Daed* an envelope of money. Isaac's family owns a furniture store in the touristy part of Lancaster County. *Daed* has some of his furniture and other things he's made on consignment."

"Why does he leave the money in the barn?" Mary also shielded her eyes from the glare.

"I'm not sure. He's always done that." She tilted her head slightly. "*Mamm* said he probably doesn't want to disturb us, which he wouldn't be." Hannah paused. "By the way, tomorrow is worship, and it happens to be at Isaac's house."

"Does he have his own house or does he live with his parents?" Mary continued to look out the window.

"He lives with his parents. I think mostly because of his father's cancer. Isaac does most of the work on their farm." Hannah stepped away from the window, hoping her cousin would do the same. But Mary didn't move, so Hannah cleared her throat. "Do you want me to help you unpack?" She waited, then said, "Mary?"

"Uh. No. It's okay. I can get it." Mary joined her by the bed, and again Hannah had an urge to straighten her cousin's *kapp*.

"Please let me know if you need anything." She folded her hands in front of her, hoping she could sneak off to her room and have a few moments to herself. It was exhausting to act normal when she was dying inside. Her grief still came in waves, and today the tide was high.

"Okay. Thanks." Mary smiled, and Hannah chose not to question Mary about her use of so much *Englisch*. And she promised herself she was going to try to have a good attitude about their cousin's visit. Maybe Mary would provide a nice distraction and eventually become a friend. She gave a quick wave, then hurried to her bedroom.

Charlotte sat down on the bed and fumbled through her purse until she found her cell phone. She scrolled through her contacts until she found Ryan's number. He answered on the first ring.

"You there, all settled in?"

"Yep. I'm here." She spoke softly as she pulled off the prayer covering and tossed it beside her on the bed, then she pulled out the bobby pins holding her hair in a tight bun. She shook her head, her blond waves falling to the middle of her back. "And it's pretty much like I thought it would be." She sighed. "Hot, no air conditioning. But they seem nice, I guess. It's hard for me to imagine that these people choose to live like this, though." She eased out of her black loafers, then her black socks, wiggling her toes. "And it's even harder for me to imagine that Ethan wanted to live like this."

As her brother's best friend, Ryan was just as anxious to find out what happened to Ethan. When she was younger, Charlotte had a crush on Ryan, but he was a few years older than her, and he and her brother had run around with an older crowd. Since Ethan's death, Charlotte had met Ryan for lunch a few times, and they'd put their heads together trying to figure out what would cause Ethan to take his life. A couple of times, Charlotte caught Ryan staring at her in a way that could have been mistaken for romantic interest, but she was pretty sure he would always see her as Ethan's little sister. She thought about how Ethan would have turned thirty this year.

"Maybe you'll get some answers while you're there."

"I'm going to try," Charlotte said as she propped the pillow up against the headboard. "Right now, I just want to take a nap." She sighed. "Although, it's so hot in here, I'm not sure that's possible. But I'm pooped."

"Okay. Well, glad you made it there safely. Keep me posted if Hannah or the others shed any light about what happened."

Charlotte swung her legs on to the bed and closed her eyes as she thought about her brother. They'd had a hard life growing up, and Ethan had battled depression over the years. But she'd thought he had found happiness here. It wasn't the ideal situation—him living with the Amish—but all she'd ever really wanted was for Ethan to be happy. Obviously, something had gone terribly wrong.

*H*annah shifted her weight to her left knee as she packed dirt around the tiny Tiger Eyes that she and her mother had seeded indoors weeks ago. She allowed her eyes to drift in Mary's direction. Their cousin didn't seem to know much about gardening, and she'd been whining all morning about the heat. Her dress was a wrinkled mess even though Hannah had put an iron in the guest bedroom. And once again, her cousin's *kapp* was lopsided.

"*Ach*, much deeper, dear." *Mamm* lifted herself up off the dewy soil and walked to where Mary was pitifully trying to plant the flowers. "Like this," *Mamm* said as she lifted the plant from its shallow burial, then dug a hole half the depth of her spade.

"Sorry." Mary hung her head for a few moments before she looked up. "I guess gardening was never really my thing. Y'all are much better at this."

No kidding. And there was that strange word again—
y'all. Hannah didn't harp on it, but let her thoughts slip
back to a year ago, when Ethan had helped her put the
garden in and plant flowers in the beds. *Mamm* had taken
ill, and for a few days Ethan had come over after his shift
at the lumberyard to help her. *I miss you every single day,
Ethan.* As sadness threatened to consume her, she forced
herself to remember that day as the happy time that it
was. She prayed often that someday she'd find comfort
in her memories and not get swallowed up by grief.

She recalled the first time she'd seen Ethan. He was
wearing blue jeans and a white T-shirt. They'd locked
eyes from across the diner where he was eating lunch
alone. Hannah rarely ate lunch in town, but a visit to the
market for more flour had taken longer than Hannah
had expected. If she hadn't been craving the diner's club
sandwich and a root beer, she might not have met the
handsome *Englisch* man who would one day propose to
her. Nor could she have foreseen his tragic death and the
hole it would leave in her heart. If Ethan hadn't come
to Pennsylvania to work on the project in Lancaster
County, and been running late himself, their chance
meeting might not have happened. The diner had been
so crowded, Ethan was near her table, eating while standing up. There was an extra chair at Hannah's table, and it
seemed rude not to offer it to him.

"I think that about finishes us up here," *Mamm* said
as she shook loose dirt from her hands and stood up.

"Hannah, you should take Mary to Paradise and the surrounding towns this afternoon. So much to do in so little time."

She'll be here a month. Hannah bit her lip and smiled. "*Ya.*" She turned to Mary. "Unless you want a day to rest from your travels."

Mary shook her head. "No, I'm fine with visiting town."

Hannah nodded, dreading having to put on a happy face. Maybe it wouldn't be so bad. Maybe her cousin liked pizza. Jacob wouldn't eat any type of tomato sauce, so Predisio's Pizzeria was never an option on the rare times that her family ate out.

"*Gut, gut,*" *Mamm* said. "You girls go and have fun today. After lunch, I'm going to finish some sewing projects."

Hannah forced another smile before she headed in to clean up. A short while later, she hitched the horse to her spring buggy.

Charlotte climbed into the topless buggy and reminded herself not to let on that this was her first time to travel this way. There was an air of excitement about the adventure, even though she was unsure if she wanted to be friends with her tour guide. But being friendly was the only way she was going to find out about Ethan.

After a bumpy ride down the gravel driveway, they turned onto a blacktop road. Riding into the breeze was refreshing until the horse began to relieve himself. She cringed, but forgot about it when she saw them approaching a highway. Bracing herself, she hoped Hannah would be able to get them safely across the busy intersection. But instead of crossing to the other side, she turned left and took up a steady trot on a narrow lane to the right of the traffic. Charlotte held her breath as cars whizzed by, and she could feel the color draining from her face as she white-knuckled the dash in front of her.

"Wow," she said as a large truck whipped past them.

Hannah picked up speed, but turned briefly toward Charlotte. "It wonders me if you are all right?"

Charlotte released the breath she was holding. "Sure. Yes. *Ya.* I'm fine." She paused as she struggled to control her erratic breathing. "We just don't usually travel on busy highways like this in our wagons." She glanced quickly at Hannah, just as another big truck almost blew them into oblivion. "Buggies." She kicked herself again. "We, uh . . . sometimes . . . we, uh . . . call them wagons."

Hannah didn't react as she steered the buggy down a road on their right. "I thought you might like to visit the Gordonville Bookstore."

Charlotte didn't care where they visited. She was just thankful to be off the highway. "*Ya,* that would be . . . *gut.*"

She stepped out of the buggy and waited in the small parking lot while Hannah tethered the horse at the hitching post. Around them were several buggies and a few cars. She took hold of the opportunity to really study the woman beside her. She was tall, several inches taller than Charlotte. And slender. Her hair was dark as coal, and her face lightly tanned. Even without makeup and her hair tucked underneath her cap, she was truly beautiful. *On the outside*, Charlotte reminded herself, and an uneasy feeling swept over her again. In Ethan's last letter to her, he said he was worried about his relationship with Hannah. He hadn't shared any details, but Charlotte wondered if maybe Hannah had called off the engagement. Had she broken Ethan's heart?

"This is where the locals shop for books and school supplies."

Charlotte nodded as she got in step beside Hannah. She knew the Amish only went to school through the eighth grade, and she couldn't help but wonder how they got away with that. In most places, children were required by law to go to school or be homeschooled until they turned seventeen. *What keeps the officers in charge of truants away from the Amish community?*

The store was obviously owned by Amish people: no lights, no air conditioning. Large skylights streamed natural lighting into the store. A lanky, older man behind the counter greeted them when they walked in. In Pennsylvania Dutch. Charlotte's chest tightened as she recalled her visits with the Amish women in Beeville. They spoke almost entirely in English. This was going to be a big problem if these Lancaster Amish people constantly reverted to this other language.

Hannah replied to him. In Dutch, of course. Then she turned to Charlotte, folded her hands in front of her, and seemed to be waiting for Charlotte to respond. "Uh, *gut . . . gut* to meet y'all," she finally said. She cut her eyes in Hannah's direction, and her brother's ex-fiancée nodded, then spoke to the owner in their language again. Based on Hannah's expression, Charlotte's response must have been okay. When Hannah started to walk around the store, Charlotte took off in another direction. She needed a few minutes to gather herself, and she'd already seen several Amish women where Hannah was headed. She didn't want to face having more conversation she wouldn't understand.

Right then, she laid eyes on a book she needed to have. *Pennsylvania German Dictionary: English to Pennsylvania Dutch.* She looked over her shoulder to make sure she was alone, then she picked up the book and thumbed through it. *Perfect.*

She tucked it under her arm, turned around, and headed toward the counter but stopped dead in her tracks, did an about-face, and went back to where she'd found the book. She placed it back on the shelf and stared at it. *Stupid, stupid.* Hannah and the owner would wonder why she was buying a book about a language she was presumed to know and understand. Glancing over her shoulder again, she pushed her purse up on her arm and had a thought.

Charlotte had never stolen anything in her life, but

if she was going to pull this off, she needed that book. One more glance behind her, then she grabbed the book and stuffed it into her purse. But the moment she'd safely gotten away with it, her stomach began to churn. She reached back into her purse and pulled out her wallet. The book was $12.99, so she pulled out a twenty and placed it on the bookshelf before she turned to leave the scene of what was almost a crime.

She ran into Hannah on the next aisle and was happy to see that she was alone. When Hannah wasn't around other Amish people, she mostly spoke English. Charlotte had no idea why, but she was thankful just the same.

"Would you like to go to Bird-in-Hand next?" Hannah smiled, and for a couple of moments, Charlotte just stared at her. She could certainly see why Ethan had been so attracted to this woman. But Charlotte would do anything if she could go back in time and talk Ethan out of ever coming here.

"Mary?"

Charlotte blinked a few times. "Uh, yeah. *Ya*. Sorry." She took a deep breath. "Sure. Bird-in-Hand. That sounds fine. *Gut*."

She wanted to ask if they would be traveling on the main highway again, and she briefly considered saying she had a stomachache so she could go back to the farmhouse. But based on the number of buggies she'd seen on the way to the bookstore, this was the prominent mode of transportation, and she was going to have to get used to it.

Hannah picked up the pace once she was on Lincoln Highway, but quickly slowed back down when the color drained from Mary's face. "Mary, are you all right?"

Her cousin nodded. "I think so." Her eyes darted back and forth between cars in front of them and the ones coming up behind them. "I'm just not used to being in a buggy with all these cars whizzing by at high speeds."

Hannah slowed down even more, although it was probably more dangerous to go so slow. "You must live in a very rural area in Texas, *ya*?"

Mary reached for the dash when Hannah hit a bump in the road. "Uh . . . I guess you could say that."

"We are turning in about half a mile, and that road is less traveled."

They were both quiet for a few minutes, but when the silence started to become awkward, Hannah began searching for something to talk about. She was curious to know if Mary had a boyfriend back home. Maybe not, since she had gawked at Isaac Miller. Her mother had already told her that their cousin wasn't married. Hannah felt like an old maid at twenty-four. Mary must feel even worse at twenty-six. But starting a conversation about relationships would only lead to talking about Ethan, and she wasn't ready to share such intimate details of her life with a stranger, cousin or not.

She finally asked Mary about her life in Texas, even

though she didn't really care. She didn't care about much of anything these days. But in an effort to keep her family from worrying, she faked her way through each day. Hannah prayed every day for Ethan's soul, but her biggest fear was still heavy on her heart. *Was Ethan in heaven?* Hannah had lost her grandmother to cancer, and she'd attended plenty of funerals over the years. But not once did she question whether or not the person had gone to their eternal rest with the Lord. But it was different with Ethan.

By the time Charlotte and Hannah got home, the last meal of the day was already laid out on the kitchen table. Charlotte nibbled, but four thirty seemed early for supper, especially since she'd eaten so much at the pizza place. She already knew the Amish called the evening meal "supper," and "dinner" was at lunchtime. And that they started their day at about four in the morning, but luckily Lena had suggested Charlotte sleep in on that first morning, assuming she was weary from her travels. By the time she'd gotten up this morning, Hannah's father and brother were already gone, and her nap last night had run past their supper hour. This meal was her first time to meet Hannah's dad and brother.

Hannah's father, Amos, was quiet. And sixteen-year-old Jacob was . . . strange. But in an interesting sort of way. Charlotte had always been fascinated with meteors, the Big Bang theory, planets outside the solar system, and anything to do with space. Jacob seemed to share that passion, even though Lena's frequent glares at her son seemed to insinuate that she didn't think it was appropriate supper conversation. A comment about the heat generated a list of factoids from young Jacob. And thankfully he spoke in English. A few times, Lena and Hannah had drifted into their native dialect, but luckily none of the conversation seemed directed at Charlotte.

"The sun is fifteen million degrees Celsius at its core, but only fifty-five hundred on the surface," Jacob said as he reached for a slice of bread. To Charlotte's horror, there was only one slice left, so she snatched it before someone else did. Full or not, she didn't think she'd ever get enough of the bread here. She was pretty sure Jacob had already had several slices. As Charlotte spread butter over the moist, warm bread, she thought about Ethan as a teenager. Her brother had always had a healthy appetite. She listened with interest to Jacob talk about moon landings, Pluto, and space debris, but when he started talking about NASA funding and the political aspects of space exploration, Lena shut him down.

"That's enough, Jacob." Lena scowled at her son.

Too bad. For Charlotte, it had been the most interesting conversation she'd had with any of them. After the meal, she excused herself. She wanted to start studying her new book.

Two hours later, she'd highlighted words and phrases she thought she could use, but she wondered if it would be enough to fake her way through a conversation. When her eyes grew heavy, she set the book aside, opting not to call Ryan till later since she couldn't stop yawning. It was too early for bed, not even seven p.m., so she'd just close her eyes for a little while.

Hannah watched her cousin walk up the stairs, and she waited until her father and Jacob had gone outside to tend to the animals before she spoke to her mother.

"What kind of Amish community is Mary from? She doesn't offer to help clean the kitchen, and we both saw what kind of gardener she is." Hannah stacked dirty plates, shaking her head at the amount of uneaten food on Mary's plate. *Wasteful.* "She talks funny too. Half the time, I'm not even sure she understands the *Deitsch.* I've been speaking to her in English."

"*Mei maedel,* remember our trip to Ohio? Things were very different there." Her mother stowed the chow-chow and butter in the refrigerator. The propane truck was scheduled to deliver the following day, thankfully. They were almost out, and the refrigerator was filled to capacity, mostly with goat milk. For as long as Hannah could remember, cows were for eating, goats were for everything else. Most of their people had milking goats and made cheeses, soaps, butter, and lotions. But *Mamm* used it for everything. Any recipe that called for milk, she used goat milk. She also made face cream for dry skin and a salve to put on wounds.

"I know that things are not always the same in other districts," Hannah finally said. "But her community must be very different."

Mamm draped the kitchen towel over her shoulder and smiled. "And this is *gut*. We can learn from her about their ways."

Hannah shrugged. "I guess." Her mother was so happy to have a new cousin that Hannah let the subject drop.

It also struck Hannah as odd that Mary didn't even inquire about daily devotions. Surely, she and her family spent time together in the evenings giving thanks and praise to God.

Charlotte only napped for about thirty minutes, but she waited until almost eleven before calling Ryan. "Sorry it's so late," she said when he answered. "I think everyone was in bed by eight, except for Jacob, the teenager. I kept hearing noises off and on, but last I peeked across the hall, his room was dark and all was quiet." She glanced at the lantern on her nightstand, then at the flashlight on her bed, which illuminated the far wall, casting a shadow from the trees outside. She wasn't planning to light the lantern. It was bad enough that there were open flames all over the house, but she wasn't going to have one in the room she was sleeping in. One fire in her life had been enough, and the first thing she'd done after that was to buy a long rope that she kept with her whenever she stayed somewhere overnight. She stowed it under the bed. She was never going to be trapped by fire again.

"It's fine. You know I stay up late. I have an early flight tomorrow, but it still wouldn't seem normal to go to bed before midnight."

Charlotte wanted to know a lot more about Ryan, but she did know that he traveled quite a bit for work and that he was a night owl. And it had worked out okay since in the time she'd been waiting for everyone to fall asleep, she'd continued her crash course in Pennsylvania Dutch. Yawning, she laid her head back against the pillow, then filled him in on her day.

Ryan was quiet for a few moments before he said, "Um . . . it almost sounds like you had a good time."

Charlotte sat up, twirled a strand of hair, and gave some thought to his comment. "Well, it's different. It's kind of an adventure. But I'm not sure I'll ever get used to riding in those buggies on busy highways." She paused and lowered her voice, even though she was sure the hum from the battery-operated fan in her room would drown out the sound. "I won't lose track of why I'm here, if you're worried about that. My sole purpose is to find out what happened to Ethan. I won't be lured into their world." It struck her that they may try to brainwash her into staying here. Maybe that's what happened to Ethan.

"There's nothing wrong with enjoying yourself while you're there. I'm just a little surprised. The Amish are known to be really . . . religious."

Charlotte folded her legs beneath her and sat taller in the darkness. "What does that have to do with anything?" Ryan knew that neither Charlotte nor Ethan had been raised in a church setting the way he had. But it sure hadn't stopped Ethan from joining up with these people.

"Nothing, really," Ryan said. "I just wondered if it made you uncomfortable. Don't they pray a lot, several times a day?"

"Yeah, I think so. I read on the Internet before I came here that most Amish families pray together at night, so I've just been excusing myself early. And I just bowed my head when they did at meals. I'm not worried about that. I can fake my way through some prayers. The problem I'm having is with the language. The ladies in Beeville spoke mostly English to me."

Ryan chuckled. "That's because they knew you didn't speak Pennsylvania Dutch. These people think you're Amish, so they're going to talk to you in their native dialect. I thought you'd practiced up on that."

"I did, but my knowledge of their language is comparable to knowing a little conversational Italian before you go to Italy. You can ask for the check or where the bathroom is, but that's about it. I should have known they would speak their language more frequently." She sighed.

"Just do the best you can."

They were both quiet for a while before Charlotte asked, "Do you think Ethan would be mad about what we're doing?"

"*We?*" He laughed again. That was one of the things Charlotte liked most about Ryan. That he laughed a lot. He'd told her over one of their lunches that she didn't laugh enough. She'd pondered that comment ever since. She'd always thought of herself as a fairly happy person. Despite the grief she was clinging to over Ethan's death, she still found joy, even if it was in limited doses. She'd battled some demons in the past, but overall, she'd trained herself to be happy. Forced happiness is what her therapist called it as he encouraged her to go deeper into herself to discover what real happiness could be. Charlotte would just nod, having no idea of the difference. Happy was happy. Sad was sad.

"Hey, just because I'm the one in the Amish clothes, you're in this too," she said jokingly, then added in a more serious tone, "You didn't argue when I said I wanted to do this. I know you are just as curious about what pushed Ethan over the edge as I am."

"Yeah, I am. But I hate that you're having to pretend to be Amish." He paused and took a deep breath. "And to answer your question, yes . . . Ethan would probably be ticked if he knew about you—I mean *us*—lying to the woman he loved and her family."

"I know. And I don't feel good about it, but I just can't shake the feeling that maybe Hannah knows something more about his death. She was engaged to the guy."

"I just wish we could have come up with a better plan."

Charlotte pointed the flashlight at the ceiling and moved it in circles above her head. "Well, I couldn't think of anything else. And the fact that Hannah is so tight-lipped makes me suspicious." She paused, thinking about her day. "And I could be way off, but I think Hannah is suspicious of *me* too. Lena is beyond excited to have me here, but sometimes I catch Hannah looking at me funny."

"Maybe you just feel guilty, and you're imagining that she's on to you. But I've always heard that the Amish like to keep to themselves. Although, they think you are Amish, so that doesn't really apply."

"I know. I read that online. But I don't believe they walk the walk like they preach, acting all holy and better than everyone else."

Ryan was quiet.

"Are you still there?"

"Yeah, I'm here. But I think you're wrong about them. They're known to be a Christ-centered group, and the reason they detach themselves from outsiders is because they believe themselves to be unequally yoked."

"*Exactly.* They think they're better than everyone else."

Ryan let out a light chuckle. "Get to know them before you judge them. Or better yet, try not to judge them. Hey, maybe you'll learn something."

"The only thing I need to learn right now is how to speak their language. Oh, and how to fall asleep without air conditioning." She smiled as she started swirling the flashlight overhead again. "But, hey, I'll take one for our team."

Ryan was quiet, and when he hadn't said anything after a long pause, she finally asked, "Having second thoughts?" She turned the flashlight off, but quickly flipped it back on. A lamp in the yard—presumably propane—shone in the distance, barely casting a faint glow against her window. She wasn't fond of the dark, and despite the heat, she felt a chill run the length of her spine.

"No second thoughts. I already faced my guilt, and even though I know God is frowning, I want to know about Ethan." He paused again. "I remember Ethan telling me at Donna and Shane's wedding that he hoped to be dancing to good music well into his eighties." Ryan sighed.

Charlotte was reminded of the dance that she and Ryan had shared at the wedding of their mutual friends. Ryan wasn't too tall, but the perfect height for someone petite like Charlotte. He kept his dark hair cut short, and he had kind, gray-blue eyes that reflected his personality. He was a good guy. But he was a little heavy on the religious stuff sometimes, and Charlotte didn't know enough about the subject to engage him in a conversation.

She only knew that the God everyone spoke about hadn't shown Himself to her. If God was God, then He could do anything. Why hadn't He helped her brother, someone who had chosen to trust Him?

"I don't know about God frowning. I'm trying to get a visual of that," she said as she rolled onto her side, keeping the flashlight on. "I'm imagining a giant super-being hovering above in the clouds looking down on you, scowling."

Another chortle from Ryan. "More of a figure of speech, but I do feel bad about the deception, and I'm sure God wouldn't approve."

"Hmm..."

Charlotte had often wondered about the friendship between Ryan and Ethan. To her knowledge, Ethan had never believed in a divine being, which had made it all the more surprising when he became Amish.

They were both quiet again. As much as Charlotte fought the urge to have a conversation about God, something was niggling at her. "Ryan, you're a good guy. But don't feel badly about what *I'm* doing. I was just teasing you. I'm the one embedding myself in a world of lies."

"Yeah, well . . . I probably should have talked you out of it."

"You wouldn't have been able to." She sighed. "Besides, I've probably already earned a spot in hell. I'm guessing there is still hope for you." She grunted, only half kidding.

"Charlotte, I don't know why you would say that. I've never known you to be anything but good-hearted."

I'm damaged. She chewed on her bottom lip, not wanting the conversation to get too deep. "Ryan, you talk a lot about God. And that's fine. But it's just . . . well, He just isn't my thing. I don't base my decisions, choices, or motivations around God."

"It's never too late to have a relationship with the Lord."

Charlotte's eyes were watering for reasons she didn't understand. She changed the subject, but couldn't quite detach herself from the God-talk. After they hung up, she lay awake for another hour . . . wishing, longing for a God, someone who loved her, no matter her faults or mistakes. Someone who would forgive her, who was preparing a place in heaven just for her, the type of paradise believers talked about.

Closing her eyes, she thought about Ethan, hoping he was in such a place.

*I*saac looked at the clock on the wall, knowing a hundred people would be piling into the house for worship service soon. Hosting church fell on each family every nine or ten months, and a lot of extra work went into getting everything ready. The house had a fresh coat of paint, the yard was freshly mowed, low tree branches trimmed, shrubs and flower beds manicured, and his mother had been hard at work on the inside. He glanced out the window at his father sitting in a rocker on the porch, then turned to his left when he heard his mother's footsteps.

"He seems to be having a good day so far," she said as she touched Isaac's arm. Anna Ruth Miller smiled, and Isaac nodded as he recalled the way their lives had been before his father got cancer. Everything had changed three years ago. Isaac remembered exactly where he was when he got the news. He'd been on his way to ask Hannah King out, finally, after years of dating other girls that weren't right for him. But Hannah had always had a long list of suitors, and for once . . . neither one of them were seeing other people. By Amish standards, they were both well overdue to get married, but following his father's diagnosis, Isaac assumed the role as head of the household, and Ethan slipped into town and stole Hannah's heart before Isaac even had a chance to try.

Sometimes, Isaac wondered if he was even worthy of Hannah's love. He'd sensed that Ethan might be in trouble, but he'd let jealousy creep into his heart and hadn't made an effort to help. Isaac believed that he'd failed God—and Hannah—by not doing more for Ethan. He knew that God had forgiven him, even if Isaac struggled to forgive himself.

He walked out onto the porch, looped his thumbs beneath his suspenders, and peered out over the yard into the pastures. Over a hundred acres to tend. It had been tough when there were two of them doing it, and now it was only Isaac. They were blessed to have good employees at the furniture store. Isaac went in once a day, but without Phyllis and Tom, he'd be lost.

"*Sohn*, everything looks *gut*. I know your *mamm* gets anxious when it's our turn to host worship." His father carefully stood up and eased toward Isaac. *Daed* was still getting used to a prosthetic leg. "You've done a fine job readying up the yard."

"Danki." Isaac had hoped that the new leg attached at his father's knee might be more comfortable and allow his father to at least do a little bit around the house. The cancer was in remission, and his *daed* seemed to have more good days than bad.

A line of buggies was heading up the driveway, and Hannah was in one of them. Just knowing that sent Isaac's heart to racing. Maybe it was time to leave the past behind him. He couldn't bring Ethan back, but he could love Hannah with all his heart if she'd let him.

"I'm going to ask out Hannah King," he said to his father, giving a taut nod. When his father didn't respond, Isaac turned to him, lifting a hand to his forehead to block the sun rising behind *Daed*.

His father was losing his footing, and if Isaac hadn't caught him by the arm, he would have fallen. He helped his father back to the rocking chair.

"I'm still a clumsy man." *Daed* shook his head, sighing. "Now, what were you saying?"

Isaac looked out at the buggies getting closer, then back at his father. "I-I was thinking about asking out Hannah." He turned to his father, who was scowling.

"I've heard that *maedel* is still brokenhearted. Probably best not to pursue her. You might end up with a broken heart as well."

"It's a chance I'm willing to take." Isaac watched Hannah stepping out of one of the buggies. He was tired of living in regret.

"I guess I could sell this place," his father said, sighing again.

Isaac looked at his father. "What? You can't do that. This farm has been in our family for four generations."

"Isaac . . ." *Daed* stroked his long gray beard. "I'm not able to tend this place on my own."

"You can't sell it." Isaac reached for his father's arm when he struggled to push himself up from the chair. Normally, Isaac's parents would have moved to the *daadi haus* on their property, but the old house was in need of repairs—repairs that should have been started on years ago. It wasn't livable anymore, and Isaac didn't know when he'd fit that into his schedule. Others in the community would lend a hand, but these days, everyone stayed busy. It was hard to make a living just farming, and many had turned to an outside source of income, the way Isaac's family had with the furniture store. Although, for the past three years, Miller's Furniture Store had been mostly dependent on consignment pieces.

"It only makes sense that you should leave here, marry, and have a family. Your *mamm* and I can make do in a small *haus*, something we can take care of."

"*Mamm* loves this place," he said softly as he watched Hannah coming up the sidewalk.

Charlotte smiled at Isaac Miller as she followed Hannah on the sidewalk. She couldn't believe she was going to have to sit on a wooden bench for three hours, listening to a church service in a foreign language, about a subject she didn't know anything about. Even someone as attractive as Isaac couldn't provide enough of a distraction for this. At least they only held church service every two weeks.

Lena introduced Charlotte to everyone, and several people spoke to Charlotte in Dutch. She quickly realized that memorizing a few words and sayings wasn't going to make her proficient overnight. And based on some of the strange expressions, she was failing miserably. Eventually, she pointed to her throat and whispered, "Sore." But she caught the look between Lena and Hannah, pretty sure they were on to her.

She spent the three hours on the bench plotting another lie, one that she hoped her pretend Amish cousins would believe. Otherwise, it was going to be a long month trying to fake her way through conversations.

Hannah and Lena headed directly to the kitchen following the worship service. All of the men left the house, and Charlotte could see most of them making their way to the barn. Charlotte shuffled into the kitchen with the other ladies, and even small children were gathering plates, food, and utensils to carry out to tables that were set up outside. *Nothing like baking in the*

August heat. She thought about Texas and how much hotter it was at home, and she made a mental note not to complain too much.

As Charlotte carried a tray of pickles outside, Hannah and Lena got in step with her. Hannah spoke to her in Dutch, then smiled. Charlotte had chatted in English with some of the other women in the kitchen earlier, so pointing to her throat wasn't going to work again. But she didn't feel like this was the time to break into the story she'd prepared. So, instead, she said, *"Gut, gut."* She realized she hadn't retained much of what she'd read in her dictionary. Hannah glanced at her mother and then at Charlotte, and she knew that she'd not given an appropriate response. Hannah nodded, then turned to her mother as they laid out food. Hannah spoke to her mother. In Dutch.

"She doesn't understand a word we are saying," Hannah said to her mother. "You heard what I asked her."

Her mother waited until Mary was out of earshot before she put her hands on her hips and whispered, "'Tis tacky for you to trick her like that."

Hannah grinned. "I thought it was funny. I asked her what her favorite color is, and she said *gut*. Because that seems to be the only word she knows."

Mamm dropped her arms to her sides and sighed.

"I'm sure there is a reason her people don't speak the
Deitsch. And the Lord would not approve of you intentionally deceiving her like that."

"He also wouldn't approve of her pretending to know
the language. That's lying." Hannah walked with her
mother back to the house. Mary brushed past them with
a tray of glasses filled with iced tea.

"We will speak with her later about this. Not now."
Mamm opened the screen door for Hannah to go in first,
but out of the corner of her eye, Hannah saw Mary walking toward Isaac. He was washing his hands at the pump.
Mary would be wasting her time with him. Several of
Hannah's friends had tried to get Isaac to take an interest
in them, but Isaac stayed busy taking care of his parents
and had no part of it. Hannah had known Isaac all her
life, and she'd watched the wonderful man he'd grown
into. But there had been opportunities in the past, before
Isaac's father became ill, for Isaac to ask Hannah out,
and he never had. Besides, Hannah's heart still ached for
Ethan. She wasn't sure when she would be ready to date
again. But if there was one man in their community that
could make Hannah consider dating again, it was surely
Isaac Miller.

Charlotte wondered if Isaac might provide a nice distraction while she was here. His muscular body was evident

beneath his blue shirt, black slacks, and suspenders that strained against his broad chest. His dark hair was cut like every other Amish man, and his cropped bangs fell above dark-blue eyes. Hannah had told her he wasn't married. But she figured that out right away because he was clean-shaven. She quickened her steps until she was right beside him, all the while hoping that he would speak to her in English.

"Hi, we haven't met. I'm Mary." She waited for Isaac to finish washing his hands before she extended hers. He stood tall and hesitated for a few seconds, but eventually wiped his palms on his black slacks and latched on with a firm grip.

"*Wie bischt?*"

Finally. A phrase she was familiar with. "I'm *gut*," she said, then quickly added, "It's hot out here, but not as hot as in Texas. That's where I'm from." She wanted to set the tone for the conversation and ensure that it would be in English.

"Do you ride horses there? Do the *Englisch* ranches have oil wells? Cowboys in big hats?" Isaac tapped a finger to his straw hat.

Charlotte smiled. Why was it that every time a Texan left the state, these questions popped up? "No. I . . ." She stopped herself before she said she lived in a high-rise apartment near downtown. "I don't ride horses. Some ranches have oil wells, but you don't see too many cowboy hats unless you're in a rural area."

He nodded and smiled. Initially, she'd only approached Isaac to see if he was just as handsome up close, which proved to be the case, but now she was thinking that Hannah wasn't the only one here who had known Ethan. Maybe Isaac and Ethan had been friends.

"So, um . . . Hannah told me that your family owns a furniture store. I'd love to see it while I'm here." Charlotte could think of worse ways to spend her time. At least Isaac was easy on the eyes.

"*Ya*, it's on the main road. I can give you directions. An *Englisch* couple runs it for us. Just ask for Phyllis or Tom." Isaac shrugged. "Or anyone working that day can help you."

Charlotte nodded, smiling a little, as she tried to think of a reason she needed Isaac to be the one to show her, but nothing came to mind.

"Nice to meet you, Mary," he said before he turned to walk away.

He'd only taken a few steps toward the barn when Mary sprinted to catch up with him. "Maybe you can show me your furniture store, and . . . we . . . uh, could have lunch . . . or something."

Isaac stopped, faced her, and scratched his cheek. "I have much work to do, but . . ."

"We can make it a quick trip." She was seizing the moment, hoping to get him to commit. "What about Saturday?"

Isaac's eyes rounded as he grinned. "*Ya*. Okay."

"How does noon sound?"

He nodded, narrowing his eyebrows, almost appearing confused. Then he pointed to the barn. "I better go join the others."

"What's going on in the barn?" she asked, getting in step with him.

He didn't say anything, but opened the barn door for her. A cloud of cigar smoke rushed at her face and into her lungs. She backed up a few steps. She coughed and waved her hand in front of her face. "I'll just see you back at the house." Charlotte backed up a few steps until she was clear of the smoke.

"They are all smoking in the barn. Is that normal?" she said to Hannah when she returned to the tables.

Hannah plucked an olive from the pickle tray but just held it as she answered. "*Ya*. They smoke cigars before the meal while we are getting things ready, and usually after the meal too. They tell jokes out there." She popped the olive in her mouth.

Really? "People in my Amish town don't smoke." *And what about all that hay? Aren't they worried about fire?*

Hannah didn't look up as she put spoons in the jams and relishes. "I only know a few men who smoke cigarettes. It's mostly cigars." She finally glanced up. "But we were in Ohio once for a cousin's wedding. They don't smoke at all, and they were very offended when some of the wedding guests did." She shrugged. "I guess it's different everywhere."

Charlotte's mouth watered as she noticed all the loaves of homemade bread. "I guess." She scanned the table until she spotted the butter. The men would be served first, and she hoped they weren't greedy with the bread. It was tempting to snatch a piece now.

"I saw you talking to Isaac." Hannah didn't look up as she placed another spoon in a bowl of chowchow.

"Yeah. Um . . . *ya*," she said as she and Hannah walked back to the house. "We're going to have lunch on Saturday, and he's going to show me his family's furniture store."

Hannah stopped walking and turned to Charlotte, blinking her eyes. "What? Like a date?"

"I guess you could call it that."

Hannah folded her arms across her chest, her eyebrows raised. "Hmm . . ."

Charlotte's skin prickled. Did her beautiful cousin think Charlotte wasn't good enough for Isaac? Just because others had tried to win Isaac didn't mean that Charlotte would fail, even though that wasn't the purpose of the so-called date. "Are you surprised?"

Hannah dropped her arms to her sides, then reached up and twirled the string of her prayer covering with one hand. "He just hasn't dated anyone that I know of since his *daed* got cancer a few years ago."

"Oh." Charlotte fell back in step with Hannah.

Her pretend cousin didn't have much to say the rest of the day. It didn't take a genius to recognize jealousy.

Charlotte kept quiet, then excused herself after supper, even though Hannah scowled. The family probably prayed together at night and wondered why Charlotte hadn't joined them.

After showering, she sat on her bed and ran a comb through her wet hair, then pulled out her journal, which was just a yellow legal pad. She'd tried recording her thoughts on her computer and her phone, but there was something about writing them out longhand that she liked. Sometimes, she wrote letters to Ethan. Other times, she didn't think Ethan would like what she had to say, so she just logged her thoughts in a journal.

August 21

Well, I managed to snag a date with an Amish fellow . . .

Isaac rushed down the stairs when he heard the commotion. At first, it was muffled rumblings, but as he got closer, he heard his mother yelling.

"Gideon, you have to try to help yourself!"

Isaac hurried through the living room and stopped at his parents' closed bedroom door. "Is everything okay?" he said in a loud voice.

Both his parents began yelling at once, but it was his father's voice that drowned out his mother's. "*Nee!* Everything is not all right."

Isaac reached for the doorknob, but the door swung open before he could grab it, and his mother came out of her bedroom wiping her cheeks. "I give up. Your father won't try to do anything to help himself." She raised her palms as her shoulders rose. "I love him with all my heart, but I won't always be able to lift him when he falls, help him to get dressed, or all the other things he depends on me for."

Isaac sympathized with his mother, but he eased past her into the bedroom as she headed to the kitchen. His father was sitting on the floor in his underwear, reaching for his prosthetic leg. When he saw Isaac, he pulled his arm back and motioned to the leg.

"*Danki, sohn.* I guess your *mamm* was just going to leave me on the floor." Scowling, his father attached the device at his knee, then stretched out his arm toward Isaac. As Isaac helped his father to his feet, he glanced at the wooden handle on the wall nearby. Isaac had installed the makeshift support so that his father could pull himself up if he fell. "I'm half a man. What does that woman expect from me?"

Isaac felt an overwhelming urge to stand up for his mother, especially since Isaac agreed that his father was too dependent on others and didn't make any effort to learn new ways to care for himself—or anything else.

But he'd never confronted his father, and now didn't seem like the best time. He could hear his mother crying from the other room.

All this time, he'd been worried about how his parents would take care of the house and the land if Isaac ever left.

Now he was wondering who would take care of them.

Charlotte reread what she'd written this evening. Even though her journal was for her eyes only, the editor in her demanded perfection. She'd recently left the publishing house she'd worked at for two years, and now she edited manuscripts from home. The biggest perk was that she could structure her jobs and free time however she chose. If there was a downside, it was her inability to turn off her editor brain and simply enjoy a book. Same with her journal, which was supposed to be a record of her feelings. She went back and revised three sentences just the same, then read it a final time, starting from the beginning.

August 21

Well, I managed to snag a date with an Amish fellow. His name is Isaac, and I'm hoping that he knew Ethan. It's a quest for information, but the guy is incredibly handsome, so even if Isaac can't shed any light on what happened to my brother, I'll just soak in his attractiveness.

Charlotte smiled, considered changing "attractiveness," but jumped when someone knocked on the door. "Hang on. Just a minute." She stood up and stuffed the legal pad between the mattresses. "Come in."

Hannah peeked her head in. "Sorry to bother you, but I need to get something from underneath the bed. I had stored some quilting odds and ends in a box, and I'd like to piece them together for a friend's baby blanket."

"Come on in." Charlotte sat down on the bed and crossed her legs beneath her, fighting the urge to play with her phone, which was supposed to be for emergencies.

She jumped again when Hannah yelled, "Ow!" followed by a thud against the bed frame. Hannah slid herself out from under the bed, but she wasn't toting any quilting supplies. Instead she was pulling out Charlotte's emergency fire rope, and before Charlotte could explain, Hannah held it up and shook it. Her face was fire-engine red, and her bottom lip trembled. "What is this? Tell me now! Why do you have this?" She threw it on the bed. "Tell me, Mary!"

Charlotte stood up and faced off with her. "Good grief. Quit yelling, and I'll tell you. It's because—"

The bedroom door flew open. "Hannah!" Lena sailed into the room. "What is going on in here? I was coming down the hall to speak with Jacob, and I heard you yelling."

Charlotte lifted her shoulders, held them there, and shook her head. "I have no idea."

Hannah was shaking all over as she pointed to the bed. "Look what she has, *Mamm*." Then Charlotte's pretend cousin grabbed both of Charlotte's arms and squeezed. "Please tell me that you are not planning to take your own life. Please tell me that you have brought this rope into our home for some other reason. Why would you hide it under the bed in this way?" She swiped at the stream of tears going down her face, and Charlotte realized the cause of Hannah's outbreak.

"No, no, no . . ." Charlotte maneuvered out of Hannah's hold. "That's not what it's for. Of course not." She stared at the floor as her own eyes filled with tears, and when she looked back at Hannah, it was impossible not to cry. "When I was a child I was trapped in my bedroom by a fire." Charlotte could still smell the smoke when she recalled the event. "I couldn't get out of the two-story house without landing on concrete. A fireman saved me at the very last minute. I take that rope everywhere I go so that I won't ever be trapped again."

Hannah buried her face in her hands and sobbed before she ran out of the room, repeatedly saying how sorry she was.

Lena put a hand on Charlotte's shoulder. "I'm so sorry that happened to you when you were a child, Mary. So very sorry." She wrapped her arms around Charlotte and squeezed for a few moments before she eased away.

"And I am very sorry, also, about Hannah's outburst." She hung her head and sighed before she looked back up at Charlotte. "We all lost someone special to us, someone we loved very much. It was about a year ago, and it was the hardest on Hannah. She was going to marry this man." She paused, and Charlotte couldn't breathe as she waited for her to go on. "He hanged himself. Not far from here. In his own backyard."

*C*harlotte stared out the bedroom window and watched Isaac walk toward the barn. She'd been looking forward to their date on Saturday, but any excitement she'd had was suspended. She'd known that Ethan had hanged himself, but hearing Lena say it and being witness to Hannah's hysteria had left Charlotte in a funk.

Hannah had apologized for her outburst two more times and seemed to want to talk, but Charlotte had stayed to herself the past couple of days. Hannah might be ready to share information about Ethan, but Charlotte wasn't sure she was ready to hear it now. Instead, she found herself recalling parts of her past that were best forgotten.

Their parents had spent the majority of Ethan's and Charlotte's childhood fighting. Their father eventually landed in jail for assaulting their mother, but after that, it was their mother who took over the beatings, and after one too many times, Charlotte had called the police, something she wouldn't have done if she could have foreseen the consequences. She had no idea where her mother was these days. And she didn't care.

Charlotte's phone call had resulted in Ethan and her being separated for nearly two years. She recalled the foster home where the fire had started, and a shiver ran up her spine—but only partly from recollections of the fire. She and Ethan never talked about those two years apart, and she'd always wondered if Ethan's foster home had been anything like the one she'd been in. She wondered if Ethan had hidden things in an empty mothball box in the closet like they'd done when they lived at home. Their mother had insisted they keep a box of mothballs in the closet, but she wouldn't even touch the boxes, saying the smell made her gag. Charlotte and Ethan had always trashed the mothballs and stored anything they didn't want her to see in the empty boxes. It wasn't until she was older that Charlotte realized that mothballs were toxic. Luckily, neither she nor Ethan had ever eaten one.

She stuffed the painful memories back in the dark part of her brain and walked downstairs. The aroma of freshly baked bread was too much to resist. She walked into the kitchen just as Hannah was taking two loaves from the oven. Lena had gone to the auction to see about purchasing more goats, and Amos and Jacob were doing whatever they did out in the fields. They came in each night smelling of hay and manure. Charlotte was thankful they both bathed before dinner—*supper,* she reminded herself.

Charlotte breathed in the smell of what had become her most favorite food in the world, then she walked to the window, just in time to catch a glimpse of Isaac leaving in his buggy.

"Are you excited about your date?" Hannah placed the loaves of bread on the cooling rack.

Hannah's tone was clipped. Clearly, Cousin Hannah wasn't in the mood to apologize anymore. Charlotte shrugged. "I guess."

Hannah leaned against the counter and folded her arms across her chest. "You will only be here for three more weeks, so I hope you won't lead Isaac on. He's a very nice man, and I'd hate to see him get hurt." Hannah raised her chin in a way that reminded Charlotte of a hair-pulling incident she'd had on the playground one time. This was a side of Hannah that Charlotte hadn't seen before.

Charlotte stuffed her hands in the pockets of her black apron as she raised an eyebrow. "Maybe. Your mother said I should extend my stay." Even though there was no way she would stay here any longer than she needed to, she was just irritated enough to meet Hannah on the playground. "We might hit it off. You never know."

Then Hannah spoke to her in Dutch, all the while wagging her finger and frowning. Charlotte recalled the story she'd made up during worship service. She had lucked out the past couple of days during meals. Jacob had done most of the talking, in English, about a space documentary that was coming on television next week. His parents were refusing to let him go to a friend's house to watch it even though he was in his running-around period, or *rumschpringe*, as they called it.

Charlotte knew she had a deer-in-the-headlights look, but she was trying to organize her thoughts before she just blurted something.

"Who are you, Mary Troyer?" Hannah took a step closer to her. "You did not understand anything I just said, and it wonders me why that might be."

Think, think. Be careful. Get it straight. She hung her head for a few moments, before she sat down in a kitchen chair and lowered her palms to the table in front of her. "I'm so sorry I've been deceitful." This was going to require the best acting she'd ever done. Normally, she despised lying. "I'm-I'm just embarrassed. I became Amish late in life, and by the time I was welcomed into my Amish family, I had a hard time latching on to the dialect. So everyone made an effort to help me out by using English around me."

Then Charlotte told Hannah the part of the story that was actually true, how her parents were abusive, but she omitted the part about having a brother or about being in foster care. She wasn't sure how much Ethan had shared with Hannah, and she feared Hannah might make the connection. "I just couldn't take it anymore, so I left. I knew my great-aunt had married an Amish man, so I ran away to their house in Texas. They took me in, and I was baptized into the faith when I was nineteen."

Hannah slipped into the chair across from Charlotte, her eyes round as saucers, and reached for Charlotte's hands. "*Ach, mei* cousin. Why didn't you tell us? How awful for you." Hannah shook her head. "I feel badly that so much of the time, you couldn't understand what we were saying. I am so ashamed for testing you."

"It's okay." Charlotte pushed the truths about her past from her mind, hoping she'd be able to keep all her lies straight.

"*Nee, nee.* It is not okay." Hannah kept her hands on Charlotte's as she spoke. "Someone very close to me was also abused by his parents, and then later at the hands of his *Englisch* caretakers. It was heartbreaking to hear him talk of his stay with strangers. Foster care, he called it." She paused, sighed. "And it's a shame that this kind of thing happens everywhere. Even here." Hannah paused again, a faraway look in her eyes. She blinked a few times, pulled her hands away, and leaned back against the chair. "He died almost a year ago. *Mamm* said she told you what happened. But before that, he said that coming here and learning about the Lord saved him." She smiled. "He used to say that I completed him, a line from one of his favorite movies, which of course I'd never seen. His name was Ethan, and he also became Amish late in life."

Saved him? He killed himself. Charlotte was surprised that Ethan had told Hannah about those two years, since he'd never talked to Charlotte about it. She wasn't sure that she wanted to know the details, but she'd always wondered. "I'm sorry about your friend. Was he . . ." She took a deep breath. "Was he, um . . . badly abused?"

Hannah nodded, and Charlotte swallowed back the knot forming in her throat.

"*Ya.* He was." Hannah looked away as a tear rolled down her cheek. "I think *Mamm* told you . . . he was my fiancé. We were to be married."

Charlotte was anxious, yet relieved, that Hannah didn't share the details about Ethan's time in foster care. "I'm-I'm sorry." She waited to see if Hannah would tell her about Ethan's death, but they were both quiet. Finally, Charlotte stood up. "If it's okay with you, I think I'd like to go lay down for a while." She wasn't tired, but she didn't want to burst into tears.

Hannah jumped from her chair, hurried around the table, and threw her arms around Charlotte. "I'm so sorry. So sorry that someone hurt you. Thank you for sharing that with me." She eased away and wiped the tears from her cheeks with both hands. "I feel so much closer to you now. And I know how blessed I am to have such a wonderful family. I don't want to take it for granted. Ethan always said we were the family he'd never had."

Charlotte doubted that was true. *I was his family.*

"We couldn't wait to be married. I still miss him."

She buried her head on Charlotte's shoulder, and Charlotte slowly wrapped her arms around Hannah, but only because it seemed awkward not to. She was starting to like Hannah, but she didn't want to get any closer to her than necessary. Charlotte had loved and lost plenty of times. No need to add Hannah to that list. And she still felt uneasy about Ethan's fiancée and hadn't been able to mentally clear Hannah from having something to do with his death.

All the tears in the world couldn't bring Ethan back. He might have had a hard childhood, but so had Charlotte. Before coming here, he'd had a good job as a roofer, a nice apartment, and lots of friends. It was his job that brought him to Pennsylvania in the first place. The company he worked for had won a bid to put a new roof on a church in Lancaster County following a storm that had caused some structural damages to several build-ings. Charlotte had known about it, but she could have never predicted that he would end up staying. Someone needed to take the blame for Ethan's death, and Hannah would have to sit in the guilty seat until Charlotte could prove her innocent. Otherwise, the loss was more than Charlotte could bear.

Hannah sat down on her bed after a cool bath, and as her wet hair lay against the back of her white nightgown, she closed her eyes and welcomed the breeze coming through the screen in her room. After a few moments, she laid back and closed her eyes.

Lord, I'm lifting up Mary with extra prayers tonight, for peace and healing. I also ask, Lord, for You to forgive me for not being kinder to Mary. Mei *cousin has been through* baremlich *times in her life, and I cannot put right in my mind how a mother or father can hurt their own* kinner. Aamen.

Hannah recalled the awful stories that Ethan had told her before he died. And to learn that Mary was also harmed at the hands of her own family . . . it was just so sad. She wanted to do something nice for Mary, to bring some joy into her life, and maybe by doing so, she could bring a small amount of happiness into her own heart. In the strangest way, she felt like Ethan was encouraging her to befriend her new cousin. She smiled, feeling comforted.

At times, Mary seemed familiar to her. Nothing Hannah could put her finger on, just a sense that maybe she'd known her from somewhere. That was impossible, but she was going to take it as a sign that she and Mary were growing closer, and for that, Hannah was grateful.

She turned up the lantern on her bedside table and pulled her knitting supplies from the bottom drawer. It would take her a couple of hours to finish the fourth potholder in the set, but she wanted Mary to have them. Hannah had been making these for her home, the one she would have shared with Ethan. Two were solid red in the shape of a heart, and two were red and pink, also shaped like hearts. She hadn't worked on finishing the last one since Ethan's death. It would feel good to give Mary the set to take home with her.

Charlotte squeezed her eyes closed and tensed as she told Ryan about her date with Isaac, even though there was no reason it should be awkward. "You know, it's just to try to get information. It's not really like a *date*."

"It kinda sounds like a date."

Charlotte frowned, even though she could picture Ryan grinning. "Well, it's not, I assure you." It was still early in the evening, and she could hear activity down the hall, so she lowered her voice. "It wouldn't matter how good-looking this guy was, or how charming he might turn out to be, I certainly couldn't live the way these people do." She dabbed at the sweat on her forehead.

"Ah-ha. So, he's a handsome fellow." Ryan chuckled. "We just never know who might step into our lives from one day to the next. Maybe this has been God's plan for you all along, to hook up with a nice Amish man."

Charlotte had listened intently in an effort to note any jealousy in Ryan's tone, but he didn't seem bothered in the least. "Very funny," she said, making a mental note that Ryan just mentioned God again. If he had any notable flaw, it was being so overt about his religion. But something was bothering her, and she decided to run with the thoughts even if it might bring on a conversation she wasn't comfortable with.

"I'm pretty sure God didn't send me here to end up with an Amish man." She sighed. "But I'm forced to sit in on the devotions now." She told Ryan the story she'd told Hannah, why she didn't know their dialect. "Hannah shared my big fat lie with everyone else, so now they rarely speak Dutch around me. And they assumed that was the reason I wasn't joining them for devotions." She paused, took another breath. "Anyway, I can't figure a way to get out of it, but all this praying is making me feel bad about myself. And I don't know why that is. It's making me think about things and feel . . . weird."

"That's not surprising. When a person first begins to develop a relationship with God, it's like a cleansing of the soul or something. I didn't find God until I was an adult, but when I did, it was like every sin I'd ever committed in my life ran through my mind as I moved toward a different and better way of life."

"I said I'm *forced* to pray with them. I don't see that as any kind of spiritual cleansing," she said softly, deciding that she didn't want to pursue this conversation after all. "I hear someone coming down the hall. I gotta go." She was drowning in sin . . . mostly lies. She didn't want to feel any worse about that than she already did. On that note, she ended the conversation.

She pulled out her yellow pad. Despite her longing to clear her mind of spiritual matters, the thoughts continued to haunt her, so she wrote them down.

God, if You exist, I'm going to need some kind of sign . . .

⌒

Hannah was surprised that Mary asked to ride into town with her the following day since the traffic on Lincoln Highway scared her so much. Hannah hoped that maybe this was a sign that Mary wanted to be friends as well as cousins, but it may have just been that she mentioned going by Miller's Furniture Store.

"Isaac is usually not at the store even though his family owns it. Besides, I thought he was going to give you a tour on your date on Saturday." Hannah glanced at her cousin as she tethered the horse to the hitching post.

"It doesn't matter. I just felt like getting out. No biggie."

Hannah wondered if maybe Mary used these strange expressions because she'd become Amish later in life. Too many of the *Englisch* ways had stuck with her.

Either way, Hannah was surprised to see Isaac behind the register when they entered the furniture store.

"*Wie bischt,* Isaac." Hannah pointed over her shoulder. "*Mei daed* asked us to drop off two small bookshelves."

64

Both pieces were solid wood and much too heavy for Hannah and Mary to carry.

"*Ya. Gut.*" Isaac eased around the corner toward the front door, then locked eyes with Hannah.

"And you remember my cousin, Mary." She pulled her gaze from Isaac when she felt her cheeks flushing. She'd always miss Ethan, but her attraction to Isaac still brought on considerable guilt. But Isaac had finally decided to start dating, and Mary was the woman he chose, so Hannah needed to support his choice.

Isaac returned carrying both bookcases as if they were no heavier than a pail of grain, his muscles straining against his short-sleeved blue shirt. Hannah turned to Mary, who was clearly smitten with Isaac. Her cousin couldn't take her eyes off of him.

"*Danki,*" Isaac said as he carried the two bookshelves past them and toward the back of the shop.

Isaac was a gentle soul, someone who loved animals, worked hard, and cherished the Lord. There was a time, long before Ethan, when Hannah had hoped things could be different between her and Isaac. They'd grown up together, and she'd witnessed his kindness for years, even when he didn't know she was watching him.

Mary walked away, presumably to take a self-guided tour of the spacious store, and when Isaac returned from the back, Hannah said, "I hear you and Mary are going out Saturday."

Isaac smiled. "*Ya.* She wanted to see the store and . . ."

He looked around until he spotted Mary. "But I guess it will just be lunch instead since she's looking around now. Phyllis and Tom took the morning off to go to one of their *kinner*'s school programs."

"I think it's *gut* that you have decided to date again. I know you've been busy taking care of your father. He looked like he was doing better at worship service."

"Some days are better than others for *Daed*." He scratched his chin. "I-I didn't exactly ask your cousin out. She wanted to see the store and have lunch. Since she's here now, I'm wondering if we will still go to lunch."

Hannah fought the urge to spout something ugly since Mary hadn't made bother to mention that she'd been the one to do the asking.

"There are some great pieces in here," Mary said when she rejoined them. "Really beautiful." She smiled. "See you Saturday. I'll bring lunch."

Hannah wondered how that might go since she'd never seen Mary prepare much of anything in the kitchen. Isaac nodded, so Hannah forced another smile and gave a quick wave good-bye.

How forward for Mary to ask a man out. She wanted to say something to her cousin when they got back into the buggy, but Hannah was afraid that Mary might notice a tinge of jealousy, so they stayed quiet for most of the trip. Right before they got home, Hannah couldn't stand it anymore.

"Isaac said that you asked him out. Is that how it's

done in Texas? Because that seems . . . odd." She straightened her back as she picked up the pace. When Mary
reached for the dashboard of the buggy, Hannah sped up
even more.

"I don't think it matters who asked whom." Mary
rolled her eyes, and even though it appeared to be a
playful gesture, it still fueled Hannah's aggravation. But
she stayed quiet as she recalled the way she'd pushed
everyone away from her since Ethan's death. She needed
a friend, someone to confide in, to be close to. How could
she fault Mary for wanting to spend time with Isaac?

She had another stop she wanted to make on the way
home. It was a place she always visited by herself, but she
wasn't sure when she would have another opportunity to
do so for the next few days, and she felt like she needed to
be somewhere she could feel close to Ethan. Her feelings
about Isaac and her cousin were confusing.

5

"o you mind if we make a stop on the way home?" Hannah asked after a few minutes of silence.

"That's fine." Charlotte couldn't shake the feeling that Hannah was judging her for asking Isaac out. Charlotte had spent the bulk of her life judging herself. She didn't need anyone else doing it. But she wanted Hannah to trust her so she would open up more about Ethan, even though a part of her was terrified to know the details. But also heavy on Charlotte's heart was the feeling that Hannah was somehow being disloyal. If she loved Ethan so much, then why was she jealous of Charlotte's upcoming date with Isaac? Or was Charlotte misreading her?

A coworker once told Charlotte that she was too quick to judge a person. Charlotte hadn't been able to argue with the woman. That was likely the reason she didn't have many friends. She glanced at Hannah and wondered what it would have been like to have Hannah as a sister-in-law. Would they have been close, like sisters? Would Ethan eventually have accepted Charlotte into his world, and vice versa?

Charlotte was lost in thought as the breeze rushed against her face, the only relief from the heat. She tried to overlook the hint of manure wafting into the buggy. She glanced at Hannah again, then back at the car in front of them. Maybe Hannah deserved a second chance at love. With Isaac? The jury was still out, depending on what she found out about Ethan while she was here. Charlotte wondered when she would get her shot at happiness. She'd dated plenty of guys over the years, but it took tremendous effort for her to get close to anyone, and she usually ended the relationship before it really got off the ground. Sometimes she felt like she could explode with all the love she'd been holding back for the right person. *So where is he?*

Of course, it wouldn't be anyone like Isaac, and she hoped that by asking him out she wasn't leading him on. But where was this love that had eluded her all her life? Maybe only good people got that idyllic life: great family, friends, spouse, children. She realized that the only person she'd ever trusted was Ethan, which made the distance that had formed between them—geographically and otherwise—so hard. Despite their awful childhoods, they'd always been close, except for the two years they'd been separated by foster care and then later when he'd ended up in Lancaster County.

Hannah clicked her tongue, picking up speed along Lincoln Highway.

Charlotte's knuckles weren't as white as last time, but her heart was still racing.

"Where are we going?"

Hannah kept her eyes straight ahead. "A special place I like to go."

Charlotte wished it was a mall. Or a hair salon so she could get her roots touched up, something she should have done before she made this trip. Her roots were going to be a problem if anyone in the King household got a look at the top of her head before she was able to use the box of hair dye she'd brought from home. She sighed, thinking how nice a pedicure sounded, knowing it would be at least a couple more weeks before she visited any of those places.

Thankfully, Hannah turned off the main highway, and she slowed the buggy to a trot down a narrow dirt road that didn't have any wheel ruts or evidence a horse had been there recently. From what Charlotte had seen of Lancaster County so far, it was rolling hills with lush fields and manicured homes. It reminded her of the Texas Hill Country, except in Texas, there were very few silos, and the tall feed containers were plentiful here.

But this stretch of road didn't resemble the pristine areas she'd passed by since her arrival. "A road less traveled," she said softly as the sun peeked over a hillside in front of them. No houses in sight, no cattle, and after only a few minutes, even the buzz of cars on Lincoln Highway became faint, then disappeared altogether. Gangly stalks of greenery on either side of the road blew in the breeze, which seemed cooler all of a sudden—so much so, that the line of sweat that ran the length of her spine chilled for a few moments. Some tree branches arched over the road, so low the buggy barely cleared them. There was something peaceful about this place, if not a bit eerie. "Where are we?"

Hannah pulled back on the reins. "Whoa." Once they were stopped in the middle of the road, Hannah stepped out of the buggy and tethered the horse to a tree. As Charlotte got out on her side, she eased up to Hannah, and again, she felt a shimmer of cool air.

"My special place." Hannah offered only a faint smile as she motioned for Charlotte to follow her. Pushing back twigs hanging on both sides, Charlotte could see a narrow path.

"What about the buggy? Can you just leave it in the middle of the road?" Charlotte stepped carefully. "Are there snakes here?"

Hannah continued to push the hanging greenery to the sides as she walked the path. "*Nee*, no one comes here. And there are no snakes."

Hannah couldn't know that for certain, so Charlotte kept her eyes peeled on the dirt path in front of her, her head ducked, and arms spread to keep from getting popped with a twig. She slapped at a spidery bug crawling on her arm. This was an adventure she could have done without. The silence was growing disturbing. Not even the sound of a bird chirping. She stopped walking and stiffened as a thought assaulted her. "Wait," she said.

Hannah stopped, turned around, and lifted an eyebrow. "What's wrong?"

Charlotte drew in a breath. "Is this the place . . . the place where . . . ?"

"What?" Hannah gave her head a little shake before she put her hands on her hips. "What place?"

"Where, uh . . . your friend . . . uh, Ethan . . . ended his life?" Charlotte didn't want to ever go to that place, and if Hannah was bringing her to Ethan's hanging tree, Charlotte was turning back.

"*Nee*. Of course not," Hannah said. "But this is where Ethan and I used to come. And I promise that once we get past these woods, you will love what you see." She turned and started walking again. "Ethan loved it here."

Charlotte couldn't imagine that she would love whatever was on the other side of the wilderness, as she brushed away a spider's web that Hannah had managed to avoid. But she was curious what her brother found so attractive here, so she marched forward in her black leather loafers that were ugly as sin, but the most comfortable shoes she'd ever worn.

The path ended, and as if walking through a doorway into another world, the forest was behind them, and Charlotte followed Hannah out onto a lush, freshly mowed clearing that looked as big as a football field. It was as lovely as any of the yards surrounding the Amish homes both in town and in the rural areas. As the sun swelled on the horizon, Charlotte brought a hand to her forehead to block the glare, but there was no denying the beauty kept secret by the thick forest surrounding this spot. "Wow," she whispered as she took in the view. "I can see why Ethan liked it here." Just saying his name caused a knot to pulse in her throat, so she pressed her lips together and kept following Hannah across the open field.

In the distance, she could see a small structure tucked into the tree line. "What's that?" She pointed to her right as she quickened her pace and caught up with Hannah.

"It's the original outhouse that belonged to the homestead that used to stand here. When Ethan tore down the house, I asked him to keep one thing that belonged to the man who used to own the property, since he was someone respected in our community. His name was Jonas Miller. He grew up in the farmhouse that used to be here, and he and his wife Irma Rose lived here for a while before they bought a house off of Black Horse Road. They both died, and this tract of land had been all but forgotten until Ethan stumbled upon it one day while out exploring."

"It's really pretty," Charlotte said, being careful not to let her voice crack. She could almost feel Ethan around her. "Was Ethan . . . um . . ." She gulped, trying to harness all the emotion bubbling to the surface. "Was Ethan going to build a house here?" This was definitely a place he would have chosen.

Hannah nodded and smiled, even though her eyes were glassy. "He went to go see Sarah Jane, Jonas's daughter. She'd forgotten about the property and happily sold it to Ethan." She slowed her pace as they neared the lone structure with a half-moon carved into the door. "Much of this was still wooded, but Ethan began working to clear it, then decided he liked it this way, surrounded by the woods."

She walked to the side of the outhouse and ran her hand along the side. There was a heart with the names Jonas and Irma Rose inside of it. Others had carved their names as well—Sarah Jane, Samuel, Lillian, Lizzie, and several others. She breathed in the freshly mowed grass. "Who keeps this mowed?"

Hannah smiled again. "I have no idea."

Charlotte frowned. "How can you not know who is taking care of your property?" *Or is it Ethan's property?* That thought brought up an interesting point. Charlotte had insisted that Ethan's body be sent home to Texas, finally hiring an attorney to make it happen. But otherwise, she knew of no possessions outside of the small savings he had in Houston and the sparse furnishings in his apartment.

"Many in our district knew that Ethan and I loved this place, and I think someone is tending it out of respect to Ethan." Hannah tucked a strand of loose hair behind her ear. "I don't know. I guess they will tire of it some-day." She ran her hand gingerly across the etched names, sighing. "Ethan and I were going to write our names here after we were married."

"What's that?" Charlotte took in a deep breath when she saw Ethan's name etched across the small cross a few yards from the outhouse.

Hannah moved toward the cross and squatted down in front of it. "Ethan's family told us we had to send his body back to Texas." She glanced up at Charlotte. "He was raised in Dallas. Is that anywhere close to where you grew up or where you live now in Beeville?"

"No," she said softly as she recalled their move from Dallas to Waco. That was when their family structure started to fall apart. Their father had an affair, and their mother never recovered from the betrayal.

"Anyway," Hannah went on, "Ethan's sister hired a lawman to make sure Ethan's body was sent to Houston, which is where she lives. Ethan and I had talked about both being buried in our family cemetery someday. When I wrote his sister a letter explaining that, I didn't even hear back from her, but the lawman got word to us."

Charlotte's shoulders had never felt heavier, like the burdens of the world rested on them as she tried to decide if Ethan would have really said he wanted to be buried here. She remembered reading that letter, but at the time, Charlotte just wanted Ethan home, and she'd placed full blame for his death on Hannah. During the first few weeks following her brother's death, she needed someone to be accountable. Over time, Charlotte's therapist had worked hard to try to convince her that Ethan was ultimately responsible for his own life. But Charlotte still struggled to accept that.

"So, is anything buried there?" Charlotte pointed to the cross.

Hannah stood up. "*Ya.* A few special things that both Ethan and I treasured. It was all I had, and I needed a place to come to mourn."

As the sun settled behind some clouds, Hannah took a few steps to her left, sat down in the grass, then laid back. "Ethan and I used to lay here and find pictures in the clouds." She looked up at Charlotte and grinned. "That must sound silly, but have you ever done that?"

Plenty of times. With Ethan. She nodded.

"Let's find pictures now." She patted the green grass beside her.

Charlotte let out a small grunt. "I was a kid when I did it. I mean . . ." She thought about Ethan lying on the grass staring up at the clouds. "Okay." Easing herself onto the ground, she felt a bit ridiculous and thought briefly about ants and other creepy crawlies, but the smell and feel of the freshly cut grass instantly took her back to happier times, before things had gone bad between her parents. She was glad that she could recall those few good memories.

"What do you see?" Hannah folded her hands across her stomach and crossed her ankles.

Charlotte felt like she was six years old again. "I don't know." *Clouds. Dark clouds.*

They were both quiet as the sun continued to fade, but Charlotte turned toward Hannah when she heard her crying. With her face covered, Hannah said, "Every time I come here, I look toward the sky for some sort of sign that Ethan went to heaven. I beg God to let me know that my Ethan is there with Him. But I see nothing. Not even pictures anymore."

Charlotte held her breath as an overwhelming need to comfort Hannah wrapped around her, but instead she just closed her eyes, knowing she wasn't going to see any formations in the clouds either. No answers. No visions. And no one to comfort her.

They were both quiet again, until Hannah sniffled and said, "Do you believe that Ethan is in heaven?"

Charlotte snapped her head to the side until she was eye to eye with Hannah. "If there is a heaven, Ethan is there."

There was no mistaking the confused expression on Hannah's face. "What do you mean, Mary? *If* there is a heaven?"

Charlotte was so tired of lying. It took way more energy than telling the truth, and one tiny web of lies was turning into a thick nest of betrayal. "Don't you ever wonder? Don't you ever doubt or question if there really is . . . a place we go after we die?"

Hannah didn't look like she was breathing as she

stared at Charlotte. "*Nee.* Not once have I wondered about that."

"Then why are you questioning if Ethan is there?"

Hannah's chest rose and fell as she drew in a deep breath, then let it out slowly. "Because some people don't think you will go to heaven if you take your own life." She turned to Charlotte again. "And I can't imagine being in heaven without Ethan."

Charlotte didn't know what to say so she refocused on the clouds as they shifted across the sky, and eventually Hannah did too.

After a few minutes, she could see a picture forming, as if an artist with a brush was creating a painting right in front of her. When she realized what it was, she put a hand over her mouth so she wouldn't gasp, but she couldn't control the tears filling her eyes. She bolted upright, shaken, but never more thankful. *Ethan is in heaven. There must be a heaven.* Charlotte wanted to shout it from the rooftops, but Hannah would want to know what she saw and how Charlotte could be so sure Ethan was with God. Then her cover would be blown.

Hannah sat up quickly. "What did you see?"

Charlotte did what she did best. And told another lie.

After supper, Charlotte had struggled through the nightly devotions with Hannah and the rest of the family. Now that she was tuned in to the possibility that there was a God and an afterlife, there seemed to be a giant overhaul of her soul underway, and it was painful and unwelcome. She thought back to what Ryan had said. *When a person first begins to develop a relationship with God, it's like a cleansing of the soul or something.*

Charlotte had no doubt that she needed a life overhaul, but at what cost? She pulled her knees to her chest and pulled her oversize white T-shirt over her knees. Rocking back and forth on the bed, she closed her eyes and reminded herself why she was here. Then she forced herself to think about Ethan dangling from a noose, hanging from a tree in his yard. And that vision was enough to get her back on the course she'd set before she arrived, no matter how painful the truth might be. She found her yellow pad between the mattresses and got comfy.

August 28

The Plain People seem to pride themselves on separating themselves from the world because of their unwavering faith in God, but what happens when one of their own takes his or her own life? Will that person go to heaven? Did Ethan go to heaven? Apparently, the Amish debate this question like many other religions. Hannah is really struggling with this, and I believe that her grief about Ethan is real, but I can't help but wonder what goes on behind closed doors here.

Charlotte paused. She'd had enough counseling to know that just because her childhood had been horrible, that didn't mean there weren't good people in the world. Her parents' way of raising children wasn't the norm.

She thought about what she saw in the clouds today.

I'm choosing to believe in God. I'm choosing to believe that Ethan is in heaven.

But if that was the case, Charlotte wondered if she would ever see her brother again. She was pretty sure there wasn't a reserved seat for her on the other side of the pearly gates.

Charlotte knew about the fund that the Amish all contributed to for medical needs, and she wondered if Ethan should have seen a counselor, and if that option had ever been offered to him.

Putting the pad beside her on the bed, she stretched her legs out in front of her, leaned against her pillow, and picked up her cell phone. When Ryan answered, she filled him in on the day.

"So, do you believe in signs?" she asked him after she told him what she'd seen in the clouds.

"I don't know. I think God sometimes gives us signs. Faith means believing in what we can't see, and God doesn't have to prove Himself. But, I have to admit, it's pretty cool that you saw that."

Charlotte still wondered if she'd created the formation in the clouds just by wishing it to be so. Or was it the sign she'd asked God for?

She jumped when she heard a noise that sounded like it was coming from outside. "Hey, I gotta go. I hear something out in the yard. I'll call you tomorrow."

Charlotte shined her flashlight on the wood floors and tiptoed to the window. She waited until the light from the propane lamp caught the shadow running through the yard and wasn't too surprised to see that it was Jacob. She'd been right when she thought she'd heard the front door opening late at night. Apparently, Amish and English teenagers had something in common.

6

Hannah stood next to her mother at the kitchen window. Mary had rushed to the barn when she saw Isaac pulling up in his buggy, and now they were smiling and laughing.

"Isaac must really like Cousin Mary. She told me that they are going on a date tomorrow." *Mamm* kept her eyes glued to the two of them, which was probably a good thing because she didn't see Hannah scowling. "I think it's wonderful that Isaac is starting to date again. He's spent so much time tending to his parents; he deserves someone special in his life."

"*Mamm* . . ." Hannah folded her arms across her chest and struggled to keep the agitation from her voice. "First of all, Mary won't be here very long. And did you know that Mary was the one who asked Isaac out?"

Her mother didn't pull her gaze away, but smiled. "I think that's just fine."

Hannah shook her head. "I don't know how you can say that. It's not appropriate." She moved away from the window, poured a cup of *kaffi*, and sat down at the kitchen table to read *die Botschaft*. She took a sip as she caught up on posts from relatives in Indiana. Anything to take her mind off of Mary and Isaac. After a few moments, her mother joined her.

"How are you and Mary getting along?" Hannah's mother pulled out the chair across the table from Hannah, but instead of coffee, her mother was sipping on goat milk, not a beverage Hannah enjoyed by itself.

Hannah marked her spot with her finger and shrugged. "We get along fine." She recalled Mary's comment about heaven. "She's different. And I still don't think a woman should ask a man out on a date. I know the *Englisch* do that sometimes, but that doesn't make it right."

"Hannah. If I didn't know better, I'd think you were jealous."

Hannah dropped her jaw. "*Mamm!* That is not true. I am still grieving for Ethan. And besides, jealousy is a sin."

"And we all sin from time to time," her mother said as she put a hand on Hannah's. "I know how much you loved Ethan, but it's been a year, Hannah. If you have an interest in Isaac, you need to talk to Mary about it since she is only here visiting."

Hannah started shaking her head as tears filled her eyes. Even all this time later, she felt guilty for considering the feelings she might have for Isaac.

Her mother leaned against the back of the chair and took a long sip of milk. "Ethan would want you to be happy. He would not begrudge you going out with Isaac. We all know that Isaac is a wonderful man."

Hannah blinked her eyes a few times as guilt and sadness turned to anger, which was possibly brought on by jealousy, making her mother right. But Hannah was not about to admit it. "No matter the situation, Isaac and Mary are going out tomorrow, and I think we owe it to both of them to see if they might have a chance together." She heard the words leap through her lips and knew it was the truth, but they left a bad taste in her mouth.

"The Lord might have put Mary in your life for a reason, Hannah. You've withdrawn so much since Ethan's death, and I think sometimes people avoid you because they don't know what to say."

Hannah knew this to be true. Even her closest friends kept their distance these days. "Maybe."

"I would like Mary to stay longer. I mentioned it to her in passing, but the subject hasn't come up again. She's already been here a week. It seems like she just got here yesterday. You know, her great-aunt and uncle aren't living anymore. And she doesn't have anyone courting her." *Mamm* took a sip of the thick milk, and it left a white mustache. Hannah smiled and pointed to her own upper lip. *Mamm* chuckled as she dabbed at the spot. "How would you feel about that?"

"I'm sure she has people in Texas to return to, but it's up

to her." Sometimes Hannah could feel a friendship forming, and maybe with more time, she'd grow even closer to Mary. Or would her cousin only grow close to Isaac?

Mamm sat taller, put her palms on the table, and smiled. "I will talk to her later." She nodded toward the window. "Maybe more than a friendship can grow and she'll end up staying here."

Hannah scowled. "*Mamm*, they're just talking."

Her mother raised an eyebrow. "You just never know who the heart will choose. Who God will choose." *Mamm* stood up and pressed her hands together in prayer, closed her eyes, and looked toward the ceiling. "I'm going to pray that both of them will find true love if it's God's will."

Hannah forced a smile, then walked to the window. Mary and Isaac were still talking. Maybe they would choose each other.

Hannah wrapped her hand around the back of her neck. *Who will ever choose me?*

Isaac chuckled at another one of Mary's stories. She'd surely experienced things that Isaac couldn't imagine, but it made him want to travel to Texas someday—to see longhorns, bluebonnets, and maybe even a cowboy. And he'd sure like to try one of the *kolaches* Mary spoke of, fluffy pastries with sweet fillings like poppy seed, prune, and apricot.

"And your *mamm* never found the baby armadillos?" he asked when Mary was done with her tale.

"Nope. My friend and I raised the four babies in an old doghouse in the backyard. They looked like pink little rats, but what could we do? They didn't have a mother." Mary looked away as she blinked her eyes a few times. The friend was Ethan, but she didn't think she should mention that she had a brother since none of Hannah's family thought she had any siblings. "That was a long time ago."

Isaac studied her for a few moments. She was pretty with golden-blond hair framing a tanned face peeking from beneath her bonnet, and she had deep-brown eyes. But when he glanced toward the house, he found himself wishing Hannah would come outside. He couldn't help but wonder if he'd read Hannah's expression wrong at the furniture store when she'd avoided making eye contact with him. She'd fidgeted with the string on her *kapp*, as if maybe she was bothered that Isaac would be going on a picnic with her cousin.

He wondered what kind of community Mary came from, where it was okay for a woman to ask out a man.

"Um . . . since you already visited our furniture store, are you . . . are we . . ."

"I would still love to go on a picnic." She took a step toward him as she spoke, smiling. Isaac glanced at the King farmhouse again, but all was quiet.

"*Gut.* Okay."

86

Isaac wanted to straighten Mary's prayer covering. It was always lopsided. But he didn't want to embarrass her.

She raised both eyebrows and smiled until tiny dimples formed on her cheeks.

"And remember, I said I'll bring the food."

They settled on a time, and Isaac went on his way, back to the store. It had been so long since Isaac had been out with a woman, he couldn't help but feel a little anxious. Even if he did wish that it was Hannah he'd be spending the day with.

Charlotte helped Hannah set the table for lunch—*dinner,* she reminded herself—while Lena finished running the clothes through the wringer washing machine.

"*Mamm* said she mentioned you staying a bit longer with us." Hannah made the statement in a way that Charlotte couldn't decipher. She wasn't sure if Hannah wanted her to stay. Would Lena or Hannah want to stay in touch when Charlotte went back to Texas? She hoped not. With each passing day, she felt worse about the lies, and to keep in touch would just be continuing the deceit.

"Oh. I don't want to inconvenience y'all." She cringed, wishing she'd remember to sound more Amish.

"It wouldn't be an inconvenience," Hannah said as she placed a fruit salad on the table. "*Mamm* enjoys having you here."

Charlotte pondered the comment.

The screen door in the living room slammed. Amos and Jacob were home for lunch. The familiar smell of sweat, manure, and hay wafted into the kitchen with the men, although it was a fraction of the odor they'd bring in at the end of the day. Despite their straw hats, both father and son sported a bronze tan, although Amos's face had a web of wrinkles from years of outdoor work.

Jacob didn't strike Charlotte as the poster child for the Amish. Not only had she caught him sneaking out of the house a couple of times, his hair was longer than most, and he rattled on about politics, space, movies, and places he wanted to go—most notably to the moon or Mars. And such conversations always drew criticism from Lena.

After they'd all prayed, Jacob said, "I bought a telescope with the money I've saved working side jobs." The sixteen-year-old sat taller and raised his chin, seeming to know that at least one of his parents would challenge him. Amos spoke up first.

"What is this telescope? A phone?" Amos bit into a slice of bread, and Charlotte hurried to nab her own piece.

"It's an instrument to look into space," Jacob answered with a mouthful of chicken.

Charlotte was aware that Amish kids were allowed some liberties when they turned sixteen. Supposedly, it was a time for them to experience the outside world, then decide if they wanted to be baptized into the Amish faith. Although, she couldn't imagine why anyone would stay here when there was an entire world, away from buggies and primitive living, to experience.

"*Nee*, that is a luxury," Lena said firmly. "What do you think the bishop would say?"

Charlotte had seen the bishop at their church services, but the way everyone talked about this guy, he was judge, jury, and executioner, so to speak.

"There is nothing wrong with me wanting to educate myself about the world we live in," Jacob said defiantly enough to draw a scowl from his father. *Go Jacob*, Charlotte thought.

"You have all the schooling you need," Lena said, huffing out the words. "I hope you didn't spend much on this space seeker."

Charlotte fought a smile and stuffed more bread in her mouth.

"It's my money to spend." Jacob spat the words out like any normal teenager.

"You return it. We don't need such worldly things here." Lena sat taller and sighed loudly.

"*Nee*, I'm not. It's coming on the package truck. And I'm keeping it."

Amos laid his fork noisily on his plate, which was still half-full of chicken, potatoes, and green beans. "You will watch your voice with your *mamm*." After directing the comment to Jacob, Amos turned to Lena. "He can keep the space seeker. He saved his money, and it won't hurt anything."

"*Nee*, Amos. What if the bishop sees it? What use is it? Why should he dabble with such things, and—"

"Stop, Lena." Amos's voice was firm as he spoke to his wife, and Charlotte held her breath for a few moments while she waited for Lena to counter. But Lena was quiet.

Huh . . . she'd learned something new about the Amish folks today. *The man of the house runs the show.*

Hannah sat up in bed, lit her lantern, then opened the drawer of her nightstand. She pulled out the cedar box with a few keepsakes from Ethan, things she hadn't buried. Even though pictures weren't allowed, she and Ethan had taken one of themselves a few weeks before he died. Their day at the Allentown Fair was one of Hannah's fondest memories, and from high up on the Ferris wheel, Ethan had held out his phone and snapped a picture of them. A flash of light lit up their faces against the darkness of night behind them. If only she could have known that only a short time later, her Ethan would be gone.

Why, Ethan? Why? She'd asked herself hundreds of times. They'd had their entire future to look forward to, and Hannah had been certain God had blessed her beyond her greatest hopes. She took out the two dried roses, the first ones Ethan had given her, ones he had grown himself. She thumbed through other keepsakes, expecting the familiar tears to build, but lately, her grief had taken a new turn. Anger. How do you love someone, commit to a lifetime with them, then leave without saying good-bye, not even a note? Nothing. Just word from a neighbor that Ethan was dead, that he had hanged himself. And now Hannah had to live with that image in her mind. Although, she was sure it wasn't as bad as the vision that Big Johnny Stoltzfus would have to carry around, since he was the one who found Ethan. She missed Ethan, but he hadn't only ended his own life, he'd taken a part of Hannah's too.

She was putting everything back in the small box when she heard a voice, and since sleep wasn't coming this evening, she picked up the lantern and eased her bedroom door open. She could see a light coming from beneath the door in Mary's room. Tiptoeing, she made her way down the hallway and knocked lightly.

"Mary, are you awake?"

"Yeah, just a minute."

"No, no, no," Charlotte whispered as she looked at her watch. She'd just finished applying the hair color she'd brought from home. Since she might be here at least another three weeks, she decided to fix her hair tonight while everyone slept. Someone was bound to notice her roots any day now—they were so obvious to her.

She was thankful for the prayer covering. She always

had her hair done at a salon, so she had no idea how to match just the roots, which is why she'd applied the dye over all her hair. Hopefully, this would be a shade of blond she could live with and that no one would notice a difference. Twice, Hannah had almost caught Charlotte without any head covering. She was sure Amish women didn't color their hair. She'd seen plenty of the women with full heads of gray hair, many who didn't even look like they'd reached forty yet.

Hannah often wore just a scarf over her head at home, and sometimes nothing at all when she was inside the house. Same with Lena. When both of the women had asked why Charlotte never took her prayer cap off, she said she wasn't comfortable doing so around Hannah's father and brother. She had no idea what the rule was, but it was all she could come up with at the time.

Ugh. Dye was going to get all over the towel, but as she wound it around her head, she decided to worry about that later.

"Hey, what's up?" she asked as she pushed the door open a few inches, shining her flashlight toward the ceiling.

"I'm sorry. I thought you took a bath earlier." Hannah held the lantern up a little higher and stared at Charlotte through the opening.

"I did. I'm just . . . well, just . . . soaking my hair."

Hannah cocked her head. "*Soaking* your hair?"

Charlotte opened the door a little wider and forced a toothy smile that she hoped might look genuine. "Oh, it's just something to make my hair shiny." She knew vanity was looked down upon, and once again, she was kicking herself for not choosing her words more carefully. "Not really shiny, just manageable. It tangles easily."

Hannah crinkled her nose as she waved a hand in front of her face. "*Ach*, it doesn't smell very *gut*, does it?"

"No. It's pretty stinky." Charlotte cleared her throat, wondering why she hadn't thought this through.

"I can't sleep and wondered if maybe we could talk."

Charlotte was just about to concoct another lie, excuse, something—when Hannah added, "I want to talk about Ethan. Something is bothering me."

"Okay." She eased the door open, glad Hannah was ready to discuss Ethan, but nervous too. She took three quick steps backward when Hannah came closer with the lantern.

"*Ach*, I'm sorry. I can snuff it out."

"No. It's okay." She sat on the side of the bed closest to the window, and Hannah put the lantern on the dresser across the room before she took a seat on the other side of the bed.

Charlotte waited, her head tingling from the dye. She turned the flashlight off and placed it on the bed. From where it was on the dresser, the lantern cast only shadows on the two of them. But that was okay. Charlotte didn't need the open flame any closer.

"Do you need to go do something with your hair?" Hannah pushed her thick, dark hair over her shoulder.

"No. *Nee*. It's fine. It has to set." She scratched her forehead. "For management. I mean, to be manageable." *Good grief. This is so exhausting.* "Anyway, you said you wanted to talk about Ethan?" She folded her legs underneath her and hoped she was ready for whatever Hannah was about to share.

"*Ya*. My feelings about Ethan have started to change lately. For some reason, I'm feeling angry at him. I've prayed for God to keep this anger away from my heart, but at times, I'm more mad than hurt. And I'm just not sure how to feel about that."

Charlotte's bottom lip trembled. Hopefully, Hannah couldn't see it in the darkness. "Why are you angry?" She heard the way she spat the words. Hannah may still be grieving Ethan's death, but Charlotte hadn't cleared Hannah of somehow being involved, even if only emotionally.

Hannah lowered her head. "*Ya*, I know. I am ashamed for feeling this way. But Ethan left me. He left me alone here, loving him and unable to be with him. Why would a person do that to someone they loved?"

Charlotte was trembling all over now as she recalled Ethan's last letter to her, still wondering if Hannah had broken Ethan's heart. She shined the flashlight directly in Hannah's face. "What happened, Hannah? Why do you think your fiancé killed himself?" Charlotte held her breath as her heart pounded. This was it, the purpose of her trip, if Hannah trusted her enough to be honest.

Hannah hung her head, shaking it back and forth as she sniffled. "He ended things with me. I have no idea why. He told me he wasn't worthy of my love, called off our wedding, and he was dead two days later."

Charlotte waited for Hannah's words to register, then forced herself to breathe. "What?"

"It just didn't make any sense." Hannah stood up and paced in the shadows between the glow from the lantern and Charlotte's flashlight. "When I tried to question him about it, he just left me standing in the middle of his living room and ran out the door. It was the last time I saw him."

As much as Charlotte hadn't wanted to visit Ethan's house, that might be the only place she would get some answers because obviously Hannah was as confused as Charlotte. "I'm so sorry, Hannah." Her stomach clenched as she thought about the way she'd been feeling lately. "You have a right to be angry. It's an awful feeling not to understand why someone you love would do this."

Hannah stood up, pulled a tissue from the pocket of her white robe, and dabbed at her eyes. "I feel like I can't move forward, like I'm stuck until I know what caused Ethan to do this." She picked up the lantern and held it up. "It's been a year. When will it stop hurting?"

Charlotte hoped she wouldn't burst into tears. Hannah wasn't her enemy, she was her ally. She shook her head and whispered into the dimly lit room. "I don't know."

Charlotte had an overwhelming urge to make a full confession. But tomorrow was lunch with Isaac, and maybe he had more information. Although, wouldn't he have already shared anything he knew with Hannah? This wasn't the time to add more grief on Hannah, so Charlotte opted to stay in the role she'd chosen, at least for now.

Hannah excused herself and made a hasty exit. Charlotte glanced at her cell phone to check the time—noticing she only had two bars left—then she sat on the bed to wait ten more minutes until her hair would be done. She'd been so wrong about the woman her brother had intended to marry, and she was more confused now than ever.

Finally, it was time to wash out the color. She eased her bedroom door open and tiptoed down the hall. As she fumbled in near darkness, she set the sink faucet to warm and did her best to rinse her hair by the light of her flashlight, trying desperately to sort things out in her mind.

But as she rewrapped her head in a clean towel, she couldn't help but wonder if she would find the answer at Ethan's house.

*C*harlotte picked up her cell phone from the nightstand and checked the time. *Ugh*. Not only was she
late for breakfast, but she was going to need a trip to town
soon to charge her phone somewhere. It was still dark
as she fumbled with the flashlight, then pulled a dark-
blue dress over her head, followed by a black apron. She
twisted her hair into a bun and put the prayer covering
on, opting to skip brushing her teeth until after breakfast.
She knew that Lena and Hannah would clean things up
right after the men finished eating, and Charlotte didn't
want to miss out. She could hear forks clinking against
plates, so she picked up the pace as she shined the flashlight down the stairs and breathed in the aroma of bacon.

"I'm sorry I'm late again," she said as she eased into
her chair and reached for a slice of bread. She was just
about to take a bite when she realized they would all be

expecting her to pray, so she bowed her head and closed her eyes. *I wish I knew You. But even though I don't really, maybe You can help me find some sort of peace about Ethan. And I'd like to pray for Hannah to have peace in her heart also.* It was the first prayer she'd said in a long time. During devotions, she'd mostly just listened, and that had been hard enough.

When she opened her eyes, no one was eating, and all eyes were on her. She grinned. "What?" She dabbed at her chin, swiped at her eyes, and wondered if there was something on her face. Then Jacob burst out laughing.

"Your hair is *green*!"

Charlotte reached up and touched the patch of exposed hair that always showed even with the prayer covering on. "What?" she said in a whisper as she glanced at Hannah, then at Lena. She'd washed the dye out in almost total darkness last night and the sun wasn't up yet this morning, but as always, the kitchen was well lit with lanterns hanging above the table and on the counters.

Hannah brought a hand to her mouth, covering it as her eyes grew round as saucers. Even quiet Amos was staring. Charlotte scooted back from the table so fast, the chair hit the wall. She fumbled with the flashlight, trying to turn it on, and ran through the living room, darting up the stairs two at a time. She didn't stop until she was in front of the mirror in the bathroom, and as she tore her prayer cap off, she pointed the light toward the mirror. She was speechless.

"We will fix this," Hannah said when she caught up to Charlotte, breathless as she lifted the lantern she was carrying. "But we must hurry before your picnic with Isaac later today." She shook her head, frowning. "Your stop-tangle tonic must not have worked like it was supposed to."

"My hair is *green*." Charlotte pulled the pins from her bun, allowing her hair to fall halfway down her back. She glanced at Hannah, who was standing with one hand on Charlotte's shoulder. "I finally have a date . . . and my hair is *green*." There hadn't been a shortage of dates in her life, but it had been awhile—so long that she couldn't even remember the last guy she'd gone out with. She'd just sort of shut down after Ethan died.

Charlotte bit her lip and held her breath until she couldn't stand it any longer. She shook loose of Hannah's hold and bent over, bursting with laughter. After she'd laughed until she had tears in her eyes, she stood up and faced off with the woman she'd been so wrong about. At first, two deep lines of worry appeared between Hannah's eyes and she shook her head. But after a few moments, she started laughing too.

"It's not funny," Charlotte said as she turned to the mirror again, but within seconds, her stomach started to hurt from holding in her giggles. When she finally composed herself, she could see in the mirror that Lena, Amos, and Jacob were all standing behind them, mouths gaping. Lena slowly eased around Hannah to Charlotte, raising her lantern higher.

"Mary, it wonders me what has happened to your hair, but I'm sure that something can be done." Lena's soft, consoling voice only caused Charlotte to laugh harder, which seemed contagious to Hannah. "I don't think the bishop would object to you going to one of those *Englisch* places that does hair," Lena added.

After another moment, Charlotte and Hannah finally pulled themselves together and convinced the others it was okay to leave. Once they were alone, Charlotte looked at Hannah for a long moment, and again, she wondered what it would have been like to have Hannah as a sister-in-law, to be a part of this family, had Ethan allowed it.

Without giving it much thought, she pulled Hannah into a hug. "I'm glad I'm here." It felt good to be truthful. She slowly eased away and grinned. "Even if I do have green hair."

"I'm glad you're here too." Hannah chuckled. "Even if you do have green hair."

Charlotte felt like she was about to start crying again. And not tears of laughter. It had been a long time since Charlotte had made a genuine friend, and it saddened her that her growing friendship with Hannah was built on nothing but lies.

Isaac tucked in his shirt, pulled his suspenders over his shoulders as he made his way downstairs, and he was almost out the door when he heard commotion from his parents' bedroom. Sighing, he glanced at the clock on the mantel, not wanting to be late for his picnic with Mary. He strained to hear what his mother was saying, but the volume of his father's voice bellowed above hers.

"Get out of here, woman. I don't need your help, and . . . I don't need *you!*"

Isaac couldn't ever recall hearing his parents fight prior to his father's cancer. Isaac had always respected his father as a faithful man who was a good provider for his family. He had a kind soul and gentle spirit. Until recently.

His mother burst out of the room crying, then halted when she saw Isaac. She grimaced after stubbing her toe on an uneven slat on the wooden floor. "I'm sorry you overheard that." She leaned down to have a better look at her toe, but quickly rose and then straightened her back. "I'm still trying to make your father do more for himself, but it wonders me why he is so resistant. I shouldn't have coddled him for so long; I should have forced him to do more on his own. And now . . . it's just hard to change things."

Isaac wanted to encourage his mother to stay strong and keep doing what she was doing, but he hated hearing his parents fight, and it was difficult to see his mother crying so much. "I know. I wish he tried harder too." Even more bothersome for Isaac was the change in his father's personality. The meanness that had crept in. The darker his father's behavior, the more Isaac thought about Ethan and the depression he'd seemed to be battling.

His mother sniffled, blew her nose, then gave her head a quick shake as if to clear any unpleasant thoughts. "Never you mind. You go on your picnic with Mary. We will be just fine."

Isaac took a few steps toward his mother. "Are you sure? I can cancel and go another time."

"*Nee, nee.*" She waved a hand toward the door. "You go. Everything will be fine."

Isaac hesitated, but he thought about how many times he had canceled plans with friends to take care of his parents, especially his father. But this time, he nodded and left.

On the way to pick up Mary, he thought about the distance growing between his parents. It made him uncomfortable, but also sad for them. He hated to see his mother so exhausted from tending to his father, but Isaac was growing more and more upset about the way his father was treating his mother.

Mary was on the porch when he pulled up in his topless spring buggy. The elders referred to it as a courting buggy, although it had been awhile since Isaac had used it for that purpose. He was prepared to get out and go to the door to get Mary, but he hadn't even come to a complete stop before she came skipping down the porch steps carting a picnic basket. She stowed it in the back and jumped into the buggy before Isaac had a chance to help her.

"I hope you like tuna salad. I made it myself. But not with eggs. I don't like hard-boiled eggs. But I eat them sometimes." She drew in a breath. "I also brought potato salad, also without the hard-boiled eggs. And pie. Coconut pie. Oh, and . . ." She took in a long breath. "That's probably too many salads. But there's bread. And chowchow, and . . ."

It was obvious she was nervous, but Isaac couldn't get past the new color of her hair. When she finally stopped talking, all he could manage was, "Your hair . . . is . . . dark now."

She brought both hands to either side of her head. "Yes. Uh, *ya.* My hair. It's a long story."

Isaac wanted to hear the story, but Mary blushed, bit her bottom lip, and cringed, so he let it go, clicked his tongue, and backed up the buggy. He wanted to reach over and straighten her *kapp,* but he didn't.

What is wrong with me? This wasn't even a real date, and yet Charlotte had never rambled on in such a way. She recalled a friend telling her that she had to have frequent dates so she wouldn't get out of practice. She hadn't bought into that theory—until now. But she couldn't help but smile as she thought about her circumstances. If anyone had told her that she would be going on a picnic with an Amish man, she would have never believed it. Taking a deep breath, she reminded herself why she was spending time with Isaac and that whether or not he took a romantic interest in her didn't matter. Probably best if he didn't.

"I brought iced tea too," she finally said as Isaac clicked his tongue again, pushing the horse into a steady trot. At the main road, they took a right. "I've never been this way. Hannah always goes to the left, toward town."

"She, uh . . . probably doesn't go this way on purpose." Isaac spoke softly, so much so that Charlotte could barely hear him with the wind in her face and the horse hooves clopping against the asphalt.

"Why not?" Charlotte kept her eyes on the handsome man beside her.

He nodded to his left. "That's where Ethan lived."

Charlotte couldn't breathe all of a sudden, as if someone had their hands around her throat, and she found herself gasp for a breath of air as she stared at the blue frame house with an overgrown lawn. She fought to control the quiver in her bottom lip. "Oh," was all she managed before her mind drifted to Ethan. She forced her thoughts into order and slowly said, "Do you know why—why he took his life?" Charlotte knew now that Hannah didn't have anything to do with it, but she still wanted someone to be accountable.

"It's hard to understand why a man would do such a thing." Isaac glanced at Charlotte, frowning. "But Hannah loved him very much. And he hurt her." He shook his head. "A cowardly thing to do."

Charlotte fought the urge to defend her brother. "Where are we going?"

"There's a park about a mile down the road." He turned to her and smiled this time. "*Englisch* mothers are sometimes there with their *kinner*, but it's pretty and shaded."

Goodness me. The man did have a smile that could melt a girl's heart. Someday, there would be a lucky Amish woman who would snag this guy, but Charlotte just planned to enjoy the view. It didn't sound like he would be able to offer up any new information about Ethan, but she'd try again later.

"That sounds good—*gut*. I like to watch children playing. Laughing children make a person feel good—*gut*."

Isaac nodded and turned into the park. Sure enough, there were several women with their children over by the slide and jungle gym. Isaac steered the horse and buggy to the far side of the park where there was a picnic table. "This okay?"

Charlotte nodded as her stomach rumbled. In the distance, a mother squatted at the end of the slide, waiting for her son to slide into her arms. The scene was postcard material, and as Charlotte looked on, she thought about her own family. What if she and Ethan had been raised by loving parents in a normal household? Would things have turned out differently for Ethan? For her?

⌒⌒

Hannah was hanging the last towel on the line when she heard a buggy coming down the road. She picked up the empty basket and raised her hand to her forehead, squinting to block the sun.

Edna Glick. Another one of Hannah's friends who hadn't come around much since Ethan's death. In truth, Hannah had withdrawn into her own little world, so she couldn't fault others for not wanting to be around her. She was thankful for Mary. Her cousin seemed to have an understanding about Ethan's death, and even though she hadn't said so, Hannah suspected Mary must have lost someone very close to her also.

"*Wie bischt,*" Edna said as she crossed the yard toting a wicker basket. Edna was known for her glazed apple cookies. Hannah couldn't remember the last time she'd had one.

"I'm sorry I haven't been by in a while." Edna stopped in front of her and smiled. "I've been spending a lot of time with John."

Hannah had heard rumor that Edna and John Dienner were going to get married, though they hadn't published it for the community to know yet. Edna was twenty-three, and most folks were surprised it had taken this long for them to get engaged. They'd been dating for a long time.

"It's fine," Hannah finally said as she eyed the basket, hoping for the apple cookies.

"These are for you." She held the basket out for Hannah. "It's a new recipe that I found in *Mammi*'s old recipe box. Cinnamon sticks. Very tasty." Edna smiled, and with her tiny dimples and small stature, she looked much younger than she was.

Hannah took the basket. "*Danki*, Edna. This is so nice of you. Jacob likes anything with cinnamon, and I know we will all enjoy these." Hannah tried to recall the last time she'd baked anything as a gift. Maybe next time she carted Widow Hostetler to town, she'd bake something for her. Then she remembered the potholder she'd finished knitting for Mary, but forgotten to give to her. "Do you want to come in for iced tea?"

"*Nee.* I must be on my way, but I wanted to bring you these, and I also wondered if you would be at Sisters' Day next week." She paused, looked down, then locked eyes with Hannah after a few moments. "Everyone really misses you."

Hannah fought the urge to cry. She hadn't been to the monthly gathering since Ethan died. And she had to admit, it felt good that she'd been missed. "I would like to go. I want everyone to meet our cousin Mary who is visiting from Texas. Did you meet her at worship service?"

Edna shook her head. "*Nee*, but I saw that your family had a guest. I meant to introduce myself, but your *mamm* was making the rounds with her, and I didn't get a chance. It would be nice for her to meet everyone next Thursday."

Hannah thanked Edna again, then headed toward the house, munching on a cinnamon stick as she walked. The glazed apple cookies now held second place to this tasty treat. She'd stash a few somewhere that Jacob couldn't find them. Maybe a late-night snack for her and Mary.

As she walked up the porch steps, she wondered how Mary's date with Isaac was going, but she couldn't help but wonder if things would have turned out differently if Isaac's father hadn't taken ill. Would Isaac have eventually asked her out? Would she have ever met Ethan? She knew better than to question the Lord's plan for her life. But there was no denying that the idea of Isaac and Mary together bothered her, even if she wasn't comfortable sharing this new feeling with anyone.

Isaac ate a little bit of everything Mary brought, although it had been a challenge. Not only were there no eggs in the tuna salad, but there was way too much relish and hardly any mayonnaise. And he wasn't sure why she'd brought potato salad to accompany the tuna salad, but it was just as bad. Maybe mothers didn't teach their daughters to cook in Texas. Or maybe they ate differently there. He was scared of the pie, but it actually turned out to be wonderful. When he commented on how great it was, Mary said Hannah had baked it. This wasn't surprising. Hannah was a good cook. Any man would be blessed to feast on her cooking on a regular basis.

Mary talked a lot. Sometimes it seemed like nervous chatter, but Isaac couldn't fault her. He hadn't been out on a date in a long time, so he'd been a bit anxious in the beginning too. She explained how she became Amish when she was nineteen, so that explained a lot. Especially her inability to speak their language.

"I like your hair that color," he said as she was packing up the leftovers, which were plentiful.

"Thank you." She smiled. "I mean, *danki*."

Isaac waited for her to tell him why she'd changed it, but when she didn't, he decided to ask. "What would make you change it?" He wasn't even sure if that was allowed.

Mary fell into a story about a hair product she'd used on her hair to make it easier to manage. She had long, thick hair, so that made sense. Then she told him about showing up at breakfast, not realizing it had turned her hair green, and they'd both laughed.

Mary was a pretty woman, but they didn't seem to have much in common. She said she didn't enjoy gardening, and Isaac thought of tending the land as a gift, a way to provide without having to rely on outsiders. And he'd discovered she didn't like to cook either, which explained today's meal.

She'd asked a lot of questions about Ethan, and it had been a challenge to answer her truthfully without giving up information he wasn't comfortable sharing. He thought he'd done pretty well sidestepping some of her inquiries. But he had a few questions of his own.

"It wonders me how Hannah is doing. Do you think she is ready to move on with someone else, or is she still grieving? We always hear that time heals, but they appeared to be so in love . . ."

Mary put the thermos of tea she'd brought into the picnic basket, closed it up, and set it aside. "I think the thing that bothers Hannah the most is not knowing why her fiancé took his life. She said it's hard for her to move forward not knowing the truth."

Isaac swallowed hard. He hated that he knew why, and he briefly wondered if he should tell Mary, who would most likely tell Hannah. But he just couldn't bring himself to. He couldn't decide if the truth would hurt Hannah even worse.

He tried to follow up with a few more questions about Hannah, but Mary wasn't sharing information either.

Charlotte folded up the blanket she'd brought and stood up. She'd learned one thing for certain on this lunch date. Isaac knew something about Ethan that he wasn't sharing. He'd danced around the issue without giving a direct answer to most of Charlotte's questions. She didn't think he was lying; he was just being evasive.

"This was nice," she said as they walked toward the

buggy. Isaac was easy on the eyes, but he wouldn't have been someone she could date even if they were both Amish or both English. They didn't have much in common. He enjoyed working on his land, building things, and eating. She liked to read books—and a host of other things she couldn't share with him—like having her hair and nails done, shopping at the mall, dinner at nice restaurants, makeup, and clothes that didn't make her look like a granny.

On the ride back, they were both quiet, but when they passed by Ethan's old house, Charlotte couldn't pull her eyes away. She would go there soon. It was a tiny house, so that must have been the reason Ethan had bought the pretty tract of land where Hannah had taken her. She wondered if Hannah had packed up Ethan's belongings. Where was she storing his things?

By the time Isaac slowed the buggy to a stop at the place she was calling home for now, she noticed that all three buggies were gone, so Lena and Hannah must have each traveled somewhere separately since she knew Jacob and Amos had left early that morning for construction supplies.

So, her date with Isaac wasn't all she'd hoped it would be. But it hadn't been a total bust. Maybe she didn't know why Ethan killed himself, but Isaac definitely knew something. And Charlotte had no doubt that Isaac had feelings for Hannah. He'd tried to act cool asking questions, but he hadn't fooled her.

Isaac stepped out of the buggy and walked around to her side. He offered her a hand stepping down.

"*Danki* for bringing the picnic. It was nice getting to know you." He looped his thumbs in his suspenders and smiled.

"It was very nice getting to know you too." She took the picnic basket and blanket when he handed them to her, and she caught him look over her shoulder twice toward the house. She considered telling him that Hannah wasn't home, but she didn't want to embarrass him. "We should do this again." Charlotte grinned. "But I'll get Hannah to help me with the food."

Isaac's face took on a flush anyway. "*Nee*, it was, um . . ."

Aw, it's sweet that he doesn't want to lie. He could be a good influence on her. "It was awful," she said, then laughed. "All but the pie."

She was trying to figure out a way to find out what else he knew, but he spoke up first. "Do you want to do this again next Saturday?"

Charlotte raised an eyebrow. "Um, yes. *Ya.* That would be nice."

"*Gut.* Then it's a date." He turned, gave a quick wave, and Charlotte watched him head down the driveway until he was out of sight.

"Uh oh." She shook her head, wondering if she'd read him wrong. Maybe all the questions about Hannah had just been to keep the conversation going. Maybe Charlotte had unintentionally led him on and now he was interested in her. It had been a long time since any man had shown an interest in her, so there was an air of flattery swirling around, even if he was Amish. She walked to the house with a bounce in her step.

8

Hannah hurried to the couch when Mary turned and headed toward the house. It had been impossible to pull her eyes from Mary and Isaac, and even though she felt guilty for watching them say good-bye, she couldn't help but wonder if he would kiss her, even if just on the cheek. Relief washed over her when that didn't happen, which only confused her more. She quickly reached for a gardening magazine on the coffee table and began thumbing through it.

Mary rushed into the living room, but stopped abruptly. "Oh. Hannah. I didn't think you were here. Where's your buggy?"

Hannah closed the magazine and placed it on the table as she sat taller. "I let Jacob borrow it. At the last minute, *Daed* needed him to deliver a piece of furniture while *Daed* went for supplies. *Mamm* had a checkup at the doctor."

"I thought you didn't like to loan Jacob your buggy because it leaves you without wheels."

Wheels? Hannah felt a flash of annoyance at Mary's Texas slang. "I'm not going to deny him use of it when he truly needs it." She could hear the clipped tone in her voice, so she took a deep breath and made her expression more pleasant. "How was your date?"

"Pretty good, I guess. He's a super nice guy." Mary sat down in the rocking chair against the far wall and pushed with her feet, kicking the rocker into motion. "We're going on another picnic next Saturday so I guess he had fun too."

Hannah picked up the magazine again and started flipping the pages. "*Ach, gut.* I'm happy for you."

They were quiet for a few moments.

"Um, you don't sound happy for me. You sound all out of whack about it." Mary crossed one leg over the other as she kept rocking.

"Why do you do that? Talk that way. It isn't appropriate."

Mary stopped rocking. "How is the way I talk inappropriate?" Her cousin frowned as she folded her arms across her chest and uncrossed her leg.

Hannah raised one shoulder and dropped it slowly, but she didn't look up and kept flipping pages in the magazine. "I would think that you would try not to use so much slang. Maybe try learning more Pennsylvania *Deitsch.*" She finally looked up at her cousin. "I don't think you should talk the way you sometimes do. It's not the way a proper Amish woman speaks. We don't say things like that. I know you didn't choose to be Amish until you were grown, but respectfully, you should behave in a way that represents who we are."

Mary rose from the chair, took a step forward, her head tipped to one side. Hannah braced herself, prepared for a lashing. But instead, Mary was quiet for a few moments, then said, "You're right. I'm sorry. I'll try to watch the way I speak."

Hannah let out a heavy sigh before she stood up. "*Nee*, it's okay." She shook her head as she searched for an explanation about her bad mood, but there was only one thing bothering her. And it didn't have anything to do with the way Mary talked. "I've just been having a rough day. Uh, Ethan. He's . . . been on my mind." *Oh dear Lord, forgive me for the lie.* Hannah realized that this was the first day in a long time that she hadn't thought of Ethan, making her fib that much worse.

Hannah was all worked up, but Charlotte suspected it didn't have anything to do with the way Charlotte was talking—or Ethan. As she sat back down in the rocker, she leaned back and settled into a slow motion, wondering if she should tell Hannah that Isaac had spent much of their time together talking about her. But Charlotte was confused now that Isaac had asked her out for next

Saturday. She didn't want to get Hannah's hopes up, and it also felt disloyal to Ethan if Charlotte encouraged anything between Hannah and Isaac. Charlotte would be gone soon enough, but she wanted one more chance to get some more information from Isaac since he'd clearly been holding back. She was still pondering Isaac's intentions when Hannah stood up.

"I have something for you, Mary. Can you wait here while I get it out of my room?"

"Okay." Charlotte couldn't imagine what it might be, but a minute later, Hannah came back down the stairs with her hands behind her back, and she was wearing a glowing smile as she approached Charlotte.

"These are for you," Hannah said as she extended her hands from behind her.

Charlotte accepted the beautiful pink-and-red potholders and tried to corral her emotions into a place that made sense. She was sure that Hannah was jealous, a bit ticked off at her, yet she chose this moment to do something nice for Charlotte.

"Did you make these?" she managed to ask before swallowing back a lump in her throat.

"*Ya*. I had planned to use them after Ethan and I were married, but I had one left to finish when he died. I finished it the other night for you." Hannah's smile quickly shifted to a frown. "Are you okay?"

"Yes. I mean, *ya*." Charlotte stared at Hannah for a while, trying to figure her out. And trying not to cry. Not only was it a lovely gift, but it was something that had sentimental value. "These are truly beautiful, Hannah. *Danki*."

"If I behaved badly, Mary, I'm sorry. It isn't fair for me to begrudge anyone love or romance just because I don't have it in my life anymore." She squatted down in front of the rocking chair where Charlotte was still sitting. "I will hope and pray that things work out for you and Isaac."

"Oh, no no. *Nee*. It's not like that. I see us more as friends."

Hannah wasn't jealous of Charlotte and Isaac . . . Hannah was jealous of the situation and regretful that she didn't have anyone in her life. Charlotte had been so wrong about Hannah, and she could see why Ethan loved her so much. Charlotte had another impulse to make a full confession.

"Sisters' Day will be soon, Mary. I would like for us to go together. I haven't been in a long time, and it would be nice for you to meet some of the women that you didn't get to meet at our worship service."

"Sisters' Day?" Charlotte wondered if there would be more praying. This soul cleansing was wearing her out.

Hannah stood up and folded her hands in front of her. "Usually, we have Sisters' Day once a month. Don't you have it in your community in Texas?"

Charlotte had never heard the Amish ladies in Beeville mention it. "Um. No. *Nee*, we don't."

"It's a time to quilt, can vegetables, or work on other fun projects. Sometimes we visit a shut-in and clean their house or cook for them." She smiled. "And it's always a time to find out what's happening in our community." Whispering, she added, "Gossip."

"Gossip?" *That's allowed?*

Hannah sighed. "*Ya,* gossip. Everyone knows it's wrong, but it finds its way into conversations. Usually, it's about an upcoming wedding, teenagers who are starting to date, or things like that. But every once in a while . . ." She grinned. "We hear something we didn't expect. It wonders me, is there no sharing of tales in your community?"

"*Ya.* I guess so."

"*Gut.* Then it's a date." Hannah pressed her palms together in front of her, smiling again. "I'm going to go ready up my bedroom, then I'll be down later, and if you'd like, we can start supper." Hannah moved toward the stairs, then took them two at a time.

Charlotte just sat there. In the rocking chair. In this surreal world that was nothing like she'd imagined.

Hannah dropped to her knees, folded her hands, and put her elbows on the bed as she bowed her head. *Lord, forgive me for my lie. And I ask that You forgive me for any ill will I might have shown Mary. Jealousy is a sin, and I've felt*

it seeping into my heart, especially now, since I'm finding myself angry with Ethan. But Lord, I hope and pray that Ethan is there with You, that You took mercy on his soul.

She stood up, sat down on the bed, and put her hands in her lap. It was hard to understand what she was feeling. She'd spent a year swallowed up by sadness, and now unwelcome emotions like anger and jealousy were slipping into her heart. Hannah reached up and touched her lips. Closing her eyes, she thought about all the kisses she'd shared with Ethan, and how wrong it was to feel attraction toward another man. After three years, Isaac was finally stepping out to date, and he'd chosen Mary. Maybe Mary would choose to stay here, a possibility her mother had mentioned.

She lay back on the bed, her thoughts shifting between Ethan and Isaac. She'd been very much in love with Ethan. And she'd grown up with Isaac. She could recall the many times she'd caught him staring at her over the years, and she'd always wished things could have been different. Isaac was kind. And brave. Hannah recalled an accident during a barn raising. Isaac had been the first one to climb to the top of the structure to help Jake Beiler, who had slipped and broken his foot. Isaac was only a teenager at the time.

Hannah closed her eyes and prayed that God would keep jealousy out of her heart.

Charlotte waited until the following Saturday to visit the small, blue-framed house with the overgrown lawn. She hadn't told Hannah she was leaving that morning, fearful Hannah might want to come along. It had been a long walk uphill to her brother's house.

After she caught her breath, she eased the waist-high gate open and walked into the yard as gnats buzzed in the tall grass all around her. She wondered why no one had mowed the yard recently.

She walked slowly up the sidewalk, careful of the deep cracks in the concrete every few feet. Turning the doorknob, she was relieved to find the house unlocked. As she pushed the door open, a rank odor shot up her nose, and she recognized the smell right away. *Skunk.* She stood at the threshold trying to decide whether or not to go in, but she recalled the skunk she'd dealt with a few years ago before she'd moved to a high-rise. It came by most days and sprayed the outside of her apartment building, a place outside of the city and near some woods. That's probably what was happening here, so she pinched her nose and left the front door open as she moved into the living room. A green lizard clung to the window on the far wall, illuminated by the sliver of sun shining onto the dusty hardwood floors.

Charlotte moved slowly about the room, still clenching her nostrils. A dark-green couch, two wooden chairs, and a small round coffee table were the only furniture in the room, unless you considered the potbelly stove in the corner. There were piles of boxes against the far wall. She eased into the kitchen as perspiration clung to her maroon dress and sweat beaded on her forehead. It took a few minutes to force open a window in the kitchen, but the hot air outside didn't do much to dissipate the skunk odor inside.

No electricity, of course. No air conditioning. More boxes were on the floor in the kitchen. A thick layer of dust covered the white kitchen counters. She crossed back through the living room, then pushed open the only other door she saw, which led to Ethan's bedroom. There were clothes piled up in the corner and the unmade bed was piled with boxes that were half-full. It looked like someone had stopped in the middle of packing.

Charlotte pulled back the flap on one of the boxes. She ran her hand across the high school emblem on the front of the yearbook before she picked it up and put it on the bed. As she thumbed through keepsakes from the past, she wondered if Ethan had been packing things up to make room for Hannah until their house was built. Or maybe Hannah had packed this after Ethan died. That seemed a more likely scenario. Maybe he was packing to go back home to Texas since Hannah had said he broke up with her. She moved to the next box, which was already open and filled with plastic glasses.

What happened, Ethan? She put one of the boxes on the floor, dusted off a spot on the bed, then sat down. The smell of skunk wasn't as bad in this room, but it was just as hot. She went and opened a window before she returned to the bed. Sighing, she glanced around, not knowing what she hoped to gain by being here. All it was doing was making her sad.

She decided to leave, but stopped short of the bedroom door and paused at the four-drawer chest against the wall. The top drawer was half-open and she could see underwear and socks inside. The second drawer was filled with folded T-shirts. Shirts that wouldn't be allowed here, but ones that represented Ethan's life and travels. She picked up the one with a picture of the Alamo on the front and recalled Ethan telling her that he and a group of guys were enjoying the Riverwalk in San Antonio and a trip to the Alamo. She flipped through Ethan's memories—Port Aransas, Galveston, Freeport. Then she got to out-of-state shirts from New York City, Atlanta, and New Jersey.

She reached back into the drawer and took out the T-shirt from Port Aransas. She and Ethan had gone to visit a distant uncle there. She could still remember her mother driving them, hoping that Uncle Phil would take them in, but he hadn't been in good health. That had been right before they were placed in different foster homes. Charlotte wanted a keepsake of Ethan's, but she stuffed the shirt back in the drawer, deciding that trip wasn't a time she wanted to remember.

She was crossing the threshold back into the living

room when she felt an invisible nudge to turn around and go back. The closet door was cracked a few inches, so Charlotte reached for the knob and opened the door wider. More boxes. She scanned the small area until her eyes landed on a mothball box in the corner, and Charlotte felt like she'd struck gold as she hurriedly reached for the box. Her heart raced as she picked it up. The box felt empty. But she opened one end and turned it upside down. A single photo fell onto the floor.

She picked up the picture and studied it. The potbelly stove was in the background, so she knew it had been taken in Ethan's house. But who was the woman in the photo? She was Amish, dressed in the traditional clothing, and holding out her palm, smiling—almost as if she didn't want her picture taken, but playfully allowing it.

Charlotte looked closer at the picture. She didn't recognize the woman. But sometimes, it was hard to tell the ladies apart since they dressed so much alike. Disappointed to not have found anything else, she started to put the photo back in the box, but on habit, flipped the picture over first. Written in blue pen was: *To my one and only. I love you* . . . in neat cursive.

She'd planned to snoop in an effort to find out more about why Ethan took his own life, and she hoped this process might help her to face her grief. But she never expected to find something like this. The skunk smell, along with this finding, was starting to overwhelm her, so she stuffed the photo in the pocket of her black apron, tossed the empty box back into the closet, and sprinted toward the front door.

But when she got to the porch, company awaited her.

9

Charlotte hurried down the road back to Hannah's, thankful it was a downhill trek. She held her breath as much as she could. She'd tried not to move when she'd met her visitor on the porch, but that didn't stop the black-and-white intruder from spraying her from head to toe. There were two things in life that Charlotte couldn't stand to smell. Hard-boiled eggs and skunks. Over the years, she'd learned to tolerate the eggs, but she would never get used to this smell.

Once the house was in view, she picked up the pace. Jacob was in the front yard, and as Charlotte got closer, she could see that his telescope had arrived. He waved as she got closer, but Charlotte stopped a good ten feet away from him. When Jacob grimaced and pinched his nostrils, she realized that she should have hung back even farther.

He rattled off a string of Dutch that Charlotte didn't understand, but he ended with a chuckle. "You're going to need a tomato bath." He let go of his nose and waved a hand in front of his face.

"Tomato bath?" Charlotte remembered that she had a date with Isaac later in the afternoon.

"*Ya*. That will help take away the smell." He laughed again. "I would ask you to come look through my telescope, but maybe, uh . . . after that bath."

Charlotte hung her head. Something in the universe was working against her when it came to Isaac. First the green hair, now this. She waved to Jacob and headed toward the house. Hannah met her on the porch.

"I was wondering where you were," Hannah said, but then her eyes grew round and she backed up until she was against the side of the house. "Skunk!"

Charlotte couldn't help but grin while she walked up the porch steps. "I went for a walk. Jacob said I need a tomato bath. Does that take the smell away?"

Hannah pinched her nose. "*Ya*. I will go gather some tomatoes and see how much sauce we have. *Mamm* usually keeps some store-bought sauce for unexpected guests or emergencies." She grinned. "And this is surely an emergency."

"Ugh. Tomatoes don't sound nearly as good as that goat-milk stuff your mom makes to put in the bathwater. I'll get out of these clothes while you find everything." Charlotte moved toward the screen door.

Hannah burst out laughing. "*Ach, nee!* You can't come in. There is an old claw-foot tub in the barn." She pointed behind Charlotte. "*Mamm* makes *Daed* and Jacob bathe outside when they are really dirty, and Jacob met up with a skunk once too. Come to think of it, maybe that's why Jacob doesn't like tomato sauce!"

Charlotte turned toward the barn, then back to Hannah. "You expect me to take a bath in an old tub in the barn?"

Hannah smiled. "Of course." She spun around and went inside.

Charlotte sat down on the porch step, longing for a spa day back in Houston, followed up by a nail and toes appointment, then finishing off at the hair salon. Getting her hair done was a necessity in her mind. The spa day was something she sprung for after she'd finished a big project. She was going to consider this entire endeavor one big project. She took a deep breath, but nearly choked on her own smell, so she held her nose and waited.

This was one bath she was not looking forward to.

About ten minutes later, Hannah supplied her with several jars of tomato sauce, some fresh tomatoes, and a water hose, and Charlotte trudged to the barn in the wake of Hannah's giggles.

She filled up the claw-foot tub, dumped everything in, then stared at the red water with clumps of tomato floating on top. After glancing around the barn, she eased one foot into the cold water, then slowly lowered herself in. Wearing nothing but her prayer covering, in an effort to keep her hair up and away from the water, she tried to relax. But this experience would forever remain in the top five grossest things she'd ever done.

After her soak, she tucked her head into the crook of her arm. All she'd done was add the aroma of tomato sauce to the skunk smell. One day she'd laugh about this. This was not that day.

After Googling other remedies to get rid of the smell, she asked Hannah to help her concoct a solution using hydrogen peroxide and baking soda. Two baths later, she could finally tolerate herself, but she wasn't going to torture Isaac by exposing him to the smell, albeit faint, of skunk pizza. So she called and canceled their picnic, hoping he wouldn't be too upset.

Isaac had surprised himself by asking Mary to go on another picnic, but he enjoyed her stories, and it would've been nice to be away from his parents and all the fighting. He was a little disappointed when she canceled, although he could certainly understand why. Even though he was more interested in spending time with Hannah, Isaac didn't think she was ready to date. Just the same, his friendly interactions with Mary made him feel a little guilty. He didn't want to lead her on.

"I caught the tail end of your conversation with

Mary," his mother said, walking into the living room. "That's terrible that she got sprayed by a skunk."

Isaac scratched his head. "*Ya*, I know. She must have scared the animal or something while she was on her walk. They aren't normally aggressive." Now that he had the day to himself, he was wondering what to do. "Where's *Daed*?"

"I don't know." His mother pushed one shoulder forward, tipped her chin down, and closed her eyes for a few moments. She held the expression long enough to make her point, then sighed. "I'm just glad he's not inside this house. It's *gut* for him to be outside busying himself."

Isaac looked out the window, but saw no sign of his father. "I hate it when the two of you fight," he finally said when he turned back to her.

"We never used to." She sat on the couch, still clutching a towel she'd brought from the kitchen. "But his cancer has been in remission for a while. I've tended to him from the beginning, and I sympathize that he lost his leg. But he didn't lose his life, and he needs to be grateful to the Lord for that, not bitter and constantly saying he is now half a man." She twisted the towel until it looked like a pretzel. "It's my fault. I should have encouraged him to do more from the beginning."

Isaac could still recall when his father was diagnosed. They'd all been devastated to learn he had bone cancer in his right leg. And even worse was the fact that *Daed*'s affected area was too large to be able to save his leg. Isaac sat down beside her. "What can I do to help?"

His mother twisted to face him and pressed her lips together as she slapped the towel to her leg. "Start the repairs on the *daadi haus*."

Isaac's jaw dropped a little. "*Mamm*. I don't know when I'll have time to . . ."

"Make time. What are you doing now? Nothing. Go down to the house and give it a good look-over and make a list of what needs to get done. You know that folks in the community will help."

It was a large undertaking. Isaac looked at his *mamm*. "Why now?"

Mamm chuckled. "Do you want to live here with us forever? Now that you're dating again, I think you need to make those repairs a priority so that your father and I can move there one day, as it should be."

He wanted to tell his mother that he wasn't exactly dating Mary, but this was the first mention of repairing the *daadi haus* in a very long time—years. This was his mother's way of encouraging him to find a *fraa*. He nodded. "Okay. I'll go find *Daed*. Maybe he'll want to help me."

"Or maybe he won't." *Mamm* put her hands on her hips. "Either way, *sohn*, I want you to work on that *haus*."

Isaac nodded again, then left to find his father. Sometimes, his *daed* went to the barn and smoked a cigar. His mother hated that habit, and sometimes Isaac thought that was the only reason his father partook in a practice that was known to cause cancer. Even though the type of cancer his father had was rare, smoking cigars wasn't healthy, and everyone knew it, despite the smoking that went on in barns before and after worship service.

He pushed the barn door wide and waited for his eyes to adjust. He spotted a figure facedown near a pile of hay. *"Daed!"*

When Isaac got to him, he fell to his knees and rolled his father onto his back, relieved when he opened his eyes. *"Daed*, what happened?" Isaac glanced at his father's leg. His prosthesis was attached. Isaac helped his father to his feet.

"I guess I must have tripped and hit my head." He pointed to the corner of his workbench as he ran his other hand across the back of his head. "Just a little bump, but enough to knock me out, I guess. *Gut* thing you came out here. Your *mamm* wouldn't have come looking for me."

There was such bitterness in his voice, Isaac almost cringed to hear him talk about his mother like that; the woman who had spent the last three years giving up so much of what she loved to make sure that his needs were met. Isaac couldn't recall the last time she'd gone to one of her quilting gatherings or to lunch at a friend's house. She used to read a lot too. The only thing she attended anymore was the monthly Sisters' Day.

"Daed, she would have come looking for you." Isaac brushed the dirt and hay from his pants. *"Mamm* wants me to work on the *daadi haus*, so I was wondering if you wanted to help me make a list so I can get started."

Scowling, his father shook his head. "We aren't taking on that project when there are so many other projects that need to be handled." He pointed to his workbench. "I have a list written down on that pad."

Isaac took a couple of steps, found the white pad of paper, and read:

1. Paint the back fence

2. Call the farrier

3. Replace boards at east end of porch and repaint porch

4. Take all money out of bank and put in new bank

Isaac paused, looked at his father. "Why are you moving your money?"

His father huffed. "Because the *Englisch* man at the bank is stealing it."

Isaac stared at his father for a few moments before he returned to the list. Mr. Franklin had been their business and personal banker for as long as Isaac could remember.

5. Replace cracked windowpane in the mudroom

Isaac hadn't even noticed that it was in need of repair.

6. Clean the fireplace

7. Chop up Anna Ruth before first freeze

Isaac's heart skipped a beat. *"Daed . . ."* He walked to his father and pointed to number seven. "Did you mean chop up *wood* before first freeze?"

His father chuckled, then broke into a full-belly laugh. *"Ya, ya.* Of course that's what I meant."

Isaac didn't laugh and went back to the list.

8. Take inventory at the furniture store

Phyllis and Tom had been doing inventory at the store for years, but Isaac kept reading.

9. Grease snow plow, general maintenance
10. Replace missing slat on east side of barn

Isaac set the pad down. *"Daed,* none of these are huge projects. I think we will still have time to work on the *daadi haus."*

His father shook his head. *"Nee, nee.* Chopping your mother up will take some time." He patted Isaac on the shoulder as he passed him and went out of the barn. Isaac sprung into step right behind him.

This time he would have to agree with his father. No time to repair the *daadi haus.* Isaac would be busy making sure his mother wasn't alone with his father.

Charlotte made her way up the stairs behind Hannah and Jacob. After devotions, they'd all splurged on a second piece of chocolate pie. Like the rest of them, Charlotte had eaten a piece following supper, but she didn't have the self-discipline to turn down a second helping when Jacob suggested it. She closed the bedroom door behind her and turned on the battery-operated fan. After she positioned it in front of the open window, she pulled her cell phone out of her purse.

"I was starting to wonder if you'd gone full Amish," Ryan said when he answered. "I hadn't heard from you in a while."

Charlotte had only talked to Ryan once since her date with Isaac. She'd told him then that she thought Isaac might know something about Ethan's death, but the conversation had ended abruptly when Ryan said someone was at his door. It was the first time Charlotte had wondered about Ryan's dating life. Was his visitor a woman? It had been a random thought, but bugged her a little just the same.

"Well . . ." She sighed as she plopped down on the bed and folded her legs underneath her. "I went to Ethan's house today."

"Hmm . . . I bet that was tough."

She thought for a few moments. "Did Ethan ever mention hiding things in an empty mothball box?" Charlotte pulled the picture from her apron pocket. "It's something we did when we were kids."

"No, why?"

Charlotte brought the picture closer to her face, then whispered, "I think Ethan might have been cheating on Hannah." She told him about her visit to the house and finding the picture. "Oh, and the price I paid for snooping . . . I got sprayed by a skunk and had to take a bath in tomato sauce in the barn." She brought her forearm to her nose and sniffed. "Then I took a couple more baths to try not to smell like a skunk pizza."

Ryan laughed.

"I thought you might find some humor in that."

"Yeah. Sorry. I just got a visual of you soaking in tomato sauce out in a barn." He paused. "But as for Ethan cheating, I don't know about that."

"Our dad was unfaithful to our mom, and Ethan swore he'd never be a cheater." She recalled her troubled childhood, then cringed. "But our mother was no picnic either. Oh, and speaking of picnics, I was supposed to go on another date with Isaac today, but I rescheduled, since I don't smell so great at the moment."

There was a long silence. "Oh. I thought that was a onetime deal."

Charlotte didn't want to play games with the one person in her life that she'd stayed truthful with. "I told you that I sensed he might know something. That's the only reason for a second picnic. Only thing is, I hope he won't think I'm leading him on."

"I'm not sure I've ever been on a picnic. If I have,

it was a long time ago and must not have been very memorable."

"It was nice. It was hot, but not like in Texas. It's not nearly as humid here."

"I hope he proves to be your answer."

She sensed some jealousy. "*He* won't be my answer. I'm hoping he *has* answers. I want to find out what happened so I can go home. It's going to be hard enough to say bye to these people. I guess I never saw that part coming—that I would grow to care about them."

"Are you going to tell them who you are before you leave?"

"I don't know. I don't think so. I was thinking maybe a letter when I got back home."

Charlotte fluffed her pillow behind her and kicked her legs up on the bed. "I wish I knew who the woman in the picture was. I'm trying to think of a way to ask Isaac, but he would wonder where I got the picture. I can't tell him Ethan's house. I'd just be adding one more lie to my long list, and it's already exhausting to keep up with them all."

"I know. I'll be glad when you get home and come clean with all of them."

Charlotte crossed her ankles. "I think under different circumstances, Hannah and I would have become good friends. She has something I'd like to have more of. Kindness." Charlotte paused, long enough for Ryan to interject, but when he didn't, she went on. "And of course, they all have this relationship with God that you speak about, and that continues to elude me. Although . . ." She was quiet.

"Although what?" Ryan said.

"Remember how we talked about a spiritual cleansing? I'm still getting that weird feeling. I feel it when they are saying devotions in the evenings, and I feel it sometimes when they are being so nice to me."

"That's the Holy Spirit, Charlotte."

She wasn't sure about that, but it provided an opening for what she really wanted to know. "I have a random question to ask you, Ryan."

"Shoot."

"Do you think Ethan is in heaven?"

Ryan was quiet for a while. "Are you asking me this because he killed himself?"

"Yeah, I guess so." She recalled what she saw in the clouds. "It worries Hannah that Ethan might not be in heaven." *It worries me too.*

"Well, I tend to think that he is, but there are plenty of people who would disagree with me. What do you think?"

Charlotte grunted and rolled her eyes. "I'm sure I'm the last person to weigh in on this, but I want to believe that Ethan is in a good place."

"Then pray about it. Pray for his soul."

Charlotte thought for a few moments. "Does that work?"

Ryan chuckled. "What? Does prayer work? Or will it get Ethan into heaven?"

"Both, I guess."

"Prayer works, Charlotte. God answers our prayers. He doesn't always answer them the way we might want Him to, but He hears us, and ultimately everything He does for us has purpose. Will praying for Ethan save his soul? I honestly don't know, but Ethan was a good man, and I choose to believe that he is with the Lord. And Charlotte . . ."

"I'm still here." She stared out at the setting sun as tears pooled in the corners of her eyes.

"Sometimes people have mental illnesses that we aren't aware of. You know that Ethan suffered on and off from depression."

"I know. So did I. But I never once thought about killing myself." She sniffled. "See, it's happening again! The waterworks, that weird feeling."

"Let Him in, Charlotte. He's knocking, and all you have to do is open the door."

"Maybe I'll just crack a window for starters," she said, only half kidding.

"Hang in there, sweet girl. I'm here for you. But I do think you need to get straight with these people, tell them who you really are. The Amish are known to be incredibly forgiving."

"I know. I remember how they forgave the guy who shot all those schoolchildren. And to this day, I don't understand how they could forgive him. I still think it would be easier to come clean in a letter, but for now, I'm hoping to find out who the woman in the picture is. I'll pay more attention at the next worship service and see if I can find her. Although, I tend to tear up there too." She sighed.

"All will be well, Charlotte. Pray."

"Despite what you might think, I have been praying. I'm 99 percent sure I'm not doing it correctly, but I'm trying."

"Sweet dreams, Charlotte."

After they'd hung up, she started to cry. Maybe it was the spiritual cleansing Ryan spoke of. She was sad about Ethan. The burden of all her lies was weighing her down. But at the core of her feelings was a desire to really belong somewhere, to have a family like Hannah's.

But when they learned the truth, would they forgive her? Ryan said they would, but it was a chance she wasn't ready to take.

10

C harlotte nodded and smiled as Hannah introduced her to the ladies at Sisters' Day. Lena followed up by telling everyone that Charlotte was baptized into the faith as a teenager, and that she didn't know much Pennsylvania Dutch. Charlotte had already met some of the women at church service, but it was hard to remember names.

"And this is Edna Glick," Lena said as she introduced the petite brunette that Charlotte instantly recognized from the picture. She was even wearing the same color dress, dark green. Even beneath the baggy dress, it was apparent that this Amish woman had a great figure, and when she smiled, she was truly beautiful, even in the plain clothes and with no makeup. Charlotte reminded herself not to judge before she knew the facts.

"Edna is engaged to John Dienner," Lena said, still

toting a coconut pie she'd brought. "They will be getting married in November. I'm glad you finally published the news. We're so happy for you."

"Congratulations. How long have you and John been dating?" Charlotte asked, thankful for the opportunity to get to know a little more about Edna.

Edna waved a hand in the air. "A long time. *Ach*, I've lost track." She glanced to an older woman standing to her left. "A year and a half, *Mamm*?"

"*Ya*. About that long."

So, what were you doing at my brother's house while you were dating this other guy?

Charlotte searched her mind for a way to bring up Ethan. She wanted to see Edna's reaction, but Lena and Hannah might think it odd. And Hannah was still fragile talking about Ethan. Charlotte didn't want to say anything to upset her. She thought about how much things had changed over the past three weeks—how much she had changed.

After the ladies had put their dishes on the kitchen table, Lena motioned for everyone to gather in a circle within the spacious living room. Charlotte quickly gave the room a once-over, noticing right away that it was more decorative than where she was temporarily living. Two colorful floral couches sat on either side of the room—pink, yellow, lime green, and pastel blue. An antique china cabinet took up most of the third wall and was filled with white china and serving dishes. And there were several decorative vases on the mantel above the fireplace. It didn't look very Amishy to Charlotte. She wondered who enforced the rules. The bishop, she supposed. *He must not get out much.*

They bowed their heads and prayed. Just thinking about God made Charlotte feel like she would explode with emotion, so she heeded Ryan's advice. *God, please don't let me cry. Whatever is happening, I'm trying to get on board, but I wish I understood why I'm reacting like this.*

Hannah had already told her that the agenda for today was to plan a schedule for tending to the elderly for the next few months, and each of the ladies had also brought copies of a favorite recipe to share. Hannah had brought her recipe for cream of carrot soup, something Charlotte hadn't expected to enjoy so much when Hannah had made it last week. And Lena was sharing her recipe for rhubarb custard bars, another favorite for Charlotte. It was hard to find rhubarb in Texas, but it was plentiful in Pennsylvania, and she loved the flavor. At first, Lena had insisted that they would copy each recipe by hand fifteen times. But Hannah convinced her it would be so much easier to go to town and make copies. Charlotte had offered to bring a recipe of her own, but Lena and Hannah declined her offer so quickly that it solidified to Charlotte that she was indeed an awful cook. She only hoped that once she got home, she'd be able to perfect making their bread.

"I'm so glad you brought the recipe for the cinnamon

sticks, Edna." Lena flipped through the various recipes in her hand. "The family enjoyed the ones you brought us."

Charlotte cut her eyes in Edna's direction, wishing there was some way to pick her brain about Ethan.

Once they'd all exchanged recipes, the four children stayed in the living room and formed a circle on the floor as the adults moved toward the kitchen. When the children began to sing softly, Charlotte wished she could stay with them. It was the sweetest, most innocent sound. *Don't cry.* Good grief, this was getting ridiculous.

The women uncovered casseroles, put spoons in salads, and lathered butter on warm loaves of bread. Charlotte eyed the offerings, knowing that this was what she'd miss most when she went back to Texas. She flipped through the recipes hoping there would be one for the bread, but there wasn't, so she slipped them in the pocket of her apron and looked around. In contrast to the living room, the kitchen was similar to Lena's, bare except for plates stacked on one corner of the counter, along with silverware, napkins, and glasses. At the other end, four canisters, a hand can opener, and a lantern. Charlotte filled her plate to capacity and ate like she didn't have a weight worry in the world, knowing there would be a hefty price to pay when she got home.

After two hours of eating, making a visitation schedule for shut-ins, and even gossiping a little, Lena, Charlotte, and Hannah packed up.

"What did you think?" Hannah asked from the front

seat of the topless buggy. Charlotte had settled into the backseat when Lena took the reins in the front. "It still wonders me why you don't have Sisters' Day in your district. I thought all communities did this."

Charlotte shook her head. "No." She'd given up trying to use their dialect. She realized how easily lies can embed themselves into a person's psyche. "Like Lena said, I was glad that Edna brought her recipe for those cinnamon sticks." Maybe this would open up some conversation about the woman.

Lena clicked her tongue and set the horse into a steady trot. "*Ya*, 'tis a *gut* recipe, but I would change a few things." Charlotte wasn't surprised. Lena really was at the top of her game when it came to cooking. "I wouldn't use store-bought bread, even though I know that's easier. And I think that I'd flavor the cream cheese with pecans and honey. That would give the recipe a nice twist." She looked over her shoulder at Charlotte. "I make all of our cream cheese from goats' milk."

Charlotte wasn't sure she wanted to know the many uses for goat milk, but she nodded and smiled. She was stuffed, and these days, she was thankful for the baggy dresses, but also wondering if she was going to fit into her clothes when she got home.

"Edna seems . . . nice." Charlotte didn't talk to Edna long enough to know that, so she added, "I mean, since she brought you the cinnamon sticks awhile back, and she was friendly today. Are you good friends with her, Hannah?"

Hannah twisted sideways in the front seat and looked at Charlotte. Something in Hannah's eyes hinted that there was a story here, but Charlotte wasn't sure she was reading Hannah's expression correctly.

Shrugging, Hannah said, "We used to be very close, but after Ethan died, I stopped doing much, and my relationships with my friends suffered." She paused, sighing. "I just didn't want to hear about boyfriends, engagements, weddings, or anything like that."

Charlotte thought about the comment Ryan made early on, how Charlotte might be wrong about the Amish. No doubt, she had been. This was a loving family with genuine faith in a God that seemed to have blessed them abundantly. *I wish I could stay here. If only I wouldn't have to become Amish . . .*

"Mary, we're so blessed to have you here," Lena said, as if reading Charlotte's mind. "It wonders us if you might consider staying."

Charlotte sat taller. "Staying?"

Lena glanced over her shoulder and smiled. "*Ya.* Live here with us. I'm sure you have friends in Texas, but you said your aunt and uncle aren't living anymore. Maybe you would like to stay with us since we're your family too." She winked at Charlotte. "Just until you find someone to share your life with. Or . . . maybe you already have?"

"Uh, no." Charlotte frowned. "I haven't found anyone to share my life with."

"Does that mean you'll move here and live with us?"

Hannah was still twisted in the seat, and she pressed her palms together and smiled. "That would be so *gut*."

If Charlotte had predicted the outcome of this trip, she could have never come up with this scenario—that she would care for this family, become close friends with Hannah, and be offered a life here. "I-I don't know. I am enjoying my time here though."

"Just think about it," Lena said. "It's been so *gut* for Hannah, having you here, and of course, you're family. We all want you to stay."

The waterworks were threatening to spill. Again. Charlotte swallowed hard. She'd never had a real family, not anything like this. But despite the love and kindness that wrapped around her, this was not her world. Her life had electricity, hair salons, cars, and trendy clothes. She glanced down at her blue dress. "I don't know, but thank you for having me here, and for the invitation to stay."

Hannah reached for Charlotte's hand. "Maybe you will marry Isaac?"

Charlotte stared at her for a while as she recalled telling Ryan that she wanted more of what Hannah had—kindness. The woman seemed to have eyes for Isaac, but she would stow it and be happy for Charlotte if something developed between them. She wanted to tell Hannah that she should pursue something with Isaac, but not quite yet. More and more, it didn't seem disloyal to Ethan, especially after finding that picture. "No, no. It's not like that." *We have nothing in common.*

Charlotte stayed quiet, but the urge to fess up was bubbling to the surface again.

❧

Hannah had just finishing mending some of Jacob's trousers when she heard her mother throwing up in the bathroom. It was the second time this week. She set the pants aside and went to the downstairs bathroom that her parents used and knocked on the door.

"*Mamm*, are you okay?"

"*Ya, ya.*" Her mother opened the door holding a towel to her mouth, but quickly pulled it away. "Something I ate must not have settled well with me."

"Maybe you just have a bug. Is there anything I can get for you?"

Mamm shook her head. "*Nee.* But I think I will lie down for a while. I'll feel better after a nap." She brushed past Hannah, then turned around. "*Ach*, I haven't milked the goats yet this afternoon. Can you do that for me?"

"*Ya*, of course."

Hannah filled a bucket with warm water and had just gotten to the barn when she heard horse hooves. They weren't expecting anyone, and the buggy was too far away to see who was driving, so she got the first goat settled in the stanchion and began washing down the teats and udder. Lucy was her mother's oldest goat that was still giving milk, so Hannah always started with her since she knew the routine.

She listened to the sound of the buggy getting closer. She didn't want to interrupt Lucy's flow, but she also didn't want anyone knocking on the door and disturbing her mother. She kept her hands on the teats, alternating back and forth, occasionally breaking to blot her face with a towel. When she heard the visitor's buggy come to a stop, she strained her neck until she could see out the barn window.

"Isaac." She stopped milking when he walked into the barn. "You're not here to drop off more money already, surely. What are you doing here?" She noticed he was carrying a paper bag with handles.

"*Mamm* said your mother left some serving pieces and a dish at Sisters' Day, so I'm just returning them." He lifted the bag and smiled. "I saw you walk into the barn, so I wondered if this might be milking time."

Hannah pushed back sweaty strands of hair that had fallen forward and eased her legs closer together since she'd been straddling the milking bucket. "*Danki. Mamm* is napping, but Mary should be inside." *Although, she naps a lot too.* "Do, um . . . do you want me to go get Mary?"

Isaac shook his head. "*Nee, nee.* I just came to drop these off." He set the bag on the workbench, then pointed at the second opening in the stanchion. "Do you want me to help you?"

Hannah kept alternating her hands on the teats. "I'm sure you have plenty to do at your *haus*." It went so much faster with two people, though. Hannah always offered to help her mother, but *Mamm* loved her babies and enjoyed milking each one of them. Her mother must be feeling really bad to ask Hannah to do this.

Isaac picked up the other milking stool and set it in front of the second stanchion. "I don't mind."

Hannah paused, reached for the other bucket, and handed it to him, deciding to accept his offer. "It's not like milking cows, you know." She resumed with Lucy while Isaac slipped a lead over one of the other goats and escorted her to the stanchion. "That's Greta. Watch out for her. She lifts her leg and tries to kick, even with her head secured."

Isaac sat down, his leg brushing against hers as he straddled the bucket. Hannah swallowed hard as her heartbeat sped up. "Are you sure you don't want me to go find Mary?"

Isaac shook his head as he reached for Greta's teats. "What's different about milking goats?" He chuckled. "I've only ever milked a cow."

"It takes a lot more strength in your arms. Even though a cow produces more milk from twice as many teats, a goat's are much tougher, and . . ."

Hannah glanced at Isaac when she heard the first splatters of milk hitting the tin bucket. He just smiled.

"I think I got it."

"*Ya*, you do," she said almost in a whisper, instantly fearful that her voice might have sounded a bit suggestive, which surely hadn't been the intent. "I think it's so *gut* that you are starting to date. Mary is a lovely person."

"Isn't she going home soon?" Isaac didn't look up or stop milking, but Hannah did.

"Isn't that a strange thing to say about the woman you are seeing?" Hannah said, turning to face him.

Isaac also stopped milking. "It's not like we're really dating. Just friends."

"I'm not understanding." She resumed her milking, shaking her head.

"She's the one who asked me out first, and I know she is going home soon. I was just being nice while she's here and also trying not to hurt her feelings. But I'm probably going to have to cancel Saturday's picnic."

"Why?" Hannah hoped her relief wasn't obvious.

Isaac sighed as he filled his pail twice as fast as Hannah's. "It's *mei daed*. *Mamm* and I have been trying to do things differently lately. I think the *Englisch* call it 'tough love.' We've been trying to get him to do more for himself and not depend on me and *Mamm* so much."

"That's a *gut* thing, though." Hannah's forearms were getting sore.

"I know. And I was going to start working on the *daadi haus*." He turned to Hannah and smiled. "In case I want to get married someday, they'll have a place to live and still be close by."

Hannah felt herself blushing as she avoided Isaac's eyes. "That also sounds like a *gut* idea."

"But now, I don't know when I'll be able to." He stopped filling the pail, pushed back the rim of his straw hat, and looked at Hannah. "There is something really wrong with *mei daed*."

Isaac told Hannah a bizarre story about his *daed's* to-do list.

"The only reason I'm here right now is because *Mamm*'s sister, *mei Aenti* Rebecca, and her two *kinner* are here for a visit today from just north of Pittsburgh. If not, I wouldn't feel *gut* leaving *Mamm* alone with *Daed*." Isaac stood up, his pail full, then motioned for Hannah to get up. "Let me finish that for you."

"*Danki*." Hannah stood up and stepped aside as Isaac's large hands took over the task. "You don't really think he would . . . hurt your *mamm*, do you?"

"They've taken to arguing a lot, but I would never have thought so." He paused and looked up at Hannah. "Maybe he's *ab im kopp*?"

"*Ach*, maybe. To write what he did on that list sounds off in the head to me. Did you show your *mudder* what he wrote?"

"*Nee*, but I told her." Isaac blew out a long breath. "At first, she slapped a hand to her chest and her eyes got big. But a few seconds later, she burst out laughing and said I was silly to worry." He handed Hannah the full pail and stood up. "What do you think?"

"I don't know." She felt herself blush again. "Maybe ask Mary. She didn't become Amish until she was older. She is more worldly than us about some things."

Isaac took a step closer to Hannah, enough so that she was aware of the onions she'd had earlier on a sandwich. "I'd rather know what you think," he said in a whisper as Hannah gazed into his eyes.

They both turned toward the barn door when they heard it being pushed open.

"Hey, you two. What are y'all up to out here?"

Hannah picked up the other pail full of milk and started toward the door without looking at Isaac or Mary. "Isaac brought back some things *Mamm* left at Sisters' Day. They are on the workbench. Can you grab them, Mary, when you come in?"

"Sure."

Hannah squeezed through the partially open barn door, sloshing milk as she hurried across the yard toward the house.

She wasn't sure what had just happened, but she realized that another day had slipped by without her thinking about Ethan, and guilt wrapped around her like a jacket that was too small. Was she growing out of her grief? Was it time to move on? What about Mary? She put the two small pails in the reserved area of the refrigerator before she rushed back to the barn, hoping that she could make up for any thoughts that God might not approve of. She burst through the door, halfway expecting to see

Mary and Isaac in an embrace, but they were standing at least ten feet away from each other. They both turned to Hannah.

"I was just telling Mary why I can't go on our picnic." Isaac smiled, and even though both Isaac and Mary insisted they were just friends, Hannah needed to clear her conscience.

"*Nee*, don't cancel. That's why I came back. I will stay with your mother while you go on your picnic. You don't have to tell her. I'll just show up for a visit, and that way you won't have to worry about her."

Hannah held her breath as Mary and Isaac exchanged looks.

But Isaac finally said, "*Ya*, okay."

Somewhere in the back of Hannah's mind, she'd hoped he wouldn't accept her offer. But since he had, all she wanted now was a sense of peace about the entire situation.

She didn't have it. How could she move forward when something so tragic had happened to Ethan? Her cousin was dating Isaac, friends or more than friends, she wasn't sure, but still.

She walked to the house and as she came inside, she heard her mother vomiting again in the bathroom. Hannah hurried to her, putting her own worries aside.

11

Isaac hoped he didn't look as bored as he was. He'd gotten word to Hannah that his *aenti* had extended her stay, so it wouldn't be necessary for Hannah to visit his mother today. He couldn't constantly be with his mother, but for today, it gave him comfort to know she wasn't alone. He was trying to decide whether or not to talk to his aunt about his fears.

After he and Mary ate at the same park as before, she rambled on about her favorite books, none of which Isaac had heard of, a few movies she'd seen, and about space and something called a geomagnetic storm. Isaac didn't understand half of what she was talking about. It didn't matter, he was lost in thoughts about Hannah.

Then, out of the clear blue, she wanted to talk about Ethan, a man she hadn't even met. At least that was something he could comment on. But he wanted to be careful how much he said.

"*Ya*, I knew Ethan. Not real *gut*, but I knew him."

"Before I turned Amish, I had a hard life, but I still couldn't imagine taking my own life."

Turned Amish? Mary talked funny sometimes, but he knew why, so he tried to overlook it.

Mary blinked her eyes a few times, and Isaac thought she might start crying, which seemed odd. "Do you think people who commit suicide go to heaven?"

"I don't know."

"If he was going to marry Hannah, he must have been a good man. Surely he is in heaven now." Mary's voice cracked. She must have known someone who had taken his or her own life.

Isaac had plenty of thoughts about Ethan, but it wasn't his place to discuss any of them with Mary. "I would like to think he is." Isaac avoided her eyes as guilt nipped at him. Once again, he wondered if he should have reached out to Ethan when he suspected that the man was going through a hard time. "A believer's sins are forgiven at the moment of salvation, so as a child of God, I think all of our sins are forgiven."

"Technically, suicide is murder. Do murderers go to heaven?"

Mary seemed stuck on this subject, and she talked for a few more minutes before Isaac had a chance to say anything.

"'For God so loved the world, that He gave His only begotten Son, that whosoever believeth in Him should not perish, but have everlasting life.'" Isaac hoped that would end the conversation about Ethan.

"That's beautiful."

Isaac sat there, waiting for her to say more. It almost sounded like she didn't realize it was Scripture. *"Ya,"* he said softly.

"Well, I'm going to choose to believe that good people, who love and know Jesus as God's Son, go to heaven." Mary stared at Isaac, and he braced himself for more talk about death. "Have you ever known anyone who got shunned?"

Isaac just stared back at her for a few seconds, wondering how they'd gone from suicide to shunning. "Uh, *ya.* Of course. *Meidung.*"

"Why were they shunned?" Mary cupped her chin in her hand.

"For, uh . . . for marrying outside of the faith."

She nodded. Isaac wished they could land on a subject of interest to both of them, but she'd already made clear her thoughts about farming, cooking, and most things their people loved. "What made you choose to be Amish?" he said.

"Well . . ."

Isaac listened with a heavy heart as Mary told him about her troubled childhood. He felt badly for her. But when she got to the part about moving in with her great-aunt and uncle, it was almost like she was making it up as she went along. There was an air of falseness in her words, like when she talked about the washing machine flooding the garage and how she had to unplug it, which led to her getting shocked. Why were her Amish aunt and uncle using electricity?

Isaac's thoughts drifted to Hannah. Mary must have sensed that he was losing interest in the conversation because she stopped midsentence. But then Isaac heard a child screaming, and he realized that was what Mary was focused on.

They both looked toward the playground. The area was empty except for a mother who was spanking her toddler as the child wailed.

"She's spanking that boy too hard," Mary said, not taking her eyes off of the woman, her voice steady.

Isaac recalled his fair share of spankings with his father's belt, some even left welts for days. "I wonder what he did." Isaac stood up.

Mary glanced at Isaac, then back at the woman who continued to hit her child on the back of his legs and behind. "It doesn't matter what he did. He couldn't be older than three or four." She took off in their direction, and Isaac reluctantly followed. This wasn't their business.

Mary slowed her pace as she got closer to the woman. The *Englisch* woman had stopped hitting the boy, but Isaac cringed when he saw the red welts on the boy's bare legs. Mary pulled a tissue out of her apron pocket and casually tossed it into a nearby trash bin, as if that had been her plan from the beginning. Then she turned around and both she and Isaac headed back to the area where they were having their picnic. But the child began to wail again, and Mary did an about-face. She hurried to the woman, although Isaac held back a few steps.

"Ma'am, I don't want to get in your business, but I feel like you might be spanking that child too hard." Mary spoke in a gentle voice as she pointed to the boy's bare legs. Isaac noticed the red welts below the child's short pants. But he was surprised that Mary was getting involved since this wasn't their way.

The large woman with dark eyes scowled and spat, "This is *my* child, and I'm disciplining him for being disobedient. And you're right . . . it's not your business."

Mary took a deep breath, let it out slowly, and said, "I understand that you are trying to teach him, but you're hitting him too hard."

The boy was still crying and clung to his mother's leg as she placed her hand on his head. "You are scaring my son," the woman said. "Go away, please."

Isaac was familiar with how hard it was to walk away, to turn the other cheek. "Mary, let's go," he said, gently tugging on her arm.

"Listen to your boyfriend, and get out of here." She grabbed her son's arm, pulling him so hard that he fell down and started to cry again. "Shut up," she said as she gave him another pop on the back of his legs. "See what you caused?"

Mary looked up at Isaac, her eyes filling with tears.

"I'm sorry." She hurried to catch up to the woman, and before she reached her, she said in a loud voice, "He will remember this, you know. Your son. He will remember what you're doing to him."

Isaac followed her, shaking his head, asking the Lord to forgive them both for what he feared might be coming. But when Mary swiped at a tear rolling down her cheek, Isaac suspected this might have more to do with her own childhood than anything else.

The woman pried her crying child from her leg and walked up to Mary, pointing a finger in her face. Opening her mouth to say something, the woman stopped, looked back at her son, then at Mary. The woman fisted both her hands, and Isaac was sure that she was about to punch Mary. He wouldn't let that happen. But suddenly, the woman dropped her hands to her sides and stared at Mary. Seconds later, the woman shoved Mary so hard that she tumbled backward, catching herself with her hands.

"Stupid Amish woman."

Isaac stepped in between them, but before he or Mary could say anything, the woman walked back to where her child was standing. Isaac helped Mary up, but he had to grab her arm when she started to bolt after the woman.

"*Nee, nee*, Mary. Let her go." He kept his hand on her arm until the woman put her son in her car and they started out of the parking lot. "Your hands are bleeding," he said, releasing his hold and noticing her bloody palms. She'd skid her hands across some gravel when she fell.

"She'll hit him again unless she gets some counseling." Mary kept her eyes on the car until it was out of sight. "Or he'll get big enough to fight back." Isaac used his handkerchief to gently dab at the nasty scrapes on Mary's hands. She cringed but didn't pull away.

Isaac wondered what Mary would have done if he hadn't held her back. "She's a cowardly woman. She knew you wouldn't fight back." Isaac grinned. "At least she didn't think you would." He took another look at Mary's hands after he'd cleared off the gravel that was stuck to them, then gave her his handkerchief. "We need to get you home so you can properly tend these wounds."

Mary clasped the rag between her palms. He caught her wincing several times. They were halfway home before Mary spoke again.

"Isaac, I'm not going to be in Paradise much longer, so I need to speak freely about something." She glanced at her hands and cringed again before she went on. "So, here goes. We both know that while some people might consider what we're doing as dating, I think we both realize that there is nothing romantic going on here."

Isaac's pulse picked up. He'd never known anyone quite like Mary—someone so forthright with her feelings. He took off his hat and put it in his lap, then scratched behind his ear, wondering where she was going with this.

"You need to ask Hannah out. Anyone can see the way you two look at each other. She doesn't think she's ready, but she is. And I'm going to tell her the same thing." Mary raised an eyebrow as if she was waiting for Isaac to respond, but he had no idea what to say.

"But . . ." She held up a finger. "I need something from you, and I'm running out of time." She looked up at the sky and closed her eyes. Isaac wondered if she was praying. "I want you to tell me about Ethan. I know you know something. Did his killing himself have anything to do with Edna Glick? If Hannah is going to move on, she needs to know what happened."

Isaac realized he was holding his breath, but this was the last thing he ever predicted Mary would ask. She carefully reached into the pocket of her apron and pulled out a picture. She handed it to him, and once he'd studied the front, she turned it over in his hand.

"How did you get this photo?" He stared at the picture and reread the note on the back.

"It doesn't matter."

Isaac thought about how long he'd kept the secret about what he saw. He'd planned to take it to his grave. But if Mary believed that knowing the truth would help Hannah be able to move forward, then maybe it was time to talk about it.

Hannah busied herself tending to chores that she normally dreaded, but she wanted to keep herself occupied so she wouldn't think about Mary and Isaac on a blanket at the park. Her parents were enjoying a breezy Saturday afternoon napping, and Hannah had no idea where Jacob was. She ran the feather duster over the mantel for the second time, but eased her way to the window when she heard a buggy coming.

Sighing, she tried to force herself away, not to look when Mary and Isaac said their good-byes, but her feet were rooted to the floor. She waited, but there was no kiss before Mary stepped out of the buggy. Isaac walked behind her, and right before she got to the porch steps, she turned around and said something to him, then came up the steps. Hannah gasped when she saw Mary holding a bloody handkerchief between her palms.

Hannah rushed toward the door. "*Ach,* Mary! What happened to you?" she asked as the screen slammed behind Mary.

"I'll let Isaac tell you." She nodded outside. "I need to get cleaned up."

"Do you need help?" Hannah eyed Mary's hands as her cousin shuffled past her, shaking her head.

"No. I'm fine."

Hannah walked out on the porch just as Isaac was heading back to his buggy, but he turned when the door shut.

"What in the world happened to Mary?" She walked toward him, holding her palms faceup. "Did she fall down?"

Isaac shook his head. "*Nee,* but an *Englisch* woman pushed her down."

Hannah gasped. "*Nee!* What happened?"

When Isaac finished the story, he added, "Mary would have gone after the woman if I hadn't held on to her arm."

"Was the woman really beating her child like that?"

"It wonders me if *beating* is the right word, but she was hitting him hard enough to leave marks."

Hannah stared at Isaac, feeling like she was seeing him for the first time. She'd been so lost in her relationship with Ethan, then in her grief, she'd forgotten how much she enjoyed being around him.

She pulled her eyes from his. "I should go check on Mary." But Hannah's feet were rooted to the ground, and as she dug her toes into the cool, moist grass, Isaac smiled. She smiled back at him, feeling like they were communicating without words. She wondered if their hearts were saying the same thing.

Charlotte lay back on the bed, thankful her hands had stopped bleeding, but wishing the throbbing would stop. She'd have to be so careful when washing her hands and doing things around the house. Not that she did all that much.

"Wow, Charlotte. I'm so sorry," Ryan said after she told him what happened.

Charlotte sighed. "I can't believe she pushed me, but

it's probably a good thing Isaac kept me from going after her. She was considerably bigger than me." Cringing, she looked down at her hands. The left one was worse than the right. "But maybe she'll think twice before she hits her kid again."

"I bet your boyfriend was shocked, but I'm not surprised he kept you from going after the woman. The Amish are passive. They don't fight. Not even in self-defense."

"You know he's not my boyfriend."

"How much longer are you staying?"

"I'm not sure. But I was right about Isaac. He did know more about Ethan than he let on. When I told him that any information he had might help Hannah to move on with her life, he spilled it. Apparently, Ethan *did* cheat on Hannah. I don't know how frequently or for how long, but Isaac saw Ethan and Edna together when they thought no one was around. And get this. You'll never believe how he stumbled upon them." She took a breath. "Isaac delivered a piece of furniture to a customer in Lancaster, about twenty minutes by car. He'd hired a driver and took the hutch in a van. After they'd delivered the furniture, the driver asked Isaac if he wanted to get lunch before they headed back. They stopped at a restaurant—coincidentally, it was called Isaac's Famous Grilled Sandwiches. Isaac had never heard of it. So, imagine his surprise when he and the driver were walking to their table and he spots Ethan and Edna holding hands across a table."

"You're kidding."

"Nope. And neither were dressed Amish. He said Ethan was wearing jeans and a T-shirt . . . and Edna had on a dress, but her hair was down, no prayer covering. And she was wearing makeup." Charlotte grunted a little. "When they looked up and saw Isaac, they released each other's hands and avoided eye contact. Guess they thought their disguises in a place not frequented by the Amish might be safe."

"Did Isaac confront them?" Charlotte could tell Ryan was hanging on her every word.

"He said he just kept walking, but a few minutes later, Ethan found him, asked to talk, then begged him not to tell anyone."

"Wow."

"I'm so disappointed in Ethan," she said as her voice cracked.

Ryan was quiet for a while. "Well, we still don't really know what happened. Maybe it was a onetime thing. A secret lunch, a couple of stolen kisses. Maybe that was it."

"I don't know." She sniffled. "Isaac said Ethan tried to downplay it, but over the next few weeks, Ethan asked Isaac several times if he was going to tell Hannah." She was quiet as she thought about how it all played out. "And the thing is, Isaac told Ethan repeatedly that he wouldn't tell anyone. But there is no mistaking the way Isaac and Hannah look at each other. He could have told her, broke them up, and maybe had a shot with her." She took a deep breath. "I don't know, though, since Isaac has spent so much time helping out his parents with the house and yard." She couldn't control the tears anymore as she told him the rest. "Isaac said that he wasn't very close to Ethan, but he could tell that Ethan was depressed. He didn't know if it was because he loved Edna, didn't want to hurt Hannah, or what. Isaac was clearly harboring some guilt, feeling like maybe he could have helped Ethan. I tried to tell him Ethan was responsible for his own life, but it was so hard not to cry listening to these details. But I'm tired, Ryan. I'm tired of the lies. No matter what happened, nothing can bring Ethan back."

"Sweetie, don't cry."

Ryan's gentle voice just made Charlotte sob harder. "And I feel terrible for thinking Hannah might have been the guilty party. Ethan left her, for whatever the reason. And he left me."

Charlotte thought about her empty apartment at home, then glanced at the ivy growing in a planter by the window. There was nothing growing in her apartment. No pets to feed. "I know I need to get home and back to work. And the sooner I get straight with these people, the better I will feel," she said softly. "But the weather is so pretty here this time of year. And I feel like I'm a part of a real family. It's going to be hard to say bye to them all, especially since I don't know if they will want anything to do with me once they know the truth."

"Don't stay gone too long. I might start missing you."

Charlotte heard the flirtiness in his voice, so she dabbed at her eyes, sniffled again, then threw it back at him. "I think you already miss me."

"I was starting to, until you latched on to that Amish boyfriend."

Charlotte couldn't help but smile. "Yeah, well . . . whatever." She glanced at her bandages. "I don't think my scraped up hands are going to get me out of church service tomorrow."

"I thought you'd started to like going to their church services."

"I also like sleeping in on Sundays." Charlotte thought for a few moments. "Actually, I like the feeling I get when I'm there, the fellowship, but I don't understand most of it. During the devotions, the family speaks English so I can understand, but the bishop and deacons don't during the worship service. And it's always awkward when someone new comes up to talk to me in Dutch, and then I have to explain, again, about how I wasn't raised Amish. I've told the same lie so many times that I've started to believe it myself."

She reached for the box of tissues on her nightstand. *Empty.* She tossed the box on the bed and walked with her arms bent at her sides and cell phone held to her ear with her shoulder, carefully turning the knob on her bedroom door. "Hey, I better let you go. I need to go down the hall to get some more tissues from the bathroom closet. I'll let you know when I decide to come home."

Charlotte pulled the door open, then gasped. Jacob was standing there.

She swallowed hard as her phone fell from her shoulder and hit the wood floor. "Jacob. How long have you been standing there?"

12

Charlotte searched Jacob's expression, but she couldn't tell if he was on to her.

"I was just coming to see if you were okay. Hannah just told us all what happened." He scrunched up his face as he leaned down and looked at her hands. "Ouch. That doesn't look *gut*. *Mamm* is mixing up some of her goat-milk stuff, her cure-all for everything. She'll be up here in a few minutes."

Charlotte had momentarily forgotten about her hands. "Um . . . have you been standing out here long?" She tried to ask the question casually, but when Jacob grinned, her heart skipped a beat.

"Long enough," he said, winking, before he walked off.

Charlotte followed him, shuffling down the hall with her arms bent at her side. "Jacob," she said in a loud whisper. "What does that mean?"

He faced her and rubbed his chin. "What do you think it means?"

They both turned toward the stairs when they heard footsteps.

"Let's have a look at those hands." Lena had a bowl of white goop in one hand and some bandages in the other, along with a washrag draped over her arm. She frowned as she took inspection. "Are you in pain?"

"A little, but I'm okay, really." Charlotte tried to smile.

Lena gently latched on to her arm. "Come, come. Let's get you on the mend."

Charlotte glanced at Jacob, but he had already turned to go to his bedroom.

Lena motioned for Charlotte to sit down on the bed, then Lena sat down beside her. "Hannah said you got upset with a woman for hitting her child." She dipped the washrag into the bowl, pulling back a gob of thick white stuff. Charlotte flinched as Lena dabbed it on her palms.

"She was beating her child."

Lena finished up quietly, and when she was done, she pushed back a few strands of Charlotte's hair and gently kissed her on the forehead. "It's not our way, Mary, to involve ourselves in other people's business, especially the *Englisch*." She paused, gazing into Charlotte's eyes. "I know it's hard to see a child being over-disciplined though."

Charlotte was tempted to show her the scar on the back of her left thigh and the smaller one on her back. Neither

were disfiguring, just a reminder of one of the many beatings she'd gotten from her mother, her foster-mother, her
father . . . and the list went on. For years, she just assumed
she was a bad girl, unlovable. It wasn't until she got older
that she realized that not every parent hits.

"Mary, it is not for you to worry about, though." Lena
must have seen that she missed a spot since she dipped
the rag in the mush again. Mush that smelled a little
like garlic, but mixed with something she couldn't quite
identify. "That woman and her child are children of God,
and He will be the one to call the woman to judgment.
It's not for us to do that."

"I know," Charlotte said, blinking back tears.

"*Ach*, sweet girl." Lena smiled. "Do you remember when
you arrived and I asked you what your special gift was?"

Charlotte nodded.

She chuckled. "I couldn't figure out what yours was.
You don't like to cook, garden, or sew." She pointed a
finger at Charlotte. "But I knew your gift would reveal
itself, and today it did." She smiled broader, even though
Charlotte couldn't imagine what Lena was about to say.

"You are a defender of goodness. A protector, someone who will stand up for justice."

Charlotte couldn't look at Lena.

"But . . ." Lena gently cupped Charlotte's chin. "We
have reasons for staying apart from the *Englisch*. We are
unequally yoked with them. And I don't say that in judgment of the *Englisch*. Many of those in the outside world

are strong Christians, as committed to their faith as we are. But the difference between them and us is that when we meet another Amish person, we *know* that person is of the same beliefs, there's no questioning it. But with the *Englisch* . . . we can't know what their value system is at first glance." Lena paused, the rag in her hand, as she looked at Charlotte. "We live by the rules of the *Ordnung*, and there's no need for us to question each other. I would think that it would be easy for you to make that comparison since you have lived in both worlds. And I also caution you against righteous anger. Even though Jesus got angry, and there are many instances of anger throughout the Bible, it is hard for us to discern between being righteously angered and being tempted by human impulse."

"She pushed me down," Charlotte said softly, knowing she sounded like a child.

Lena dropped her hand and smiled. "And if you were five years old, we would be having this same conversation. If you had not approached the woman—had remained separated—this would not have happened. But since it did happen, the right thing to do would have been to walk away. I'm sure your Amish family instilled these beliefs in you from the time you chose to be baptized into the faith. It sounds like Isaac had to keep you from making the situation even worse."

Charlotte knew she was being disciplined, although she'd never had anyone do it without yelling and hitting.

Lena was mothering her, and Charlotte wished more and more that she could just stay in this bubble of love forever.

"God's love is more powerful than any misgivings we might have about righteousness, ours or others'," Lena said. "The best thing that you can do for that woman and her child is to pray for them."

"And ask for what?" Charlotte blurted out without thinking. But her hands throbbed, and now Lena's words were making her feel even worse. Not to mention that simmering on the back burner of her mind was how much of her conversation with Ryan that Jacob had heard.

"You ask for God's grace, for His mercy." She cupped Charlotte's cheek. "You should ask for that in everything you do."

A tear rolled down Charlotte's cheek. "Lena . . ."

"*Ya?*"

Charlotte sniffled, unable to choke back the tears in her throat. She put her arms around Lena's neck. "Thank you for having me here." *I love you.*

Following a long nap, Charlotte joined the family for supper. As much as she loved the homemade bread, even a warm, buttered slice wasn't enough to cheer her up, and she was keenly aware that Amos was watching her. Several times, she'd made eye contact with the head of the household, but he'd scowled and looked away. She'd tried to connect with Jacob, but he wouldn't look at her, adding to her worry that he'd heard enough of her conversation with Ryan to implicate her entirely. Did Lena and Amos know that Jacob was sneaking out at night? Maybe that was her ace in the hole.

Charlotte's thoughts were starting to carry her back to the real world. Even though she'd notified the editors she worked with that she would be taking a month's vacation, she'd started getting requests via e-mail to schedule more jobs for when she returned, which meant her time here was coming to a close if she planned to stay employed.

She couldn't stay in Lancaster County forever. She'd been paying her bills on her cell phone, and Ryan had checked on her apartment a couple of times, but sadly, life had gone on without her with barely a notice. She'd put away money over the past few years, so she wasn't at risk of depleting her savings. But she was going to prolong her stay a little longer, pretend to be a good person and a part of this family. Plus, she still had one more person to talk to before she left. Charlotte had to confront Edna Glick.

Charlotte also wanted to talk to Hannah about several things, so she struggled through supper and Amos's glares, biding her time. After supper, she helped Lena and Hannah clean the kitchen as best she could with her injured hands, something she hadn't been very good about doing in the past. Devotion time was forthcoming, so she asked Hannah if she wanted to sit on the front porch for a while to enjoy the cooler weather.

"Is there something you want to talk about?" Hannah kicked her rocker into motion with her bare feet. Charlotte had put on some socks earlier in the day. She'd loved the freedom of walking around barefoot when it was warmer, following Hannah and Lena's lead, but the wood floors were cool in the evening now.

"Your father is really mad at me. I could see it on his face all through supper." Charlotte hadn't realized until this evening how much Amos's approval mattered to her. She crossed one leg over the other and settled into a gentle rocking. Pulling snug the sweater she borrowed from Hannah, she looked at the clear sky filled with thousands of stars. She would miss this, too, when she went home. The only twinkling lights she could see at home were flickering atop the high-rises surrounding her apartment building.

"I think that with each generation, we tend to get a bit more liberal about some things, but violence of any kind is still looked down upon, and *Daed* especially doesn't like it." Hannah turned to her and smiled. "Thankfully, you didn't go after the woman, but he knows this wouldn't have happened if you hadn't approached her. But he will get past this, Mary, so please don't worry about it. How are your hands?"

Charlotte glanced at her bandages. "I think your mom's miracle mush actually helped."

Hannah smiled. "Surprisingly, it always seems to."

They were quiet for a few moments. Charlotte had several things on her mind, but she was sorting her thoughts into an order that made sense.

"Did you ever want to leave here? I mean, you had the opportunity when you were a teenager, right? Since I was older when I was baptized into the faith, I'd already experienced the world, so it wasn't really an issue." Her lies were festering like an infection, and there was no chance of healing until she came clean about everything, and even then . . . she wondered if there would be scars. She thought again about Jacob. She was going to have to find out exactly what he'd overheard, if anything.

Hannah shook her head. "*Nee*, I never wanted to leave. *Mamm* and *Daed* gave me a chance to experience some of the *Englisch* world, but *Daed* also kept a firm hand on what I did. He is stricter than some of the other fathers in our district, but he doesn't seem as strict with Jacob as he was with me."

"What is it that made you stay?" Charlotte twisted in her chair to see Hannah, shading her eyes from the setting sun to her right.

"What is it that made *you* stay?" Hannah raised one eyebrow as she threw the question back at Charlotte.

Charlotte sighed, wondering if there was a version of the truth she could offer up since she was so tired of all the lies. "It's safe here," she finally said. Even though Hannah had told her that family violence and other unpleasant acts happened even within the safety net of their community.

"You mean, it's safe in your district in Texas? Or you feel safer here, with us?"

Charlotte scratched her forehead. "Both," she said. "Safer than on the outside—in the English world."

"I wouldn't think that's enough to convert." Hannah obviously had as many questions as Charlotte. "I can understand you wanting to be away from your *mamm*, to start a life free of abuse, but surely there were chances for you to do that in the *Englisch* world."

Charlotte needed to get away from this conversation thread, to ask Hannah what she really wanted to know, but she responded with another lie, a fib that she wished was true. "I wanted to find a more spiritual life, to have a true relationship with God." In her mind, she tried to justify what she'd just said by using the relationship she was finding here and now.

Hannah smiled. "Kind of like Ethan."

Perfect. Now Charlotte didn't have to figure out a way to start a conversation about her brother. But so much had happened, she wasn't sure if she could hear any more without crying.

"Ethan was a surprise in so many ways," Hannah said, looking out over the green, lush yard. "When we first met, I could have never imagined that he would be interested in me, in being baptized into our faith, or in marrying me." She paused, a faraway look in her eyes.

"Ethan was funny. He made me laugh. And he was very compassionate, about people, animals, strangers, and causes. I fell in love with him very quickly." She blinked her eyes a few times. "But he was his own . . . hmm . . . I think the *Englisch* say it like this . . . he was his own worst enemy. Ethan was hard on himself. He never expected anyone else to be perfect, but he seemed to demand it of himself. And sometimes, when things didn't go like he thought they should, he would get very sad."

"I hope you will find someone else," Charlotte said, it being the most truthful thing she'd said all day.

"I hope so too."

They both turned toward the door when the hinges on the screen creaked. Hannah stood up and pulled the screen door wide so Jacob could maneuver his telescope onto the porch, then Hannah helped him carry it down the steps. Luckily it was on rollers, and Jacob pulled the telescope out to the middle of the yard, citing something about a planetary alignment later in the night. It wasn't even dark yet, but Lena would be calling them in for devotions soon.

"*Mamm* hates that thing," Hannah said with her hand to her forehead, blocking the sun's rays. "Jacob is so interested in anything to do with space, *Mamm* is fearful that he will leave the community to pursue his interests."

Charlotte watched Jacob setting up and positioning the telescope. It was as big around as some of the trees in the yard and about four feet tall. Charlotte assumed he'd saved quite a bit for the purchase.

"Um . . . Isaac drove me by your fiancé's house—by Ethan's house." She kept her eyes on Jacob, forcing herself to sound casual.

Hannah leaned her head back against the rocking chair and sighed. "I avoid driving by there since that is where Ethan took his life, but maybe I shouldn't. We also had some wonderful memories there." She glanced at Charlotte and smiled. "One of the first things we did was to put out bird feeders. Ethan loved anything that flew. Birds, butterflies, and even bats. He had a small bat house, but I made him put it on the far side of the yard. Bats aren't my favorite of God's creatures, but Ethan found them fascinating."

Charlotte smiled, knowing this to be true. Especially about the butterflies.

Hannah scowled. "His sister owns the house, but I don't even know if she knows that."

Charlotte's breath caught in her throat. "Oh," she managed to say.

"Ethan had the papers drawn up to deed it to his sister before he died. He said that once we moved to our new *haus*, he was hoping it would force her to come for a visit, to either sell the house—or stay awhile and get to know everyone. But we didn't go out of our way to tell her. And maybe that was wrong of us because Ethan loved his sister. But she was awful to me and my family after he died. I already knew that Ethan wanted to be buried here, but when we tried to explain that, the next thing we knew, she had the lawman threatening us if we didn't allow his body to be sent back to Houston."

Charlotte felt a muscle flick in her jaw. "She probably just loved her brother and wanted him buried close so she could visit him." She hoped Hannah couldn't see her lip trembling.

Hannah shrugged. "I guess. I think she should have thought about what her *bruder* would have wanted though." She paused, tapping her chin. "Ethan's sister wasn't happy with his choice to convert his faith, so I'm sure she wasn't happy that he was planning to marry me either. He'd asked her to visit several times, but she declined, and that hurt him. He very much wanted to have her in his life even though she was *Englisch*. But he said she had a lot of problems."

The hair on Charlotte's neck began to prickle. "Like, what kind of problems?" Even though Charlotte was still trying to adjust to the fact that she owned the little blue house, she couldn't imagine what Ethan might have told Hannah.

"He just said she was bitter, misdirected, and didn't have any faith."

Charlotte grunted. "How could he know that? She might have had all kinds of untapped faith that she just didn't understand." She quickly looked at Hannah, regretful of her revealing outburst.

Hannah frowned. "*Untapped* faith? What is that?"

Finally. A chance to tell the truth. "When a person

knows there is something else out there, a deity, a reason for living, but they've never been educated in a way to understand that it's God." She wondered if Hannah would get it. "That's how it was with me before I became Amish." *Okay, so a tiny lie at the end.*

"I don't know. I wish I could have known her since Ethan loved her so much, but it was clear that she didn't want anything to do with us." Hannah sighed, raising her shoulders, then slowly lowering them. "And maybe it's for the best. I don't think I would have liked her."

"Why? Just because she wanted her brother's body returned home?"

Hannah turned to Charlotte. "This *was* his home."

Charlotte had to give her that, but her mind was awhirl with other thoughts.

"His sister asked all kinds of questions after he died, and maybe I should have done more to help her find peace," Hannah said before she sighed. "But I didn't understand either. Ethan would get depressed, feel better, then get sad again. But we'd been happy for a long time. I wrote her back that I didn't know why he had taken his life, and when I saw phone calls coming from a number I didn't know, I just didn't answer."

Glancing at Hannah, Charlotte fought the bitterness trying to worm its way into her emotions, but she really couldn't blame Hannah for thinking she wouldn't like Ethan's sister. Charlotte didn't like herself sometimes. But things were changing, and she was looking forward to putting the past behind her, making a full confession about all the lies, and basking in the new friendships she'd made here. Thankfully, the Amish were a forgiving bunch. She might not see them as often as she'd like, but at least she'd be able to call and write letters. Charlotte was also encouraged about her developing relationship with God, and thankful that it was something that would travel home with her. And then there was Ryan . . . she wondered where that connection might lead as well.

J'm sorry it took me so long to call you. My battery went dead, and I had to get to town. There's a coffee shop that Hannah and I go to sometimes, and we get a muffin and charge our phones." Charlotte snuggled into the covers on her bed.

"Do all the Amish people have phones?" Ryan asked.

"Pretty much. I guess they can't bypass all technology. Hannah told me about a few people who absolutely will not own a cell phone. They have these little shacks that are like phone booths. They call them shanties, and several families will share one. Hannah said some of the phones are still rotary dial."

"I can barely hear you. Where are you?"

"I'm in my room. I have the fan on high, but I'm still trying to be quiet because I don't know if Jacob is asleep. He stays up late sometimes. He was standing outside my door last time I was talking to you. And now I'm worried how much he might have heard."

"Did he say anything?"

"No. Not to me. And he isn't acting any differently, but it was just odd."

"How are your hands?"

"Better. They look awful but feel better. Lena put something on them, some concoction she makes out of goat milk. It smells weird, but it helps with the pain. And she told me I won't have scars if I keep them covered and alternate between applying Vaseline and her goat stuff. I asked her if I should let them dry out and scab, and you should have seen the look on her face. She said absolutely not, that a cut or scrape should never be allowed to dry out. She said that's what causes a scar."

Ryan grunted. "Wow. And we were taught to let a wound go uncovered so it will scab."

"I know. The things you learn in Amish Country." She chuckled. "But I'm doing what she said, and it's already looking better."

"Did you decide when you're coming home?"

"I haven't even looked at flights. I know I need to start thinking about that. But, guess what? Apparently I am the owner of Ethan's little house here in Paradise, Pennsylvania." She filled him in on her conversation with Hannah this afternoon, talking as softly as she could. "So, I was thinking about maybe fixing up the place. After I tell them all the truth, of course."

"Then you'll put it on the market?"

"Yeah. I briefly thought about keeping it, fixing it up, and having my own little vacation spot, but considering what happened there . . . I think I should just sell it." Charlotte fluffed her pillow, shined her flashlight on the far wall, and wished there was a way she could get her sheets to smell like this at home, cottony fresh. But there wasn't the luxury of a clothesline at her apartment complex. She breathed in the freshness and wished she could bottle the aroma and take it home with her.

"I really thought you'd be home by now, but since you're not . . . I have to be in Harrisburg on Monday for a meeting. It's a short trip, and I need to get back to Houston, but there's this cute little Amish girl I was hoping to take to dinner."

Charlotte sat taller. "You're kidding me." She brought a hand to her chest. Ryan traveled quite a bit for work. He was contracted by the Department of Homeland Security and oversaw the installation of security equipment in government buildings.

"Nope. I Googled it, and it looks like you're about an hour from Harrisburg. Early dinner?"

"Yes, yes." Charlotte didn't realize until that moment how much she wanted to see Ryan. They'd had several long phone conversations and their friendship had grown more personal since she'd come to Paradise. "I would love that."

She jumped out of bed when she heard a noise. "Hang

on. Either a very confused bird just slammed into my window—at night—or . . ." She peered out her window. "There's someone down there."

"Probably the boyfriend wanting you to come out and play." Ryan laughed.

"Ha, ha," Charlotte said sarcastically and strained to get a better look. "It's Jacob," she said as a small rock tapped against her window again. "No idea why he's throwing rocks at my window instead of coming in like a normal person. I better go see what he wants. I'll talk to you tomorrow."

"I can't wait to see you."

Charlotte smiled at the tenderness in his voice, then borrowed a line from one of her favorite movies. "Ditto."

She walked to the corner of her room where several dresses were hanging on a rack. She pulled off her nightgown, threw on a dark-green dress, and tiptoed downstairs. The moment she opened the door, the cool night air hit her. She slipped her feet into Amos's big boots, then clunked her way down the porch steps, shining the flashlight in front of her.

"Jacob!" she said in a loud whisper. "Lucky for you that you didn't break a window. What are you doing?"

"Sorry. This is positioned in exactly the right spot based on the coordinates I have, and I wanted you to come see."

"So, you couldn't have come in the house and gotten me?"

He rubbed his hands together, grinning. "Where's your sense of adventure?"

"Upstairs tucked in bed about to go to sleep." She was relieved that he was acting like nothing happened, so she had to assume that he hadn't overheard anything.

"Look." He pointed up, then eased his eye away from the small hole he was looking through. "You can see Mars and Saturn."

Charlotte had always wanted a telescope, even as a kid. She squeezed one eye shut and peered through the hole, then stood and looked at Jacob. "I see sky. Darkness. That's it."

Jacob gently pushed her to the side. "This thing is so sensitive. If you even barely touch it with your face, it moves." He adjusted some dials on the side while Charlotte waited.

"There." He backed away and pointed to the telescope. "Look again, but don't touch it, even with an eyelash."

Charlotte grinned and handed him her flashlight this time. There was a small amount of light coming from a propane lamp in the yard, but otherwise, it was a clear night sky filled with stars. She got as close as she could, careful not to touch the eyepiece.

"Do you see them? They're both to the right of Antares, which is a star, it's red."

Charlotte kept looking through the hole. "I know what Antares is." She let out a small gasp. "I see them, both of them." She stared in amazement for a few more seconds before she stood straight. "Wow, that is pretty cool."

Jacob smiled. "I thought you'd like to see that. You're the only one in the family who would appreciate it."

Charlotte felt a warm glow flow through her. *I am part of this family.* "Thank you for showing me. It was worth the trip out of bed. Can I look again?" She heard her voice crack slightly and hoped Jacob didn't notice.

"*Ya*, sure."

He didn't seem to, so Charlotte took another look.

"There was only one other person around here who cared anything about astronomy, and it was Ethan, Hannah's boyfriend."

Charlotte visibly bumped the telescope. "Oops. Sorry." She stood up and stepped away, almost falling down as she tripped in Amos's big boots.

Jacob adjusted the dials, then announced that he had the planets in focus again. Charlotte appreciated the viewing, but twice was enough. "Were you close to Ethan?"

Jacob had wet hair from his shower and was dressed in black sweatpants and a white T-shirt. Except for his cropped bangs, he looked like any other teenager. He rubbed his nose, sighed, and said, "*Ya*, in the beginning. But not toward the end. It turned out he wasn't a very *gut* guy."

"Oh? Why do you say that? Your mother seems to have loved him as much as Hannah." This must have something to do with Edna Glick.

"That's because they didn't know him, not the real Ethan."

Charlotte's heart was racing. "Why do you say that?" she asked again.

Jacob shrugged. "What does it matter? You didn't

even know him." Jacob pulled the lens from the telescope and put it in a bag that was hanging from one side. "We'll be able to see Venus in October, if you're still here."

Charlotte didn't care about the planetary movements at the moment. "Now, you've got my curiosity up about Ethan. Hannah doesn't seem like she'd fall in love with someone, and plan to marry him, if he wasn't a good—*gut*—guy."

"I didn't find out about him until right before he died. I would have told Hannah what I thought, but after he passed, I just didn't see the good in saying anything. It would have only hurt her more than she was already hurting." He paused, and even in the dim light, Charlotte could see him scowling. "You're not going to tell her, are you?"

"Tell her what? I don't know anything. I'm just . . . uh, guessing—he must have cheated on her."

Jacob didn't respond but started to roll the telescope through the grass and toward the porch. "Only reason I called you out here is because I can't get this thing up the stairs by myself." He snickered as they got to the steps.

"That's probably true." She lifted one side while Jacob picked up the other side, and they carried it up the four steps.

"Try not to let the door slam on the way back in, like you did on the way out. I'm sure you woke up *Mamm* and *Daed*."

Charlotte thought for a few moments, knowing she needed some insurance. "I guess I wouldn't be very good at *sneaking* out of the house late at night."

Jacob got close to her ear and spoke softly. "I guess you wouldn't . . . *Mary.*"

Then he grinned and turned toward the stairs. Once he was out of sight, Charlotte let out the breath she was holding. *He knows.*

Hannah was glad to see Mary in time for breakfast. She missed more breakfasts than she made it in time for. She'd decided that it just wasn't in Mary's nature to be an early riser. They obviously didn't start their days as early in Texas. Maybe her cousin's motivation to get up early today had something to do with teaching her how to bake bread. Hannah had never seen a person eat as much bread as Mary, except for maybe Jacob. She noticed that her mother hadn't eaten much these past few days.

After *Daed* and Jacob left and the dishes were washed, Mary sat down and helped herself to another piece of buttered bread, and *Mamm* sat down and lathered up her hands with her goat-milk lotion.

Hannah tossed the dish towel over her shoulder and leaned against the counter. "*Mamm,* are you all right? You aren't eating much."

Her mother massaged the lotion up her arms almost to her elbows. "*Ya, ya.* I'm fine. I've just been a little sick to my stomach the past few days. If it's not better soon, I'll visit the doctor."

Hannah's mother rarely went to the doctor. She'd even used a midwife to deliver both Hannah and Jacob, right here in the house. Thinking back, she couldn't think of a time when her mother had ever been sick with more than a cold that she'd say was just allergies.

"You were at the doctor recently. Was everything okay then?"

Mamm nodded. "*Ya, ya.* I had to have some tests run." She smiled as she winked at Hannah. "I'm getting old, and that's what happens when you get old."

"*Nee*, you're not old, *Mamm*." Hannah studied her mother's face. It was ashen, and for the first time, Hannah noticed the dark circles under her eyes.

"Well, you don't look well." Hannah sat down at the kitchen table.

Mary stood and pressed her hand against *Mamm*'s forehead. "No fever," she said with bread still in her mouth.

"*Nee*, I don't feel feverish, and I don't really feel all that bad. I'm just a bit sick to my stomach, especially in the mornings." She lifted herself from the chair. "Hannah, can you feed the goats for me and take care of the milking? I think I need to lie down for a while."

"*Ya*, of course. Do you need anything?"

"*Nee*, dear. But *danki*. I just need to rest and get over this bug."

Hannah waited until she heard her mother's bedroom door shut, then wide-eyed, she looked at Mary. "Are you thinking what I'm thinking?"

Her cousin nodded. "Yep. Pregnant." Then she got up and slathered butter on yet another piece of bread. Hannah noticed that despite her bandages, Mary was doing better with the use of her hands, not so stiff. *Mamm's* miracle concoction.

"Well, you're the one eating like you are pregnant," Hannah said before she giggled.

Mary smiled with a mouthful. "Well, I assure you, I'm not. But it sure seems like your mom is."

Hannah sat down across from Mary. "Can that happen? I mean, at her age?"

"How old is she?"

Hannah tipped her head back, squeezed one eye shut, and counted by fives on her fingers. "Forty-seven. That's kind of old to be getting pregnant."

"But very possible," Mary added.

"I wonder if she's having her, you know, monthlies anymore."

"Ask her," Mary said.

"*Ach*, I don't know if I should." Hannah grinned. "Exactly how much bread do you plan to eat?"

Mary laughed, and when she did, she spit bread out of her mouth, some of the moist pieces sticking to Hannah's black apron. Hannah looked down at herself as her jaw dropped. "You spit on me."

Mary then quickly slammed a hand to her mouth as her eyes grew rounder beneath raised eyebrows. "Oops."

Hannah laughed out loud. It was something she

hadn't done much of before Mary arrived. She was really going to miss her cousin when she went back to Texas. But she instantly got quiet when she heard something. "Listen," she said.

They both didn't move for a few seconds.

"Aw, it sounds like she's throwing up." Mary stood up. "Maybe one of us should go check on her. Why don't you get the stuff out to make bread, and I'll go see if your mom needs anything."

Hannah nodded. "Okay."

Charlotte gently knocked on Lena's bedroom door, but when no one answered, she eased the door open.

She walked past the four-poster bed that Amos had made. Charlotte recalled the first time she'd seen the bed, how ornate it was. Amos was clearly a great carpenter, she was just surprised since the Amish pride themselves on simplicity, and the bed was anything but plain. She tapped on the closed door to the bathroom.

"Lena, are you okay?"

"*Ya.* I'm okay, Mary. *Danki* for checking."

Charlotte stood there quietly for a few moments while Lena threw up again. When she seemed to be gasping for air, Charlotte opened the door. Lena's prayer covering was on the floor beside her, and most of her hair had fallen from the bun on top of her head. She was sweating a lot, trembling, and her face was flushed. Charlotte found a washrag, wet it with cold water, and immediately dabbed at Lena's forehead, then her cheeks.

"You are going to bed." Charlotte spoke with authority, knowing Lena would argue.

"*Nee, nee.* I think it's all over. I'm fine." She eased the wet rag from Charlotte's hand. "But you are sweet to come see about me."

"Lena, have you had your period recently? Are you still having them regularly?" Charlotte didn't know much about menopause, but she didn't think it made you sick to your stomach like this. But maybe Lena did just have a bug.

"I-I don't usually talk about such things." Lena pulled her eyes from Charlotte's.

"Sorry. But I was just wondering if you might be pregnant. If there's even that possibility, you need to get to a doctor pretty soon. You do know that having a baby at your age presents some risks, right?"

Lena nodded. "*Ya,* I know. And, since you asked, *ya* . . . I am still having my monthlies."

Charlotte breathed a sigh of relief. "Oh, good. Then you're not pregnant."

Lena sighed. "I just haven't had one in the past three months."

anki for doing this, Hannah." Charlotte smiled, wishing there was a need to perfect the dialect, but she wouldn't need it soon.

Hannah rolled the dough over and over before she kneaded it for the second time. "I'm happy to show you how to make bread, but it wonders me how you couldn't know this."

Charlotte kept her eyes on the soon-to-be bread, not wanting to miss a step. "Since I wasn't raised Amish, I really didn't learn how to cook."

She hated the lies more than ever, but the worst part was, she wanted to believe them. She'd been trying to help out more with cleaning and cooking. She knew how to clean, even though she wasn't a big fan, but the cooking continued to be a challenge. Despite what she'd learned about Ethan, she'd be leaving this place knowing that she wouldn't be alone ever again. She'd never been so grateful to have something pushed upon her as she was about her newfound knowledge of the Lord. She was terrified, though, that her new family would toss her out on the street once they found out who she really was. But Ryan had assured her repeatedly that it wasn't their way to be unforgiving.

"This has to rise for a while," Hannah said as she nodded to the mound of dough. "Let's sit."

Once they were both at the kitchen table, Hannah pushed back several strands of hair that had fallen from beneath her prayer covering, which left a floury residue on her cheek. "What are you doing?"

"A crossword puzzle. I had this on the plane to keep me entertained when I didn't feel like reading. But I'm stuck on one."

"What is it?"

"A type of soup." Charlotte rolled her eyes. "Soup is soup. I don't think the clue is referring to a kind of soup, though—like chicken, potato, or whatever. It starts with a *P* and ends with an *E*."

"Puree," Hannah said, smiling.

Charlotte wrote in the letters. "Yep. That's it. What about this one?" She pointed to another clue she was stuck on, and together they spent the next thirty minutes finishing the crossword puzzle. Maybe it would be easiest to first tell Hannah the truth about her identity, then let her break it to the rest of the family.

Hannah pointed to one of the words in the crossword puzzle, one Charlotte had filled in earlier. "What does that mean?"

Charlotte glanced at the sister-in-law she would have had under different circumstances and said, "Infidelity."

Hannah twirled the string on her prayer covering. "Um . . . what does that mean?"

Charlotte disagreed with the Amish choice to only educate their children through the eighth grade. Hannah's limited vocabulary was a prime example. "It means cheating, adultery."

Hannah scowled, still twirling the string. "That's one thing I never had to worry about with Ethan. He said his father cheated on his mother and that he could never do anything like that."

Charlotte thought about what Isaac had told her. Prior to finding the picture, Charlotte couldn't have imagined her brother ever cheating either. Her stomach churned with a burning desire to tell Hannah the truth about Ethan, but she wasn't sure if it would help Hannah to move on or destroy her.

"After Ethan died, I didn't think I would ever find someone else." Hannah sat back down, elbows on the table as she cupped her cheeks in her hands. "But maybe someday."

"You know, I think your mom might be pregnant." Charlotte wiggled her toes underneath the table. Her feet had never been so dirty, but she loved the freedom of running around barefoot. Soon, it would be too cold, even during the day. "She hasn't had a period in three months."

"*Ach.* I'm not sure how she'll feel about that even though a child is always a gift from God."

"She probably needs to find out for sure, one way or the other." Charlotte tapped the pencil against the table. "And I should probably start thinking about going back to Texas." The thought instantly depressed her.

Hannah reached over and touched Charlotte's hand. "I'm really going to miss you."

As had become the norm, Charlotte started to tear up. "I've enjoyed my time here."

Hannah sat taller as she placed both palms flat on the table, smiling. "There's no rule that says you can't stay."

Oh, if you only knew. Charlotte thought about Ryan. He'd be the only one who might miss her. Working from home doing editing had been great in the beginning, but she'd slowly become her own best friend. "Oh, can you give me the number for the driver you hire sometimes? A friend—an English friend—will be in Harrisburg, and I'm going to meet him for supper since he'll be so close."

Hannah smiled. "*Ya,* of course. He?"

"Yes, it's a man I've known for a long time. His name is—" Charlotte stopped herself. Ethan might have mentioned Ryan at some point. "John. He's just a good friend," she said. When this was all over, she was going to spend every extra moment asking God to forgive her lies.

She excused herself, worried that she would start to cry. Again.

Hannah kneaded the bread one more time, then put two loaves in the oven. It had been baking for about ten minutes when Mary returned. "It needed one more round of kneading, and I just put both pans in the oven."

"I saw from my bedroom window your mother leaving. She was in a car."

Hannah took off the oven mitts and set them on the counter. "*Ya*, she's going to the doctor in Lancaster. I offered to go with her, but she said she'd rather I tend to the goats."

She heard a buggy coming, then watched as Isaac turned into the driveway. He stopped near the fence surrounding the yard, tethered his horse, and headed to the barn. A few minutes later he walked out carrying a wooden rocker, which explained the small trailer he was pulling behind the buggy.

"Isaac is here picking up some rocking chairs *Daed* made," Hannah said as she watched him carting the chair as if it weighed no more than a pound or two. "You go visit with him. I'll keep an eye on the bread." She walked to the counter where two more loaves of dough were rising. "He's having a lot of trouble with his parents. Maybe you can help him know what to do."

"What kind of trouble?" Mary walked to the window, watching Isaac.

Hannah wasn't sure it was her place to tell Mary since Isaac had obviously chosen not to, but she did anyway since things sounded so bad at his house.

"That sounds like it might be a medication problem, especially if he's normal some of the time, then seems off at other times. Maybe some of his medicines don't play well together."

"Maybe go tell him that. Hopefully, he won't be upset that I told you."

Mary folded her hands across her chest and grinned. "You are the one he chose to confide in, so I think you should go talk to him."

Hannah shook her head. "*Nee*, I . . ."

Mary huffed. "Go talk to him, Hannah. I'll keep an eye on the bread."

Hannah blushed. "*Ya*, okay."

∽

Charlotte watched Hannah and Isaac from the window in the kitchen, wishing she would be around to see how things panned out for the two of them, but in her heart, she knew they'd end up together. Such news would have infuriated her five weeks ago, but now it just warmed her heart.

She picked up one of the Amish newspapers and

started scanning it. It read like a series of letters from various Amish communities in different states, updating about marriages, births, deaths, and other stuff that Charlotte didn't find very interesting. She could faintly hear her phone ringing upstairs. Normally, she left the ringer off, but she'd been waiting for a call from Ryan to firm up their dinner plans and had meant to put the phone in her apron pocket. She bolted up the stairs, but by the time she got to her bedroom, the phone wasn't ringing so she called him back.

He was already in town and had done the legwork of finding a place to eat, so they set a time. Charlotte was wondering what she would wear, but when she glanced at the rack on her wall, she chuckled. Her choices were blue, maroon, or pine green with her lovely black apron. Shoes—the usual black loafers. But after they hung up, she rummaged through the bottom of her suitcase until she found her bag of makeup that she hadn't taken out the entire time she'd been there. At least she could put some makeup on in the car on the way to the restaurant. And if she curled her hair before she stuffed it underneath her prayer covering, she could let the waves fall freely.

As she sorted things out, she became more and more excited to see Ryan again. She couldn't help but be optimistic that something more than friendship was blooming.

Hannah told Isaac what Mary said. "She knows so many things from her time in the *Englisch* world, so maybe it is your *daed*'s medications that are causing him problems. I hope you don't mind me telling her."

"*Nee*, I don't mind. I thought about mentioning it to her, but she always seems to have so much on her mind. I finally talked to my *aenti*, the one who visited from up near Pittsburgh, and she has been spending more time with us, so that helps us some. *Mamm* thinks we are making too much of things."

"I hope your father is feeling better soon." Hannah walked alongside Isaac to his buggy as he carried the last rocker. "Please tell her I said hello and to let me know if there is anything she needs."

Isaac nodded as he strapped the rocking chair onto the small flatbed trailer.

"Mary is talking about leaving. I'm sure you'll miss her." Hannah wasn't sure why she kept testing the waters, but she needed to be certain that she wasn't interfering in a possible relationship between them, even though they'd both said they were only friends. And Hannah was pretty sure she and Isaac had shared a special moment on Saturday.

"Mary is a *gut* person." Isaac positioned the rocker, checked the strap, then turned to Hannah. "She has a *gut* heart."

Hannah avoided his eyes. "*Ya*, she does."

She jumped when Isaac gently cupped her chin. "But

she's not the one I've been interested in, Hannah. But I wasn't sure if you were ready to date again. I wasn't sure if I was ready. But Mary is actually the one who talked to me about this." He lowered his hand. "If I can get things figured out with *mei* parents, would you be interested in spending more time together?"

For the first time in a few days, Ethan's face flashed in her mind's eye, and the familiar grief bubbled, but only for a few moments. Ethan would want her to be happy. She nodded, but then they both heard a scream and immediately started running toward the back of the house.

Mary was barefoot, didn't have her *kapp* on, and was dangling from a rope that was hanging out her window. Even though they rushed, they didn't get to her before she slid down and landed on her rear end.

"Fire!" She was breathless as she pointed. "Fire. There's a fire. I smell smoke."

Isaac took off around the corner. Hannah looked at Mary's hands, blood seeping through the white bandages. Rope burn must have reopened her wounds. "Mary, did you remember to take the bread from the oven?"

"Oh no." Mary flinched as Hannah took a handkerchief from her pocket and double-wrapped Mary's right hand—the one bleeding through the gauze. "The smoke is probably the burning bread. Come on." Hannah helped Mary to her feet, and they both scurried around to the front of the house. Everything must have been okay since the hose was still outside, but she could see smoke billowing from all the kitchen windows. Isaac walked out carrying what was left of the bread—two crispy, smoldering blobs.

"Are you okay?" he asked Mary.

"Not really." She cringed as she lifted her bloody hands, then raised an eyebrow, before turning to Hannah. "I hope your mom has plenty of that goat goop because at this rate, I'm going to need a steady supply."

"Let's get you doctored up," Hannah said as she glanced at Isaac.

"I got it, I got it. I panicked and thought there was a fire. Is everything okay inside?"

"Everything but the bread." Isaac set the two loaves on the porch and looped his thumbs beneath his suspenders.

Mary stomped her foot and grumbled under her breath as she marched across the yard, waving a hand in front of her face as smoke floated out of the kitchen window.

"It wonders me what would make her slide down a rope like that." Isaac shook his head.

Hannah told him about how Mary had been trapped by a fire before. "I better go get the kitchen aired out and tend to her."

She turned around twice on her way to the house, and both times, Isaac was smiling and watching her. For the first time in a long time, she saw happiness in her future.

◦◦◦

An hour later, Charlotte and Hannah were still trying to get the smoky smell out of the house. They had every battery-operated fan they owned blowing toward a window.

"It wonders me if we're ever going to get this smell out of here." Hannah lit several candles and placed them around the kitchen.

"Scentsies," Charlotte said without thinking.

"What?"

"Oh, nothing. Never mind." The plug-in air fresheners that melted wax cubes needed electricity. "Potpourri." She glanced at Hannah, who frowned. "It's a mixture of dried flower petals and spices."

"*Ya*, I've heard of that. I will make some."

"Or just buy a bag at the Dollar Store," Charlotte said, shrugging.

"Well, that would be a very *Englisch* thing to do." She grinned and they both looked toward the door when they heard footsteps.

Charlotte leapt to her feet. "It was my fault," she said to Lena when she walked into the kitchen. "I was supposed to be keeping an eye on the bread, and I went upstairs, and . . ."

"It is a small thing, Mary. I'm going to rest. Hannah, maybe make chicken salad for lunch. And don't forget to leave the chopped eggs on the side since Mary doesn't like them." She waved over her shoulder as she headed toward her bedroom.

"*Mamm*, wait." Hannah walked to where her mother

was standing. "What did the doctor say? Are you with child?"

Lena shook her head, barely smiling. "*Nee*, no baby. I'm just a little sick, and I need to rest." She closed her bedroom door behind her.

"Well, that's *gut* news. I know a *boppli* would have been a blessing, but I would have worried about *Mamm* having one at her age."

Charlotte waited until the bedroom door shut before she spoke. "There are two loaves of burnt bread on the porch, and the whole downstairs is still smoky . . ." She paused, tipping her head to one side. "But your mother sure didn't have much reaction about it. She must really feel bad."

"I know," Hannah said softly as both she and Charlotte stared toward the bedroom door. Then Charlotte had a horrible, selfish thought. *No bread today.*

"I guess I need to get cleaned up and call a driver. I'm meeting my friend for supper tonight."

"*Ach*, I remember." Hannah sighed as she folded her hands in front of her. "Your friend is going to think we've treated you badly." She nodded at Charlotte's hands. "Where are you meeting him?"

"In Lancaster. I think that's about twenty minutes by car from here, right? And he will take a cab from Harrisburg."

"Harrisburg is a bit farther, maybe forty minutes. What restaurant?"

"Um . . . I have it written down upstairs. Blue something. Blue . . ."

Hannah gasped. "You're not meeting him at Blue Pacific, are you?"

"Yes." Charlotte smiled. "That's it. What's wrong with Blue Pacific?"

Hannah stepped closer and touched Charlotte on the arm. "You mustn't eat there."

"Oh no. Is it bad?" Charlotte tried to straighten her hands a little bit more beneath the bandages, but cringed and hoped Lena had more miracle goop in the fridge.

Hannah brought her hand to her side, raised her chin a bit, and stood taller. "Well, it is said to be one of the finest restaurants in Lancaster County, but you still don't want to eat there."

Charlotte narrowed her eyebrows. "Why not? Because it's expensive?"

"I don't know about that, but what I do know is . . . they don't cook much of their food." She shriveled her face up as her eyes grew wide.

"Raw food? Oh, you mean they serve sushi?"

"*Nee*, they serve *raw* fish!"

Despite the fact that her hands burned, she laughed. "I'm really going to miss you, sweet Hannah. Sushi is a type of raw fish that's considered a delicacy in the English world. It'll be fine, I promise."

Hannah was still scowling. "Suit yourself, but don't say I didn't warn you."

Charlotte went upstairs to get ready. She had so much more to tell Ryan, and she'd sensed that there might be more to this date than just a friendly dinner. She was eager to find out.

15

On the way to meet Ryan, Charlotte pulled her makeup bag from her purse and found her compact, glad it lit up since it was starting to get dark outside. She opened her bottle of foundation, dabbed a little on her finger, then stared at herself in the mirror. It had been so long since she'd applied any makeup, she had gotten used to how she looked without it. Continuing to look at herself, she realized she wasn't the same person as when she'd left, and she closed the compact, wiped the liquid that was on her finger on a tissue, then stuffed everything back in her purse.

"I'm pretty sure you are the first Amish woman I've taken to the Blue Pacific. Is this a special occasion?" The driver was someone that Hannah's family used often, and Hannah had already told Charlotte that she was a chatty woman about Lena's age.

"I guess it's sort of a special occasion. A friend is visiting the area, and we're meeting for din—supper."

The woman nodded, and Charlotte was thinking that it was probably a good thing she didn't walk into the restaurant in Amish clothes, full makeup, and her hair hung loose and curled. She'd decided to keep her curls under her prayer covering, which somewhere along the line had taken on a new meaning—her *kapp*. She wondered how Ryan would react to her new Amish look. She'd already warned him about how she'd be dressed.

"They have great food there," the woman said. "They're known for their sushi, but they also have eclectic choices on the menu, and—" She glanced over her shoulder. "Do you know what that means, hon? Eclectic?"

Charlotte was taken aback, but remembered that the Amish didn't get as much education as most people, so she stayed in character when she responded. "*Ya*, I do. I'm looking forward to eating there. I'm from Texas."

"I thought I heard a bit of a Southern accent in your voice. What brings you to Lancaster County? Family? They don't have a lot of Amish in Texas, do they?"

Charlotte wished she could just clamp her lips closed and not answer, and she was searching for a way to answer this woman truthfully. She was never going to tell another lie when she left this place.

"I'm just visiting for a while, and no, there aren't many Amish communities in Texas." *Ah, the truth.*

From that moment on, the woman—Mindy—did

most of the talking. Charlotte answered politely when the conversation called for it, but her stomach was churning, and not from hunger. She glanced at her bandaged hands. She'd let go of the rope about halfway down, when the pain had become too much to bear. She had a bruise on her hip from where she landed, but it could have been a lot worse, for her hands and her hip.

When the woman pulled up in front of the Blue Pacific, Charlotte paid her, looked at her cell phone, and realized she was a few minutes late, so she hurried to the door.

"I'm meeting someone," she said to the hostess as she propped her black purse up on her shoulder, then put a hand across her stomach, hoping it would settle down. "His name is Ryan Hanemann," she added.

"Yes. He's here. Please follow me."

Charlotte followed the woman through what felt like a maze, and once they got to the very back of the restaurant, she saw Ryan stand up. It took every ounce of restraint she had not to run into his arms, and she certainly hadn't expected to tear up when she saw him, but her emotions lived permanently on her sleeve these days.

"You make a beautiful Amish woman." He eased his arms around her and kissed her on the forehead, and she held on to him tightly for a few seconds before easing away. Ryan pulled out her chair, then moved to the other side of the small table.

"*Danki*, sir," she said as she slid into the chair, unable to keep her heart from dancing even though she was still fighting tears. "I'm so happy to see you. I hate that it has to be like this."

Ignoring her nod at her attire, Ryan reached over and gently grabbed her wrists, turning her palms faceup. "Still hurting?"

She nodded. "They were getting better until I slid on a rope out of my window, like an idiot."

His touch was gentle as he rubbed his thumb along the top of her bandaged hands. "This is a good look for Charlotte Dolinsky." He winked at her. "Minus the bandages."

"Wow, I haven't heard my first and last name in a really long time."

He leaned back against the chair. "You look different. And I don't mean because you're wearing Amish clothes or that you don't have on any makeup. But you look different, in a good way. And I like the new hair color I see peeking out from beneath your prayer covering."

"Well, I was thinking of dressing this way from now on," she said, grinning. "And I told you what happened with my hair." She paused. "But maybe I'll keep this color."

Ryan continued to study her for a few moments until the waitress walked up to take their order. After the woman left, Ryan refocused his gaze on Charlotte. "No, I'm serious. You're very pretty."

Charlotte could feel her cheeks turning pink. "I'm fatter." She smiled broadly.

Ryan's gray-blue eyes twinkled in the dimly lit space,

a single candle burning between them. "No, that's not it. You've always been a gorgeous woman, but you have a glow now."

Charlotte was still basking in the compliment when Ryan went on.

"You look . . . happy."

Charlotte took a sip from her glass of water that was already on the table when she arrived. "You know, I expected not to like Hannah or any of them. But they are the closest thing to family I've ever had. Except for Ethan, of course."

"I hope you'll be able to stay in touch with them after you leave." Ryan loosened the knot in a grayish-blue tie that matched his eyes. "Do you think Ethan killed himself because he felt guilty about having an affair with Edna?"

"I think there's only one person who might be able to answer that question. And that's really the last piece of the puzzle. Then I'll know." She shrugged, sighing. "And then I'll go home. I still think that I will wait and write a long letter explaining everything once I'm back in Texas."

They were quiet while the waitress placed their appetizer on the table. "This trip has never been about Ethan." Ryan reached for a pot sticker from the plate between them. Charlotte took one of the fried chicken dumplings as she waited for Ryan to explain. "You always said that you felt unsettled because you didn't know why Ethan killed himself. You said you couldn't move forward. Am I right?"

"Right." Charlotte glanced around the table for a dipping sauce but she didn't see one.

"Charlotte, you're never going to know for sure what demons Ethan was carrying around to make him take his own life. Maybe it was guilt. Or something else. And I admit that I wanted answers too. But I don't think that I realized until this moment that these past few weeks have really been about you." He smiled. "You found your family."

Charlotte finished chewing her bite. "Wait, wait. I love those people. I really do. But they might not even speak to me after they learn the truth. I found out what having a family feels like, but I don't get to keep them as my own."

Ryan tipped his head to the side. "Charlotte . . . you *did* find your family. You found your Father, and in Him, you've found your family and the missing piece of yourself that always left you feeling unsettled." He reached over and touched her hand again. "So many times, we step onto a path with our own intentions guiding the way, but even if we are being led by God, many times the destination is by His design, not ours."

Charlotte picked up her napkin and dabbed at her eyes. "I really am happy!" She gently pressed her bandaged palms against the table, half laughing, half crying.

"I'm happy for you. And I'm happy to be here with you."

Finally. Is this my shot at happiness, God?

❧

Isaac dropped his dirty boots by the front door when he got home from work since he'd managed to step in a puddle where the garden hose was leaking, leaving a muddy mess. *One more thing to fix around here.*

"*Wie bischt?*" His mother met him near the door. "Where's your *daed*?"

Isaac hung his hat on the rack by the door. "*Daed* insisted that we supervise the inventory this year, so he's still at the store with Phyllis and Tom. I came home so I can tend to the animals before it gets too late. Tom said he'll bring *Daed* home later." He shook his head as he made his way to the kitchen for something to drink. His mother was on his heels. "Phyllis and Tom have always done a fine job, so it wonders me why *Daed* thinks they need our help this year."

"Probably the same reason he wants to cut me into firewood."

Isaac closed the refrigerator after he found the iced tea and spun around to face his mother, glowering. "*Mamm*, that's not funny."

She covered her mouth with her hand, but her shoulders bounced a little as she stifled her giggle. "I know," she finally said. "But I talked to your *daed*'s doctor today and told him what was going on, that your father had been so mean . . . and saying crazy things. He does think there could be a problem with his medications, and he is calling in some adjusted prescriptions for two of them. So, hopefully he will stop wanting to turn me into firewood." She giggled this time.

Isaac shook his head, but he couldn't help but smile, feeling hopeful about this new information. "I hope that's the problem."

"Me too. Please thank your friend, Mary, for forwarding that suggestion."

Isaac took several swigs of tea before he lifted the lid from a simmering pot on the oven. *Pork roast.* He took a deep breath, savoring the aroma. "*Ya*, I will." He put the lid back, leaving it cracked like his mother had. "I'm going to feed the animals."

"So . . . will you be having any more picnics with Mary?" His mother leaned against the kitchen counter and smiled.

"*Nee.*" He turned to go, but she called his name. He knew where this conversation was going.

"She seems very nice. Why not?"

"Mary doesn't even live here. You know that. Eventually, she will go back to Texas. We're just friends."

His mother sighed. "Well, I believe her to be an angel sent from God. She was at least able to get you out on a real date. Do you think you'll stay in touch with her?"

Isaac glanced out the window into the darkness, then back at his mother. "I don't know, *Mamm*, but I need to tend to the critters."

"Isaac." She walked up to him and put a hand on

his arm. "When your father was first sick, I admit that I needed your help that first year. But despite his leg, your father is able to take care of himself now. You can't base your future on us. Do you hear me? If you don't get that *daadi haus* livable, I'm going to hire someone. Someone *Englisch*." She grinned as she slapped him playfully on the arm. "So. Unless you want an *Englisch* carpenter underfoot for weeks, you best make that a priority."

"*Mamm*, you don't know if it's *Daed's* meds making him all loopy in the head. What if it's not?" Isaac thought about Ethan and his depression. He didn't want his *daed* struggling with the same thing.

"Sweet boy." She shook her head. "Even if it isn't, we will get it figured out." A smiled filled her face. "Unless he turns me into firewood." She bent over laughing, then looked up at Isaac, who was too stunned to move. "Chop, chop!" she said. Then she laughed so hard that Isaac couldn't help but laugh with her.

Finally, he gathered himself. "It really isn't funny, *Mamm*."

"Of course it is," she said as she pulled a tissue from her apron pocket. "Your father and I have been married for thirty-four years. We squabble. And he's gotten lazy the past year. But he'd never hurt me. And I plan to keep pushing him to do more for himself." She poked him in the arm. "So, you best get out there and find yourself a *fraa* before you are an old man."

Isaac knew who he wanted to marry, but he just

nodded and went outside. He was going to stay close to his mother until he knew for certain his father wasn't losing his mind. And he wasn't going to ask out Hannah until Mary went back to Texas, out of respect.

✑

Charlotte lined out all the sushi she'd brought home for everyone to try, glad she'd gotten home before everyone went to bed. She was still basking in the aftermath of the most wonderful date she'd ever had. There was no good-night kiss, only a hug, but she could feel something happening between them. And he'd graciously offered to buy extra sushi when Charlotte had shared with him what Hannah said.

"There." She pointed to four plates she'd put the sushi on. "Try some of each." She smiled at Amos, Lena, Jacob, and Hannah who were all lined up in the kitchen. But no one was moving.

Amos folded his arms across his chest and frowned. "That is fish that is not cooked?"

Charlotte picked up a slice with her fingers. "Yes. And it's very good. Try this one." She offered it to Amos on a napkin. "It's caterpillar *maki*."

Amos locked eyes with Charlotte. "I'm not eating a bug."

Charlotte laughed. "No, no. It's not really caterpillar. It's eel, cucumber, rice, and—"

Amos shook his head, waved his hand, and took a step backward as he rambled off something in Dutch. Then he left the kitchen.

"Jacob, I know you'll try anything." She handed him the same slice, and he smelled it before he popped it in his mouth. "Ugh." He scrunched his face, then spit it back into the napkin. "*Nee*. You can keep your caterpillar eel food."

"Don't give up." Charlotte chose a double salmon thinking Jacob might like that better. He didn't eat anything with tomato sauce, but otherwise, she wasn't sure she'd ever seen him turn down food. "You just have to find one you like."

Hannah laughed when Jacob spit out the second bite into the napkin. "*Nee. Danki*, Mary, but *nee*."

Lena crinkled her nose, reminded Charlotte that she'd been sick, then she, too, left the kitchen.

Charlotte slammed her hands to her hips. "Hannah. Don't disappoint me. I know you will try a few of these." She reached for another slice. "This one is grasshopper, but I promise it doesn't have grasshoppers in it. It has shrimp, asparagus, and . . . other stuff." She decided not to mention the eel this time.

Hannah brought the food to her nose like Jacob had, then stared at it. "Maybe they should give different names to these foods." She slowly chewed it, and Charlotte waited for it to hit the napkin as Hannah twisted her mouth into an awful expression. But Hannah swallowed. She wadded up the napkin. "*Danki* to your friend John for buying these for us to try, but . . ." She crinkled her nose.

"Y'all don't have good taste. These are great." Charlotte was too full to eat one more thing, but she piled the sushi back in the to-go containers and stashed them in the refrigerator.

"Better be nice or I won't write down that bread recipe for you to take home." Hannah winked. "And I'm pretty sure you think we have pretty *gut* taste when it comes to that."

Charlotte nodded. "I promise, I'll be good."

They said their good-nights, and Charlotte went to bed at nine thirty, the earliest since she'd gotten there. So, she wasn't too surprised when she woke up at four o'clock the next morning. She got dressed and tiptoed down the stairs to the kitchen. Everyone would be shocked if she started breakfast this morning, but not as shocked as Charlotte when she eyed all the sushi boxes piled on the counter.

All empty.

16

C harlotte threw away the empty containers and was frying bacon when Lena and Hannah came downstairs. Hannah said something to Lena in Pennsylvania Dutch, and Lena chuckled, which was nice to hear since Lena had been feeling so poorly lately.

"Not fair. You know I can't understand you." Charlotte grinned as she glanced over her shoulder, then finished flipping the bacon.

"Hannah said that your people in Texas are going to be surprised if we send you back knowing how to cook. And she said something else, but it's a surprise we will share with you later. That's why she spoke the *Deitsch.*"

"I love surprises."

Jacob clomped down the stairs in his heavy boots. And Amos went straight to the table and sat down while Lena started coffee in the percolator, another thing that tasted better in Amish Country.

"Speaking of surprises," Charlotte said as she laid out the bacon on a plate lined with paper towels. She turned around when she was done, grinning. "Did someone get hungry in the middle of the night?" Her eyes landed on Jacob as she crossed her arms. He must have decided the sushi wasn't so bad after all. Maybe he'd gotten a snack while he was sneaking out of the house.

"Don't look at me." Jacob shrugged, shaking his head. "That stuff is right up there with tomato sauce."

Amos cleared his throat. "I ate your bug rolls."

Charlotte's jaw dropped, but Lena was the one who burst out laughing again.

"Amos, you ate them all?"

He opened up the newspaper and started scanning the pages. "*Ya.* I ate them all." He lifted his eyes to Charlotte. "I woke up hungry, and there was nothing else in the refrigerator but goat milk cheese and your bug rolls."

"That was a lot of food," Lena said, still smiling.

Amos held a palm up to silence them. "I do not want to know what I ate, what they were called, or anything else about them. They were *gut*, though."

They all started laughing, and Charlotte was sure she was going to burst with a joy that she hadn't even known was possible. She silently thanked God for His many blessings, for Hannah and this wonderful family, and then she thanked Him again before breakfast.

It was later that morning when Charlotte told Hannah again that she was going to need to go back to Texas soon.

"You can't leave yet!" Hannah bounced up on her toes. "The Gordonville mud sale is in two weeks. It's held at the fire station, and it's great fun. Do you have mud sales in Texas?"

"Sure we do." Maybe the Amish ladies in Beeville went to mud sales. With each passing day, the lies seeped deeper into her bloodstream like a virus that might kill her if she didn't come clean. "I-I don't know if I can stay that long, Hannah."

Hannah frowned. "I'm going to miss you so much." She pointed a finger at Charlotte. "Now, don't cry when I give you your surprise. I was going to wait for *Mamm*, but she's taking a nap, and I can't wait."

Charlotte took a deep breath. This new relationship with God was great, but the spiritual cleansing that came with it had been both joyous—and painful. "Okay, I won't cry."

"This is for you." Hannah handed her a small box. "*Mamm* and I filled it with all of our favorite recipes. With the exception of baking bread, you haven't shown much interest in learning to cook." She giggled. "But you've shown a large interest in eating. And whether or not you stayed in our community or went back to Texas, we both wanted you to have our favorite recipes with hopes that you'll think of us fondly from wherever you are."

Charlotte put the small box on the kitchen table and

threw her arms around Hannah. "I'm going to miss you the most. I love you, and I can see why Ethan—" She stopped herself just before she blew her cover. "I just love you."

Hannah eased away, cupped Charlotte's cheeks, and smiled. "*Ach*, my dearest Mary, I am going to miss you very much too."

Charlotte hung her head, choked back her tears, and picked up the recipe box. "I will cherish this forever." She smiled, wondering if Ryan would be her food guinea pig when she got home.

∾

Hannah walked into the mudroom that afternoon and waited for her mother to run a blue dress through the washer. "Are you sure you feel up to doing this?" They'd skipped doing the laundry yesterday since Hannah's mother hadn't been feeling well.

"*Ya*. I feel much better. Whatever bug had latched on to me must have flown away."

"*Ach, gut*. Is this the last of the clothes?"

Her mother tossed the wet dress into the laundry basket. "*Ya*. But Mary usually brings her sheets down when she knows we'll be doing the wash. I don't see them."

"I told her we would catch the wash today, but she's used to us doing laundry on Monday, so she probably forgot. I'll go get them." She took two steps but stopped and turned around. "*Ach*, by the way, I gave Mary the recipe box. She started talking about going home, and I wanted her to have it. I asked her to please stay until the mud sale in Gordonville in a couple of weeks, but I don't know if she will."

"I know you're going to miss her." *Mamm* worked a white shirt through the washer. "I will miss her too. God sent her here at the perfect time. She's been so *gut* for you."

"*Ya*. It's been like having a sister." She grabbed the extra laundry basket. "I'll go get the sheets."

As Hannah pulled the pillowcases off, she smiled. Mary was never around on laundry day. She thought about the things that had irritated her about her cousin in the beginning, but her cousin's quirkiness and ability to care deeply had made up for her lack of knowledge about cooking, gardening, and cleaning. She wondered if Mary wasn't good at these things because of the type of child-hood she'd had before moving in with her aunt and uncle.

She tossed the top sheet on the floor with the pillow-cases, then lifted a corner of the fitted sheet. When she did, she saw something yellow between the mattresses. She lifted the mattress up and pulled out a yellow pad of paper. She read a few sentences, then sat down on the bed . . . before she fell down.

Despite the cooler temperatures, Charlotte dripped with sweat inside Ethan's house, and the skunk smell still lingered in the air. She tried to hurry and make a list of repairs, and she took lots of pictures with her phone to reference when she got home. She would need to hire a contractor and get the house on the market.

She made one last run through Ethan's things, without actually unpacking all the boxes, and decided that she wasn't going to discover anything new about his death. She was a little worried that her black-and-white friend might still be lurking around, and being here made her sad, so she took one last look before closing the door behind her.

She looked around outside, and when she didn't see her smelly intruder, she sat down on a porch step. As she stared out at the trees in the yard, she couldn't help but wonder which one Ethan had chosen. She dialed Ryan's number.

After reiterating how much she'd enjoyed dinner, Charlotte got to what was on her mind. "I've been thinking . . . if Ethan hadn't died, I would have never come here."

"Probably not."

"Or if I had come here, it would have been for a short visit, and I probably wouldn't have found a family of friends. Or a relationship with God. It makes me believe that Ethan's death wasn't in vain. Do you think that sometimes God allows a life to be taken because He knows that a person's passing will have a positive impact on other people's lives?"

"I don't know, but He gave His only Son for all of us,

so I guess it's probably true. Scripture says we all live a complete life. I try to remind myself of this when I see a young child die. For some people, it takes eighty or ninety years to live a complete life. For others, they might live a complete life in four years, but still accomplish all they were supposed to. So, it stands to reason that Ethan lived a complete life as well."

"But did he? What if by using his free will, Ethan interrupted God's plan for his life?"

Ryan was quiet for a few moments. "Charlotte, my first thought is that you need to pray about this. We all have questions. We all have worries. And depending on who you talk to, you can get a host of responses from well-intentioned, godly people."

"Something else is still bothering me." She stretched her legs out across the two lower steps. "I'm pretty sure Jacob knows that I'm not Amish. I don't think he knows I'm Ethan's sister, but I think he might have heard just enough to know I've been lying."

"Uh oh."

"But, if he overheard, he's staying quiet about it. I sort of hinted that I knew he snuck out of the house sometimes, so maybe that's why he is keeping my secret. I think Amos and Lena would be furious if they knew what he was doing." She paused. "Although, they do have this thing they call a *rumschpringe*. When a person turns sixteen, they get to run around and experience the outside world. Hannah told me that parents tend to look the other way. Although Hannah also said that Amos was pretty strict with her, so I don't know."

"Well, you're going to tell them soon enough, and if Jacob hasn't said anything before now, he probably won't."

"Hannah wants me to stay for something called a mud sale in a couple of weeks, but I don't know. I think I'd fold before then and tell them the truth. I am never going to tell another lie again in my life."

Ryan chuckled. "Yeah, you will. Even if it's a tiny white lie that just slips out. But I think it's great that you feel that way."

"I'm just terrified about how they will react when they find out I'm Ethan's sister."

"I don't know. If I had to guess, I'd say they will be really mad at first, but then they will forgive you. It's their way. And once you tell them the reasoning behind your lies, they'll understand. I'm sure they've grown to love the Charlotte the rest of us know and love."

Charlotte's heart did a little dance. It wasn't exactly an admission of Ryan's affection for her, but there did seem to be some sort of subtext in his comment. She let out a heavy breath. "I hope you're right. I'm not looking forward to having that conversation with them." She stood up, took a last look at the house, then stepped down off the porch. "I guess I better go. I'll let you know when I book a flight."

She ended the call, then started back down the road toward home. She liked the way that sounded, even though she knew it wasn't her true home. She was considering staying for the mud sale in Gordonville. It seemed important to Hannah, although she was also anxious to spend some time with Ryan and see where that might go. And freelance projects were coming in that she'd better start soon.

She glanced up at the sky, recalling the image she'd seen form in the clouds. No way was that a coincidence. She was choosing to believe that Ethan was in heaven. That would be the one good thing that would come out of telling them all the truth—she could tell Hannah what she saw, and anyone who knew Ethan well would know the significance of this sign. She wasn't sure whether or not to tell Hannah about the picture of Edna Glick and what she'd learned. Whether or not it was a one-night stand or an ongoing relationship, it seemed cruel to tell Hannah over a year later when she was starting to move forward with her life.

By the time she got home, she'd worked up an appetite, and Hannah's cookies were calling her name. Charlotte was glad they didn't keep a scale in the house. She'd face her own scale when she got home, then get back on a schedule at the gym. She'd have her memories to take with her. And God. It amazed her how Ethan had found this place, these people. *Why would you leave all this?*

Charlotte saw that Jacob and Amos were home early. Their large work boots were by the front door when she walked in, and the familiar smell of manure and hay wafted up her nose. But she'd barely closed the door behind her when she gasped and stopped in her tracks.

Amos, Lena, Jacob, and Hannah were all standing together. And beside them were Charlotte's suitcases.

Charlotte looked at each family member. Lena and Hannah were sniffling, but wouldn't look at her. Jacob had his arms folded across his chest, and he was having no trouble looking at Charlotte—glaring at her. As usual, Amos's expression was unreadable, but he took a step toward her and handed her the yellow pad. Charlotte wished the floor would swallow her up as she took the tablet. Maybe she should have felt relief that she wouldn't have to lie anymore, but her heart raced as panic set in.

"I know this looks bad, and I've wanted to tell you all the truth for a long time." It had been a good while since she'd written a letter to Ethan, and she was frantically trying to remember what was on the yellow pad. Tears filled her eyes so that as she flipped through the first few pages, she could barely read anything. Her bottom lip trembled as she caught bits and pieces.

I've sent letters to Hannah, and while your fiancée did write me back, her notes were brief and offered no explanation. None of my phone calls were answered or returned either. Since I'm not getting any answers, I've decided to spend some time in Lancaster County, to live among the Amish, as one of them. Yes, it's deceitful, but I have to know the truth. From what I've read about the Amish, they aren't very trusting and aren't fond of outsiders. Maybe this is why, after you became a member of their group, you detached yourself from the people who love you. Either way, I'm not above playing dress-up and telling a few lies to find out what happened to my only brother.

"I wanted to tell you the truth," she said again, ". . . that I'm not Amish, but then I grew to love all of you." She paused as a tear slipped down her cheek. "I learned about God while being here. I've made friends." She pointed to Hannah, but Hannah wouldn't look at her. Even Jacob turned away from her. But Amos's eyes fired daggers at her.

"You will leave our home now. We have called a car for you." Amos held up a hand when Charlotte opened her mouth to speak, shaking his head. "No more upset for my family."

Charlotte looked at Hannah, noticing she was holding the recipe box, along with the heart-shaped potholders. "Hannah, please . . ."

"You will go!" Amos took a forceful step toward her.

She thought about all the times Ryan had said the Amish were forgiving. "What about forgiveness? Don't you even want to know why I'm here, why I came here under disguise?"

Jacob tossed something at her feet. "We know who you are."

Charlotte reached down and picked up her driver's license as tears poured down her cheeks. "I wanted to know why my brother hanged himself. You can't fault me for that! That's all I ever wanted to know."

Amos took another step toward her and pointed to the door, and Jacob picked up two of her suitcases. "Your secret was a lot bigger than mine," he said in an angry whisper as he brushed past her.

"Why didn't you just ask us?" Hannah asked in a loud voice. Lena put a hand on her daughter's arm, shaking her head.

"Because I didn't know what happened," Charlotte said, desperate for them to understand. "I didn't know if you broke up with Ethan, if you broke his heart so badly that he killed himself. I just wanted to understand and—"

"Leave here!" Amos was directly in front of her. "Go now."

Charlotte eased around Amos to Hannah. "I'm so sorry. Please, Hannah."

"You need to go, Mary." Lena sighed. "I mean, *Charlotte.*"

Hannah wouldn't look at Charlotte, and after a few moments, she ran upstairs. With the exception of when Ethan died, Charlotte hadn't felt this bad since she and Ethan had been separated and sent to different foster homes.

Once Jacob had put the last of her things out in the grass, he came back inside and stood beside his father, both with arms folded across their chests, scowling. Lena dabbed at her eyes with a tissue, stared long and hard at Charlotte, then she also went upstairs.

"I'm sorry," Charlotte said in a choked whisper. "For everything . . ." She finally spun around and ran out the door. Sitting down on one of her suitcases, she buried her face in her hands and wept, wondering if the outcome would have been different if Charlotte had confessed before they'd found out. At least they wouldn't have read her letters to Ethan and private journal entries.

She stood up, tempted to go back inside and make a final plea, but the look on Amos's face as he stood on the other side of the screen door kept her from moving. She glanced up toward the second story and saw Hannah. Even in the distance Charlotte could see her sobbing. "I'm sorry!" she yelled upward to Hannah. It was then that Amos slammed the door.

Forgiving? Really, Ryan? They can forgive people who murder their children, but they can't forgive me? She looked up at the clouds. *Why, God? Why did You let this happen?* She wondered if God would be with her when she left this place, or if He would forsake her as well. She turned around when she heard the door open. It was Hannah, carrying something. Charlotte hoped it was the recipe box and potholders. But as Hannah got closer, Charlotte could see that she was carrying a small book.

"Here." Hannah handed it to Charlotte. "Since you seem to believe that you are your brother's only keeper, maybe this will make sense to you."

Charlotte held the book in her hands, then instinctively held it to her nose, as if she might breathe in the scent of Ethan. "His Bible?"

Hannah wasn't crying anymore as she shook her head. "*Nee.* I don't know what it is. I found the book at his house, but it must be in another language. Maybe you will know how to read it. Maybe it will give you the answers you are looking for."

Charlotte studied the brown leather book, then looked up at Hannah, knowing she would drop to her knees and beg if Hannah would forgive her. Instead, she opened the book to the first page, and right away she knew that it was meant for her, or at the very least . . . it was not meant for Hannah.

"You went to a lot of trouble and told a lot of lies to find out why Ethan killed himself. It must be very important to you to understand."

"Of course it is. Don't you want to know?" Charlotte thought about the picture and the note on the back.

Hannah offered a weak smile. "I don't think any of us truly knows what goes on inside someone's head . . . or heart." She paused. "I'm sorry things worked out this way. You could have just walked up to the door, said you were Ethan's sister, and I would have told you anything you wanted to know."

Charlotte hung her head, kicking the grass with her black loafer, knowing it would be the last time she'd wear the shoes. "I thought maybe you'd brainwashed him somehow." She looked up. "It wasn't until I spent time here that I realized that . . . that your people . . . well, you're the real deal. I didn't know God before I got here." When Hannah didn't say anything, Charlotte went on. "Why can't you and your family forgive me, like you talk about in devotions, how God forgives all of our sins?" Charlotte was surprised when a tear slid down her cheek since she was sure she didn't have any left.

"We're human, Mary." Hannah sighed. "I mean Charlotte. In time, we will forgive. I will be praying about it—and for you—constantly. Ethan loved you very much. I'd always wanted to meet you. At least I did before he died and you forced us to send his body to you against his wishes."

Charlotte swiped at her eyes, longing for a hug, but knowing one wasn't coming. She turned toward the road when she heard a car coming. "I guess that's my ride."

Hannah blinked back tears. "*Ya.* God's peace, Charlotte." And she headed toward the house.

Charlotte turned away from Hannah and waited for the blue car. But then she remembered something and spun around. "Hannah, wait."

Hannah stopped and slowly turned around.

"The day we looked for pictures in the clouds, I saw something."

Hannah took a few steps closer to her, but didn't say anything.

"You said you've always wondered if Ethan was in

heaven, and for me . . . at that time . . . I wasn't even sure there was a God or heaven. But all of a sudden, the clouds seemed to split open and plain as day I saw butterflies, and I knew it was Ethan telling me that he was in heaven. I couldn't tell you at the time, but anyone who knows Ethan knows that—"

"Butterflies are always around him," Hannah said as her eyes filled with tears. "They used to land on him all the time." She took a few steps toward Charlotte. "Did you really see that? Or are you just trying to make this all better?"

"I saw it. I believe it's a sign that Ethan is with God." Charlotte turned toward the car when she heard the door slam.

"Someone called for a driver?" An elderly man walked toward Charlotte's suitcases, and she nodded.

Charlotte waited until the man was stowing the suitcases in the trunk before she spoke. "Anyway, I just wanted you to know . . . about what I saw. So, I'll leave with you all hating me, and I wouldn't say I know God very well, but it is a step in the right direction that might not have happened if things had unfolded differently. I just regret that I'm no longer part of this family."

"You never were," she said slowly, and Charlotte could feel the knife piercing her heart as Hannah turned and walked back to the house.

17

Hannah waved off her mother when she walked back into the living room. "I don't want to talk right now." She hurried up the stairs, taking them two at a time, and she closed her bedroom door behind her. After she fell onto the bed, she buried her head in her pillow and sobbed until her head was splitting. She forced back the tears and sat up. She opened the drawer of her nightstand and took out the picture she'd found while packing Charlotte's things. And for the hundredth time, she read the inscription on the back. *To my one and only. I love you . . .*

She wasn't sure which blow to her heart hurt the most—Charlotte's lies, Ethan's death, or the picture of Edna. *Ethan, why?* Hannah wondered if Charlotte had brought the picture from home or if maybe she'd gone to Ethan's house when she went on her walks. Most likely, Charlotte had found the photo at Ethan's house.

After another hour of crying, wondering, and praying, she dried her tears. Ethan was gone. And Charlotte was gone. But Edna was right around the corner.

∽

Charlotte tearfully told Ryan the whole story as she lay on the bed in her hotel room. As upset as she was, at least she wasn't sweating. The first thing she'd done when she got to her room was to turn the air conditioning on high.

"So, I booked a flight home for tomorrow morning," she said, unable to control the tears.

"Sweetie, I'm so sorry things turned out this way."

Charlotte cried even harder at the sound of Ryan's soothing voice and endearment. "I just want to come home."

"I think that the journal entries and letters to Ethan they found just added salt to an open wound. But maybe in time they will heal and let you back into their lives. I know how much you grew to care about them."

"They are so real—so loving and genuine. I don't know how to explain it. And I'd do anything to have a family like that. *Anything.*"

Ryan promised to call her later, and after she'd showered, cried some more, and squeezed into a pair of blue jeans and a T-shirt, she sat down on the bed, realizing she already missed her Amish clothes. After another ten minutes of feeling sorry for herself, she rummaged through her suitcases and piled her dresses, black socks, prayer coverings, and extra pair of black shoes on the bed. She hated to throw good clothes away, so she decided that tomorrow morning, she'd just leave them on the bed. Maybe someone from housekeeping could find a home for them.

She slipped on a pair of flip-flops, then repacked what was left, which wasn't much. It all fit in one suitcase. Then a jolt of adrenaline spiked, and she hurriedly started pulling everything out again as she searched for the picture of Edna.

Oh no. Hannah had been hurt enough, but after Charlotte searched and searched again through her things, she knew that Hannah or Lena must have found the photo. She dumped her purse on the bed, but no picture.

Isaac guided his buggy up the driveway to Hannah's house. Mary's voice mail was confusing, but her message said that Hannah would explain everything. Isaac had been hesitant to leave his mother, but she was going to run errands anyway, and she insisted that Isaac's father was much better since the doctors had adjusted his medications. Isaac was still keeping a close eye on both of them.

Lena met Isaac at the door, then went and got Hannah.

"*Wie bischt?* Can we talk?" Isaac stepped outside when Hannah pushed the screen door open. "Are you okay? I got a confusing voice mail message from Mary."

Hannah pulled a tissue from her apron pocket and

dabbed at her eyes. "I'm okay. I think. But Mary isn't that woman's real name."

Isaac stayed beside Hannah as they walked down the porch steps to a bench near the garden. Once they'd sat down, Hannah burst into tears. Isaac put his arm around her as she told the strange tale about Mary—Charlotte. *So, that's why she'd asked so many questions about Ethan.*

"It's all so awful," Hannah said, sniffling. "And now I'm also left wondering if Ethan was in love with someone else." She pulled a picture from her pocket and handed it to Isaac.

His chest tightened when he read the note on the back of the photo, wanting to choose his words carefully so he wouldn't upset her even more. But it certainly appeared that Ethan and Edna had been carrying on in an inappropriate way for her to write a note like that. He'd tried to talk himself out of that notion when he'd first seen them together at the restaurant. But this seemed like proof that they'd become romantically involved. Posed pictures were mostly forbidden. It wouldn't get a person shunned or anything, but it was looked down upon.

He handed the photo back to Hannah. "I'm not sure what to think about that." She was so upset that Isaac wondered if she really was ready to move on. And Isaac was still processing everything she'd told him.

"Charlotte was like my sister. We'd grown very close. It's a toss-up as to what I'm the most hurt about." Hannah paused. "After thinking about it, in some ways, her coming here was good. She said she found the Lord while she was here." She blotted her eyes again as Isaac kept his arm around her, gently rubbing her shoulder. Then she offered a weak smile. "Like Ethan. He always said we saved him. Maybe we saved Charlotte, too, and it was all part of God's plan."

Isaac was at a loss for words. Charlotte had asked a lot of questions, some of which Isaac had answered. He wasn't going to lie to Hannah, but he hoped she didn't ask if Isaac knew anything about Ethan and Edna. Isaac didn't want to be the one to confirm her suspicions.

"Are you going to ask Edna about the photo?" Isaac thought about the mess it would stir up if Edna's fiancé found out. But, right or wrong, it didn't seem fair for Edna to have contributed to something that caused so much pain for so many people.

"I don't know." Hannah sniffled as she locked eyes with him. "I'm glad you're here, Isaac." She put her head on his shoulder and found his hand, latching on tightly.

As good as it felt to have her near him, clinging to him, he didn't want secrets between them, and his stomach was churning with anxiety. He eased her away, keeping hold of her hand. "I need to tell you something."

"*Ach, nee.*" She let go of his hand and brought it to her chest. "You sound so serious, and I'm not sure my heart can take anything else."

Since there was no good way to tell her, Isaac just blurted it out. "I saw Ethan and Edna together once."

Hannah stared across the yard, a faraway look in her eyes. "Did everyone know that Ethan and Edna were carrying on? Everyone but me?"

"*Nee*, not that I know of. I only saw them together one time. I didn't feel like it was my place to say anything." He touched her chin and gently turned her to face him. "But I never thought Ethan was worthy of your love after that. And because of that, I never reached out to Ethan when I could tell that he was depressed, in need of a friend. Maybe if I had, he wouldn't have felt so hopeless."

Hannah was quiet for a while. "I think maybe Jacob knew something. He seemed to like Ethan in the beginning, but later in our relationship, Jacob stopped wanting to be around him." She made fists with both her hands and gently hit her knees. "I don't know who to trust! I'm mad. I'm hurt. And . . ." She searched Isaac's eyes, needing answers, but Isaac didn't have them.

"I promise you can trust me, Hannah."

Isaac's heart sank when she resumed staring, the faraway look in her eyes again. He knew he couldn't expect her to blindly trust anymore. He'd have to earn it.

Charlotte stowed her purse underneath the seat in front of her and fastened her seat belt. She was thankful for a window seat, and in three hours, Pennsylvania, Hannah,

Isaac, and all they represented would be behind her. She was hopeful that God was traveling home with her.

In her heart, she knew He was, but she was having a hard time understanding how God had let things fall apart like this. Her first conclusion, that God was punishing her. For all the lies and deceptions. She'd asked for His forgiveness repeatedly, and through the Amish worship services she'd attended, she knew that God forgave you the moment you asked Him. So, in hindsight, maybe God had forgiven her, and the horrific pain she felt was her inability to forgive herself. She wasn't the same person she'd been when she first arrived in Paradise, so she was going to choose to believe the latter, that God had forgiven her. Forgiving herself might take time.

Either way, she was going home. Back to the life she'd had before she knew what it was like to have a loving family, a sister, and a place to belong. She leaned her head back against the seat as the pilot fired up the engines. Normally, she'd be nervous until the plane was off the ground and leveled out, but today, other worries consumed her, and crashing into the ocean didn't sound so bad. Right away, she thought about Ethan and regretted her thought. She was sad, but she didn't want to die.

Following an unusually rough takeoff, Charlotte waited until her pulse got back to normal, then she reached into her purse and took out the small book Hannah had given her. She tapped her finger against the brown leather, nervous to read it. Would it make her feel better or worse? Then she tapped some more, but when the man next to her cleared his throat, she stopped. "Sorry," she whispered.

The older man cleared his throat two more times, and Charlotte realized it didn't have anything to do with her. Then he coughed. Again and again until his face turned bright red.

"Sir, are you okay?" Charlotte turned to her right, but felt her jaw drop a bit when the man's dark hair . . . moved. The elderly man looked to be in his late seventies, but there wasn't a gray hair on his head, and a dark blob of hair danced around on the top of his head. The harder he coughed, the more dancing, and Charlotte was sure it was going to flop right off his head and into her lap.

She twisted around and looked over her seat, but she didn't see a flight attendant anywhere. This guy needed something to drink. His cough was deep and raspy, and Charlotte strained to look around him and down the aisle. No food or beverage cart in sight. Then the coughing stopped.

"Well, that was bothersome." The man shook his head, and again, Charlotte feared his hairpiece was going to fly off. "So sorry. I'm sure that couldn't have been pleasant for you."

Charlotte smiled. "No, it's fine. But you had me worried for a minute."

"My name is Nicholas, and it is my pleasure to be sitting next to someone as lovely as yourself."

If the guy hadn't been old enough to be her grandfather, Charlotte might have found him a bit creepy, but he had a warm smile, even though his breath hinted that he might have had garlic recently.

"Thank you. That's very sweet. I'm Charlotte."

Nicholas nodded, and Charlotte refocused on Ethan's book. She was going to read what he'd written, it was just a matter of when. But it would take awhile to decipher, and Charlotte's head was splitting. She was worried about Hannah, what she was thinking, if she for sure had the photo of Edna, if she'd confronted Edna. Maybe she'd never know the whole story, only the little bit that Isaac had told her, confirmed in a photo that Ethan and Edna had shared at least one instance of intimacy. Charlotte hoped that's all it was, a lapse in judgment, a weak moment. Mostly, she hoped Hannah didn't have the picture.

She tapped a finger, lightly this time, against the cover, knowing that once she'd read it, she couldn't unknow what it said. The knowledge would be hers, for better or worse. Leaning back against the seat, she closed her eyes. *Ethan, what should I do?* Again, she wondered if what he'd written was for her. So she'd understand. Before she could give it much more thought, Nicholas elbowed her. She opened her eyes and turned toward him.

"My bad." He chuckled. "So sorry. I was just trying to reach down into my bag to retrieve my book."

Charlotte smiled at his use of slang—*my bad*. "No problem."

"Be glad that you are not a fat person. It is cumbersome." He shook his head. "There are more overweight people in the world than ever before. You would think that the airlines would make bigger seats." He laughed again, and Charlotte noticed his pearly whites on the top and bottom, too perfect to be real. She fought the urge to reach up and straighten his toupee.

Charlotte didn't think he looked very overweight, a bit chunky, but not really all that heavy. She wasn't sure what to say, so she just smiled and asked, "Do you want me to hand you your bag?"

"Certainly. Yes, oh yes. Could you please? I'd hate to further harm you with my elbow."

"No problem." Charlotte maneuvered her arm in front of his knees and was able to latch on to a black plastic shopping bag. "Here you go."

"Wonderful good." He reached into the bag and pulled out a hardback book, and Charlotte leaned her head against the back of the seat again, closing her eyes. Not a minute later, Nicholas's elbow found its way into her arm again, and she jumped. "Oops," he said, cringing. "Oopsie doopsie."

Charlotte bit her bottom lip to keep from laughing, then said, "It's okay." She glanced at the book he was reading. *My Life as a Butterfly.* She was glad she told Hannah about the butterflies in the clouds, and she hoped it would give her some peace eventually.

"I am an avid reader. I read five books per week. Never

four, never six. Always five." He winked at Charlotte. "I've read this one three times, though. It's a favorite. Horace Potts is a favorite author of mine. Have you read any of his books?"

Charlotte shook her head. "No, I haven't." She decided this wouldn't be a sleeping flight.

"He's a wonderful author. He has the capacity to take you inside the presumed mind of some of God's most interesting creatures. He's written *My Life as a Lizard, My Life as a Toad, My Life as a White Shark,* and lots more." Nicholas frowned. "And then, out of the blue, he wrote *My Life as an Underwear Model,* and he lost me on that one."

Charlotte laughed out loud, which felt good. "That's quite a shift."

Nicholas raised his shoulders as he shook his head, chuckling. "I know!" He settled back against the seat, still laughing. "Bizarre, I tell you. *My Life as a Butterfly* remains my favorite. Did you know that most butterflies only live for one week? The exception being the monarch, of course. The monarch can live up to six months."

"No, I didn't know that." Charlotte paused, thinking of Ethan. "My brother used to always have butterflies around him. Even when we were kids, they would land on him all the time."

"Our lives mirror the butterfly, a creature of true transformation, emerging from caterpillar to cocoon, and then finally to the beautiful winged beauties that bless our surroundings. Some even say that the butterfly may be an angel or a messenger from a deceased loved one."

"Really? I didn't know that." And two months ago, Charlotte wouldn't have given much thought about angels, God, or an afterlife. Even if what the man said was just folklore, it was a beautiful idea. Hannah had said that Ethan told her that Hannah and her family had saved him. She hoped that when Ethan took his last breath, he realized that Jesus is the only person who can save us.

"Does your brother still have this wonderful connection with the butterflies?"

Charlotte shook her head. "He . . . he died about a year ago."

"I'm very sorry for your loss. How did he die?"

Charlotte wasn't comfortable with the direction of this conversation, but she answered—truthfully—which felt good. "He took his own life."

"Oh my. Oh dear." Nicholas shook his head, tossing the hairpiece around. "I'm assuming he was a young man?"

"Yes. He would be thirty now."

"Do you mind me asking, why do you think he ended his time here on earth?"

Charlotte shrugged, searching for a way to change the subject. "I don't know."

"I can see this is uncomfortable for you, so let me ask . . . what are you reading?" Nicholas pointed to the small book in Charlotte's lap.

"Oh, this isn't a novel or anything. It's actually . . .
my brother's book, maybe a journal of sorts. I'm hoping
that it will shed some light on why he killed himself. I'm
returning to Texas after a long visit in Amish Country.
My brother had moved there and had plans to marry an
Amish woman."

"Interesting folks, the Amish."

"Do you live in Pennsylvania, or maybe Texas?"

He smiled broadly. "I live where the wind takes me.
I float on the whimsical clouds of life, dance with the
crickets on a starlit night, and sing in the shower when I
see fit to take one."

Charlotte didn't think she could wipe the smile off of
her face if she tried. *Who is this guy?* "It sounds like you
enjoy life."

"Life is a gift; how we choose to live it is a choice."

Charlotte looked down at the small book. "There's
a part of me that doesn't want to know what was going
on in my brother's head. But as sure as I'm sitting here,
I know I'll read it." She surprised herself by voicing her
thoughts to this stranger.

"But you will rise at some point to go to the bathroom.
At least you will if you're like me. Then, you won't be sitting there, so does that make you sure of anything at all?"

Charlotte smiled again. "You are an interesting person, Nicholas."

"I know." He giggled. "I really am. So, I will give you
my two cents' worth of sidewalk psychiatry. Will reading

your brother's notebook bring you peace or cause you further upset?"

"I've asked myself that same question repeatedly. That's why I've just stared at the book and not read it. But it is too tempting, to have it in my possession and not read it . . . eventually."

"Ah, temptation, our prelude to sin. Are you familiar with the Lord's Prayer?"

It was the only prayer she knew by heart. "Yes."

"Well, allow me to share the fact that the King James Version of the Bible uses the word *temptation* in translation for the Greek word *peirasmos*, and this Greek word has nothing to do with temptation the way we know it, but instead it simply means 'being put to the test.' So, by what means will you be tested? Will the journey be worth the destination?"

"I don't know." She looked at this unusual man, and his piercing blue eyes challenged her to look deep within herself. "But I don't think I can have a book of my brother's private thoughts, and not read it, in light of . . . you know." She shrugged. "I need to know. And I think he meant for me to have it."

"My bladder says it's time to take a walk to the back of this air bus." He smiled, then groaned as he lifted himself out of the chair. He put the book in his seat, and eased into the aisle. Charlotte noticed he had a slight limp as he moved slowly to the back of the plane. He'd given her plenty to think about, but she was emotionally exhausted. If she was going to have any chance of sleep, she needed to close her eyes now, while Nicholas was away. She did so and didn't wake up until her ears started to pop, so she knew they were descending. Nicholas's book was still in the seat next to her, but she didn't see him anywhere. *Maybe I was snoring.* There were lots of empty seats on the plane.

"Ma'am." Charlotte reached across Nicholas's seat and tapped the arm of the flight attendant who was standing nearby in the aisle. "Do you know where the man who was sitting here went? He left his book in this chair."

"He asked to be moved up front to one of the exit seats with more leg room. I can take him the book." The woman reached for the book.

"No, no. I enjoyed talking to him, and I'd like to thumb through the book, then return it myself when the plane lands. Can you just tell him that?"

"Sure."

Charlotte picked up the book, opened it where the bookmark was, and read:

My beauty as a butterfly is evident by my bright colors, but what most people don't know is that those same bright colors fend off predators like birds, snakes, lizards, rats, wasps, and ants. Simply because I don't taste good. I tell you this to use as a comparison within your own species analysis. Are you as pretty on the inside as you are on the outside, and does it draw goodness or repel it?

Hannah's name flew into the forefront of Charlotte's thoughts. But despite her goodness, Hannah hadn't been able to forgive Charlotte, nor had the rest of her family. She recalled what Lena had told her. *You are a defender of goodness. A protector, compassionate, and someone people tend to trust right away.* Charlotte felt sure that Lena and the entire family were ruing the day they'd ever trusted Charlotte.

She continued reading.

We often hear that beauty is in the eye of the beholder, but in my case, it is my beauty that keeps me from being lunch. Ugly butterflies are gobbled up by the aforementioned predators. In that regard, I'm thankful I'm pretty. I repel my enemies.

Charlotte stopped reading, forcing a yawn so her ears would pop again, thinking what an odd book this was. But Horace Potts must be a popular author to have an entire series dedicated to his life as animals and insects.

So, I ask, do you see butterflies? Do they land on you? Go back and reread this page—the part about drawing goodness or repelling it.

Charlotte turned the page.

If I show up with a lot of my friends, we are working very hard to get you to take a good look at what's going on in your life. Is a transformation underway? Do you need to make changes? And you just thought I was around to look pretty.

Charlotte smiled, closed the book, and brought her seat to an upright position when she heard the flight attendant instructing people to do so.

Once the plane was on the ground, she turned her phone on. No voice mails or texts. It took another twenty minutes before she was able to work her way into the aisle and toward the exit. On the way, she looked for Nicholas to see if he was waiting in one of the seats. When she stepped off the plane and onto the tarmac, she waited, but she never saw him. She looked down at the book, waited a while longer, then finally eased the book into her carry-on bag and headed toward baggage claim.

There was lots of luggage, and she was keeping her eyes peeled for her two black suitcases that were empty and her red suitcase, when she felt breath on her neck and jumped. "Hello, stranger."

"Ryan! Oh, wow. I can't believe you're here." She threw her arms around his neck and held on for dear life.

He smelled freshly showered, with a hint of spicy cologne. When he cupped the back of her head and pulled her closer, she felt like she could stay in his arms forever. He seemed to be absorbing all the hurt in one simple hug, and Charlotte started to relax for the first time in a while. "Thank you," she whispered as she leaned up and kissed him on the cheek.

He brushed away a strand of hair that was across her face. "Good to see you smiling." Then he shook his head. "I'd forgotten how beautiful you are."

Charlotte could feel herself blushing. "I don't even have any makeup on, so I'm doubting that comment."

"I told you over dinner the other night, you don't need any." He eased away. "Let's get your stuff and get you home."

"I'm ready."

Charlotte grabbed her chest, and for a few seconds, she couldn't breathe. She ripped into her carry-on bag, then dumped her purse right there on the floor. "No, no, no!"

Ryan squatted down beside her. "What is it? What's wrong?"

"I must have left Ethan's book, his journal, on the plane."

Hannah knocked on Edna's door, the picture in the pocket of her apron.

"*Wie bischt*, Hannah? What a nice surprise." Edna pushed the screen door open and stepped aside. "I just finished making a batch of *yummasetti*."

Hannah regretted that she hadn't made *yummasetti* for Mary, or Charlotte, since it was a traditional Pennsylvania *Deitsch* casserole. She doubted that they had that in Texas. Hannah wondered if she would ever stop thinking about the cousin she'd thought she had, and whom she'd grown to love like a sister.

But right now, she had other business to take care of. Edna lived in a small house on the back of her parents' property. Most likely, it would become the *daadi haus* someday, where her parents would live when she and John got married. Assuming they still got married after

Hannah showed her the picture. Would Edna feel like she had to confess to her fiancé?

"I need an explanation for this," Hannah said tearfully as she handed Edna the photo.

Edna stared at the picture for a while before she looked back at Hannah. "Where did you get this?"

Hannah was barely over the threshold, but when Edna moved to the couch and sat down, Hannah took a few steps into the living room, but stayed standing. "Were you and Ethan . . ." She swallowed back the lump in her throat. "Were you and Ethan . . . involved?"

Edna jumped off the couch, her eyes round, mouth open. "Hannah! Of course not. Is that what you think?"

Hannah felt relief wash over her, but she still needed an explanation. "But the note on the back . . ."

Edna turned the photo over, then smiled. "*Ach*, I can see why you might have thought that, but dear Hannah . . ." Edna stood up and walked to her. "Do you really think I would do that?"

Hannah raised her shoulders, then dropped them slowly.

"I wondered what happened to this photo after Ethan died. If I tell you something, please don't tell anyone."

Hannah wasn't sure she could promise that, so she didn't say anything.

"I know pictures are forbidden, but do you remember when John was leaving for Ohio? He was gone almost two months to help his cousins rebuild their house after a fire."

Hannah nodded.

"I wanted him to have a picture of me to take with him. Do you remember the day at worship service when Ethan said he used to be very *gut* on a computer?"

"*Nee*, not really."

"You were standing there when we talked about it. Later, I went to his house and asked if he would take a picture of me. I had planned to just put it in a small frame to give to John. But Ethan said he could crop the photo to just my face since my hand was in the air. He asked if I wanted him to print a saying across the front, and I said yes. I wrote that on the back of the photo. But Ethan died before he was able to do it, and I never knew where the picture was. Where did you find it?"

Hannah sighed. "It was in his house." She hoped she wasn't telling a lie since she could only presume that's where Charlotte had found the photo. Hannah didn't feel like going into a long explanation about Charlotte. The community would find out eventually, but not today.

Edna smiled. "I asked him not to tell anyone." She looked back at Hannah as her smile faded. "I am so sorry for what you must have thought."

Hannah sat down on the couch and rubbed her forehead, then she tearfully looked at Edna. "Someone told me that they saw you and Ethan holding hands. Is that true?"

"*Ach*, Hannah. If someone saw Ethan and me being affectionate, it was just a genuine thank-you for his help, nothing more."

"I thought maybe there had been a romance between the two of you, that maybe Ethan felt guilty and that's why he killed himself." She felt relieved, but still left wondering why an affair with Edna would lead Ethan to take his life.

Edna sat down beside her. "*Nee*, Hannah. I would never have done that. Never."

"I'm sorry for thinking that."

Edna shook her head. "Don't apologize. I would have thought the same thing. But you do believe me, *ya*?"

Hannah's stomach was still tied in knots, but she wanted to believe Edna, so she nodded. Edna got them each a cup of coffee and a slice of pecan pie, and they chatted about things that had nothing to do with the photo or Ethan. Mostly, Edna talked about her wedding in November. But Hannah's mind kept drifting and her stomach churning. Something wasn't right, and she couldn't quite put her finger on what it was. After a while, she told Edna that she needed to go. She was walking down the porch steps toward her buggy when Edna called out, then hurried to catch up with her.

"*Ya?*" Hannah turned to face her.

"Um . . . can I please have the picture?" She held out her hand, smiling. "You know, for John and all. Maybe I can get someone else to crop it for the frame."

Hannah reached into her pocket as her stomach began to act up again. She handed the photo to Edna, then turned and left without saying anything else.

When she got home, Jacob was in the rocking chair on the porch. She tethered her horse and crossed the yard. "Can you maybe get the horse and buggy put up for me? I'll do one of your chores. I'm just so tired." She walked toward the front door, turning around when he didn't answer. "Please."

Jacob took off his hat, ran a hand through his hair, and nodded. "*Ya*, I'll take care of it."

Hannah started walking again, but slowed her step and turned around. "Are you okay?"

Jacob didn't answer right away. Finally, he said, "I guess."

Hannah went back and sat in the other rocking chair. She should have thought about how much Charlotte's betrayal would have affected Jacob too. They'd seemed to get along well. "What's wrong, Jacob?"

Since Jacob had hit his teenage years, he and Hannah had drifted apart a little. She knew it was his time to experience the *Englisch* world, and that he was growing and maturing, but she could still tell when something was bothering him.

Her brother shrugged. "I don't know. It's just . . . I thought I overheard Mary talking on the phone and saying something about lies and maybe not being Amish. But I wasn't sure, and I guess I should have said something."

"When?"

"Not that long ago. I just didn't want to believe that she might be lying to us, so I didn't really try to find out anything. But I could tell that she thought I overheard something. Now I know I should have spoken up." He sighed before he went on. "It's just, you seemed to get along so *gut* with her. And for the first time in a long time, you looked happy."

"The outcome would have been the same, Jacob. And she probably would have lied to you anyway and said you misunderstood what you'd heard. She obviously had no plans to tell us who she really was, and I can't help but wonder how long she would have kept going with the lie."

"Must run in the family."

Hannah scowled. "What is that supposed to mean?"

Jacob shrugged again. "Never mind. It doesn't matter anyway."

Hannah wanted to let this go. She was exhausted, but she didn't need one more thing to worry over. "Are you calling Ethan a liar?"

"*Nee*. I said never mind. Maybe now that Mary—I mean Charlotte—is gone, you can date Isaac. He's always liked you. Everyone can see that. I never did understand why he was taking Mary Charlotte on picnics." He paused, sighing again. "At least Isaac is a *gut* man."

"Quit doing that, Jacob! If you have something to say about Ethan, just say it."

Jacob was quiet.

"Does it have anything to do with Edna Glick?" Maybe Edna had lied after all, and Jacob knew something Hannah didn't.

Jacob scowled. "Huh? Why would you ask about Edna?"

Hannah told her brother about the picture she'd found and about Edna's response.

"*Ach*, well . . . I doubt she would have told you the truth if they *were* seeing each other."

"If you know something, you must tell me. Why are you talking like Ethan wasn't a *gut* man?" Hannah wasn't sure she could handle one more thing, but it was too late to turn back. "Tell me, Jacob."

"I don't know anything." Jacob bolted from the chair and went inside.

Hannah wished she had someone to talk to about Edna, about Jacob . . . She missed her cousin, her friend.

She rushed into the house and followed Jacob to the top of the stairs. "You have to tell me if you know something," she said in a whisper, not wanting either of her parents to hear.

"It doesn't really matter."

Hannah stomped a foot. "It does to me."

Jacob put his hands on his hips and stared at the floor, then looked up at her. "I heard him on his cell phone one time, whispering. And I heard him tell someone *I love you, baby.*"

Hannah folded her arms across her chest, then grinned. "For your information, Jacob, Ethan used to call me *baby* quite often. Remember, he used to be *Englisch* and that's a common term of endearment."

Jacob took off his straw hat and rubbed his forehead. "*Ya*, well, at the time he said it, you were standing across the room talking to *Daed*. And you weren't on any phone at the time."

"Ethan loved me!" She didn't care who heard her as another knot formed in her throat. Edna was her friend. She'd known her for her entire life, and she believed her. Isaac misread what he'd seen. And Ethan could have been talking to anyone. "You just never liked him, Jacob!"

Hannah was desperate for something to hold on to. She wasn't sure how she'd survive if Ethan hadn't loved her. She was confused about who to trust. And the irony was, she wished that Charlotte was here, the person who had lied to Hannah the most, yet ultimately was the only one she trusted to tell her the truth about Ethan.

She would pray that Charlotte found answers in the book Hannah gave her.

Ryan stayed with Charlotte's luggage as she walked with a security guard back to the arrival gate. They wouldn't let her back on the plane, but the flight attendant said she would go look for the book.

"I was in seat 26-A. It's a small brown leather book. It's very important to me. Thank you so much."

"Be back shortly," the flight attendant said as she disappeared behind the closed door of the tarmac.

"I cannot believe I've lost that book."

The young security guard said, "You'd be surprised at all the things people leave on a plane. LeAnn will find it. It's probably under the seat."

"I hope so."

The flight attendant—LeAnn—returned about ten minutes later. "I'm sorry. I can't find anything. I looked under the seats, in the pocket on the back of the seat, but there wasn't anything there."

Charlotte blinked back tears and shook her head.

"There's a form you can fill out for lost and found with a place for the description of the item and your address and phone number in case someone turns it in."

Charlotte nodded, feeling sick to her stomach. She followed LeAnn to lost and found and scribbled her name and phone number on the form with a description that read: *Small brown leather book lost on flight from Pittsburgh to Houston. Sentimental value.* Then she remembered that it had a design on the front, so she added: *Cover has emblem of Alpha and Omega.* She drew the two symbols as best she could.

Ryan was holding two Starbucks coffees when she got back. "Did you get it?"

She shook her head. "So, I'll never know what was going on in Ethan's head when he killed himself."

"Maybe you're not supposed to know," Ryan said as he handed her one of the cups. "Vanilla latte with whipped cream, right?"

"Thank you." She took a sip. "I feel sick. How could I have left that book on the plane?"

"Maybe someone will find it and turn it in."

Ryan piled the two empty suitcases and her full red one on a rack and they started toward the parking garage. "It's not worth anything to anyone but me, and I doubt there is an address, phone number, or anything inside. My only hope is that someone turns it in at the airport. I'll call and check for the next few days. The security guard said there is a lost and found, and he gave me the number."

"It was nice of Hannah to give you the diary. Is that what we're calling it, a diary?"

Charlotte frowned. "I don't know for sure what it is." She grunted a little. "I should have tried to read at least some of it on the plane. I just had such a bad headache, then I fell asleep."

"Well, I think if it's meant to be, someone will find that book and get it back to you."

"I guess." Although, if it didn't show up, she would wonder for the rest of her life what was written in that book.

Hannah and Jacob sat quietly on the couch in the living room, waiting on their parents to come out of their bedroom. Their father had called a family meeting. It had been a week since Charlotte left, and Hannah presumed this meeting would be about the importance of forgiveness. But Hannah and Jacob had been waiting for a half hour, and they could hear muffled voices coming from their parents' bedroom.

"You think this is about Charlotte?" Jacob leaned back against the couch, then yawned.

"Maybe it's about you sneaking out at night to go see Annie."

Jacob stiffened as he leaned forward. "Do you think they know?"

Hannah shrugged. "I don't know."

"How'd you know, about Annie?"

Hannah tipped her head to one side as she folded her arms across her chest. "Because you're noisy, and the third stair creaks. I can't believe you haven't gotten caught before now, but I'm not sure that's what this meeting is about."

The bedroom door opened, so they both turned their attention to their parents. Usually, their father led these family meetings, but their mother cleared her throat.

"I know that we are all still upset about Mar—I mean Charlotte. It will take us some time to recover since we all grew to care about her very much. So, I ask you to keep your heart open to forgiveness. But I'm afraid I have some other news to share, some news I received from my doctor yesterday."

Hannah had noticed that her mother was very quiet the day before, but she didn't think that much of it. "*Mamm*, what's wrong?"

Their mother took a deep breath. "I have breast

cancer." She squeezed her eyes closed, but held a palm toward Hannah and Jacob. "And before you get upset, let me just say that the doctor said my chances of beating this are very *gut*."

Hannah thought about Isaac's father, how he'd been in remission for a while now. But she remembered how sick he'd been from all of the chemotherapy and radiation. "Will you have to have chemotherapy?" Hannah bit her bottom lip and tried to keep her breathing steady. She wanted to be strong for her mother.

"*Ya*, I will. The doctor called my cancer a stage three, so I will travel to Houston where they have a hospital called MD Anderson. He says it's the best and they have something called clinical trials that I might want to see about. Just in case I need that."

Hannah looked back and forth between her father and Jacob. Her brother's lip trembled. "That's where Charlotte lives," Hannah said. "I saw her address on her driving license." Hannah had actually copied the address down.

"I know, but not a concern one way or the other. I will speak with some of the women here to see if they can help with things while I am away. And of course, we know they will. I'm sure there will be plenty of meals brought over and help with whatever else you all need."

Hannah wasn't worried about the increase in chores. She was worried about her mother. And to her knowledge, her mother had never been out of Pennsylvania, except for their one trip to Ohio to visit family. "*Mamm,*

I should go with you." She glanced at her father. "Or *Daed* should."

Her mother shook her head. "*Nee.* Your father needs to work, and Hannah, even with help from others, you will still have your hands full with washing, sewing, keeping the house clean, and taking care of my goats. I don't want to worry about my family while I am away."

"How long will you be gone?" Hannah was wondering why there seemed to be a string of upsets in her life, one thing after the other. The only recent good thing had been the time she'd spent with Isaac this past week, and she could see things moving in a positive direction, even though she was approaching any opportunity at romance with caution.

"I don't know how long I'll be gone."

Despite her confident and steady voice, Hannah knew this was well-rehearsed in an effort not to scare her and Jacob. Hannah knew stage three wasn't the worst, but it wasn't good either. She remembered that Isaac's father was a stage three when he was diagnosed. Even though his cancer had been rare, he ended up with a fake leg. She could see the fear in her mother's eyes, and even more frightening—in her father's.

Isaac listened to Hannah for over an hour, barely getting in a word. And that was just fine with him. He could watch and listen to her all day long and never tire of it. Being with Hannah was so different than the time he'd spent with Mary Charlotte—that's what they were calling her now since no one felt comfortable calling her just Charlotte—because they enjoyed the same things. Normally Hannah flinched at the mention of Mary Charlotte. Today their former friend was the topic of conversation.

"So, what do you think? Should I write Mary Charlotte a letter about *Mamm*?" Hannah reached for a slice of pepperoni pizza on the table between them. Isaac wanted to start new traditions with Hannah, so instead of a picnic, this was their second time eating at Predisio's Pizzeria. It was a favorite for both of them, and they'd chosen a booth in the back of the restaurant to call their own.

"When Mary Charlotte and I were, uh . . ." Isaac paused, searching Hannah's eyes for a reaction. "Dating." He stopped and locked eyes with her. "Does it bother you for me to say that? I mean we weren't really dating. It was more like friends."

"Oh, sure," Hannah said, grinning as she took a bite.

He smiled back at her. "Anyway, when I was spending time with my *gut* friend Mary Charlotte, she asked a lot of questions about God, and at the time, I thought it was weird. Then I found out she wasn't baptized into our faith until she was nineteen, so that explained a lot."

"But she *wasn't* baptized into our faith."

"*Ya*, I know that now, but back then, she seemed to be

searching for something. She was kind of lost. I guess her *bruder*'s death was still heavy on her heart." The moment he said it, Isaac wondered about Hannah, if Ethan was still heavy on her heart. But she didn't say anything. Instead, she took a big bite of pizza. They hadn't talked about Ethan in a while. Hannah completely believed Edna's tale about the picture, so Isaac went along with her, even though he knew what he saw was more than an affectionate gesture for a job well done.

"*Mei daed* had his cancer treatments in Philadelphia. Why can't your *mamm* do that?"

"I'm not sure. She said her doctor was sending her to a special hospital in Houston. I'm just worried. *Mamm* has only been on a plane one time to go to Ohio, and I don't think she's ever even stayed in a hotel. I haven't either. When we went to visit cousins . . . *cousins* in Ohio, we stayed at their *haus*."

"You miss her, don't you?" Isaac was reading between the lines.

She set her slice of pizza down. "I don't miss Charlotte. I miss Mary. Or the person I thought to be Mary."

Isaac swallowed, wiped his mouth with his napkin. "I read in an *Englisch* book one time that some people are in our lives for a season, some forever. I think God had a plan for you and Mary Charlotte. As for me and Mary Charlotte, she was interested in getting information about Ethan. What I wanted to know from her is if you were ready to move on with your life without Ethan. But there was never anything more than friendship there, for either one of us. But to answer your question, I think you should write her. You need to for yourself, and I think Mary Charlotte would take care of your mother while she was in Houston. Do you think your *mamm* could see past everything that happened to let Charlotte help her?"

"I don't know. Maybe. It's *mei* father who might forbid it."

"If it helped your *mudder*, I think he might allow it."

"I think *Daed* should go with her, but *Mamm* said she doesn't want them to have to take any more than they need out of the community health fund. They want to pay as much as they can on their own, so she wants *Daed* to continue to build furniture and keep things running here. And Jacob has been sneaking out to see Annie. I think *Mamm* knows and is looking the other way. I don't know about *Daed*. I don't think they want to leave Jacob with just me."

It was late in the evening when Hannah finally decided to write Charlotte. She wasn't even sure if she would mail the letter, but she hoped it would make her feel better. She'd cried herself to sleep the past two nights, worried about her mother. She didn't see how their family could function without her. Surely, God wouldn't take away someone else she loved.

Hannah opened the bottom drawer of her dresser where she kept books, and she took out her dictionary. Charlotte was obviously educated, and Hannah didn't want her eighth-grade education to stick out too much if she could help it.

Dear Charlotte,

It is a strange feeling for me to call you by this name, when to me you are still Mary, our cousin from Beeville. I wish that I could write to you and say that our feelings are no longer sad, but that would be a lie. My heart hurts, and I wish that the Mary who was my friend and cousin were back. I know by your tears that you are sad, too, and I must thank you again for telling me about the butterflies in the clouds. I will always miss Ethan, but I have been spending a lot of time with Isaac.

I want to tell you that I had a visit with Edna Glick. She did not have a romantic time with Ethan. It is a bit much to write here, but I know Edna is telling the truth.

She tapped the pencil to her chin, knowing that she could never be positive that Edna was telling the truth, but she had to believe that Ethan was when he said he loved her.

My cause for writing you today is that I must ask a favor. Even though there have been many lies between us, my family did grow to love you. Mamm has cancer. It is the bad kind in the third stage. She will be going to Houston sometime in the days or weeks coming, and maybe it will be in your heart to visit her or maybe give her a ride to or from the airport. She is going to be afraid since she has only been out of our state one time, and she has never traveled on her own. If you do not want to do this, do not worry. If you do, please write me back.

Sending you blessings,
Hannah

She reread the letter, then put it in an oversize envelope, along with the potholders and the recipe box.

Ryan eased down on the couch beside Charlotte, following a Weight Watchers' version of meat loaf she'd cooked for them. It wasn't nearly as tasty as what Lena used to make, but Charlotte's scale in her bathroom was no longer her friend, and she was trying to undo some of the damage she'd done feasting on the food in Amish Country. Even though she missed the food, and especially the bread, she missed her family the most.

"I got this in the mail today." She handed Ryan the letter she'd received from Hannah. "I read it about a dozen times." After he'd had time to read it, she showed him the potholders and recipe box, explaining the significance of each.

Ryan had been over to visit every night since Charlotte got back, and things were definitely moving in the direction of an official relationship.

"I know both of these items mean a lot to you," he said as he handed the box and potholders back to her. "And I caught the part about Hannah hooking up with your ex-boyfriend."

"He was never my boyfriend." She nudged him with her elbow.

He handed the letter back to her. "I'm glad she seems to be finding some happiness with Isaac, after everything with Ethan and all. I know you're glad she reached out to you, but that's awful about her mother."

"I know." She read the part about the cancer again. "I have an editing project to finish up tomorrow morning, then I'm going to write her back. I'm wondering if Lena knows that Hannah wrote to me. I'd like to offer for Lena to stay here during her treatments. My schedule is flexible enough to work around her appointments, give her rides, or whatever else she needs."

"That's a big job, caring for someone going through chemo. You sure you're up for that? I'll help you any way I can."

Charlotte leaned her head on his shoulder. "Aw. I know you would." After a few moments, she eased away a little and turned to face him. "I'm going to make the offer for all of that, but not because I'm trying to make up for all the lies." She cringed. "Okay, well, maybe that's part of it. But Lena was more like a mother to me during those weeks than my own mother ever was. I want to help their family if I can. Ethan would want me to."

"Are you going to tell her you lost that little book?"

Charlotte sighed. "I don't know." She grunted, slapping her hand to her leg. "I cannot believe I did that. I am so mad at myself. When I was reading that man's butterfly book, I must have set Ethan's notebook on the seat beside me, or it fell on the floor—something. Speaking of, I need to try to get that book back to that sweet old man." Frowning, she shook her head. "I bet the flight attendant didn't look very hard. But to answer your question, no, I don't think I'll tell Hannah that just yet, even in a letter. She's got enough going on with her mother. I'm going to, um . . . I'm going to pray about it." Smiling at Ryan, she added, "I do a lot of that these days. And I am never going to tell another lie for the rest of my life."

"We talked about that. Sometimes it's hard." Ryan leaned over and kissed her on the cheek. "I'll pray about it too. But for now, I gotta go."

"So soon?" Charlotte stood up when he did and walked with him to the front door of her apartment.

"Yeah, I've got an early meeting in the morning I need to get ready for this evening, and you have work to do. Dinner was fantastic." He kissed her gently, lingering as he put his hand around the back of her neck. "But I'm still waiting on some homemade bread."

"That was a low-calorie dinner. But I promise I'll make you some bread soon now that I have the recipe. Although, no guarantees. I learned a few things from

Lena and Hannah toward the end of my stay, but I'm still no expert in the kitchen."

"I'll call you later." He kissed her again before he left.

Charlotte decided not to wait until tomorrow to write Hannah back. After she'd showered and wrapped up her editorial notes, she crawled into bed and positioned on her lap the same yellow pad she'd used in Pennsylvania. How was she ever going to be able to articulate how she felt? Once again, she prayed. This time for God to give her the words.

Dear Hannah,

I was so happy to receive your letter, but also very sad to hear about your mother. Please know that I am willing and able to do whatever you might need me to do. Lena is welcome to stay with me. I'll take her to her treatments at the hospital, and care for her. Please let me do this. I know I can't make up for the lies I told you and your family, but I care deeply about all of you. I miss you. I knew I couldn't stay there forever, but you were the closest thing to a real family I've ever had. And for what it's worth, I can completely understand why Ethan wanted to be there.

She paused, fearing that Ethan's reason for taking his life would haunt her forever.

I know now that we can reach out to God from anywhere on the planet, but for me . . . I met the Lord and got to know Him while I was in Pennsylvania, so your home and family will always hold a special place in my heart. I wanted so badly to blame someone for Ethan's death, to believe that he'd been brainwashed. I know now how wrong I was. I am begging for your forgiveness.

It gives me great comfort to know that Ethan wasn't romantically involved with Edna. I just didn't think it was in Ethan's DNA to cheat. Someday, you'll have to tell me what the picture was all about. And I am also glad that things are working out with you and Isaac. He was a friend to me, and he seems to be a really good guy. I am spending a lot of time with my friend Ryan, and just like you and Isaac, we have known each other for years.

I don't feel like the same person that I was when I arrived in Pennsylvania. I'd like to feel that I'm a better person, or at the least, working hard to be a better person. I want very much to help your mother. And I would very much like for us to be friends. I think that would have made Ethan happy, and I miss you. Please call me.

Many blessings and love,
Charlotte

She leaned back against her pillow and closed her eyes, knowing there would come a point when Hannah would ask if Charlotte read the book. And since Charlotte was determined not to lie, maybe it was best she'd lost it. The old Charlotte would have thought that God was punishing her somehow by denying her resolve about Ethan. But even though Ethan's reasons for killing himself might linger for a long time, she knew that God wasn't punishing her. He wanted her to be happy, for all of His children to be happy, and through free will, that was possible. Somehow, her not knowing about Ethan was part of His overall plan, and she'd have to live with that, trusting that God knew what was best.

The next morning, she checked her e-mail and then decided to take a walk to the nearby park. She felt lighter than usual, almost as if through prayer, God was slowly lifting her burdens, making it easier to walk without the weight of worry and fear on her shoulders. She was dedicated to staying in the light of the Lord, where no matter what happened, she was determined to keep her trust in Him, that He always had a plan.

She slipped the letter to Hannah in the outgoing mail slot outside her apartment building, and when she saw a butterfly near her, she held her arms parallel to the ground, surprised that it landed on her hand. She couldn't help but wonder if the butterfly brought a message, was an angel, or just a reminder of the beauty that surrounds all of us.

After her walk, Charlotte stopped at the cluster of mailboxes for her complex, and turned the key in her personal mailbox, grumbling under her breath at the way the mailman had stuffed a package into the small space, a package that should have been left at the manager's office for Charlotte to pick up. Once she wrangled it out, she saw that the return address was Bush Continental Airport in Houston, and her heart leapt from her chest as she ripped it open.

"Ethan's journal," she whispered as she unfolded the letter she'd almost ripped in half during the process. She gingerly ran her hand over the symbols on the front. Ryan had told her at the airport when she'd described the book to him that Alpha and Omega were derived from the statement said by Jesus in Revelation about being the Alpha and Omega, the First and the Last, the Beginning and the End.

Charlotte held the book, the letter, and the envelope to her chest, and ran back to her apartment, pushing the elevator button repeatedly until it dinged to go up. Barely over the threshold, she dropped her purse, keys, envelope, and letter on the floor before she kicked the door closed behind her. She went straight to her computer, something Hannah could have done if she'd known how.

She went to Google and typed in: Pig Latin to English Translator, and several sites pulled up. Her heart raced as she thought about all the times she and Ethan had played the word game when they were kids, even though their mother hated it. She could recall getting a hard slap across the face for using it because her mother couldn't understand what they were saying to each other.

Recalling the rules, a consonant or consonant cluster at the beginning of a word got moved to the end of the word and "ay" was added. She could have figured all of this out on her own but it would have taken forever. This way she could just type it into the translator, which was still going to take some time, but not nearly as long as deciphering the code manually after all these years. She opened to the first page, then chose a translator online. She typed in the first few sentences and hit Enter. And right away, she knew that things had not been as they'd seemed.

Isaac stood alongside his mother, both of them watching Isaac's father on the plow, guiding the mules in preparation of the fall harvest. It was the first time in over three years that his father had been on the plow.

"What made him decide to tackle this by himself all of a sudden?" Isaac stared in wonderment and thanks. Maybe Isaac could start on the *daadi haus*, especially since things were progressing with him and Hannah. There would be several weddings coming up following the harvest, and weddings always seemed to ignite romance for the ladies. He was in love with Hannah, but he hadn't told her yet. He hoped that this time next year they would be getting ready for their own wedding.

Isaac's mother sighed, shaking her head. "Maybe he

got tired of plotting and planning to chop me up for firewood." She laughed out loud and playfully slapped Isaac on the arm.

"*Mamm*, you laugh every time you say that out loud, but it's really not funny." He scowled, but couldn't help but grin when she laughed again.

"First of all, your father just needed a dose of tough love to realize that he wasn't half a man, the way he always referred to himself. And his medication did seem to be playing with his head. He hasn't mentioned chopping me up in weeks." She bent at the waist and snorted as she laughed, then quickly straightened, forced composure, and smoothed the wrinkles in her black apron. "Besides, I would have kicked that fake leg of his right out from underneath him if he'd come at me with an axe."

Isaac had noticed a playfulness between his parents lately, so he was going to assume that it was okay for his mother to laugh about his father's comment, since it sure tickled her something fierce every time it was mentioned.

"*Ach*, so tell me . . . how are things with you and the King girl?" His mother pulled a feather duster and busied herself at the knickknacks on the fireplace mantel.

"*Gut*. We will be going to John and Edna's wedding together." Isaac wished he didn't have to attend the event. Every time he saw Edna, he envisioned her with Ethan at the restaurant that day. He'd questioned what he saw a hundred times, but Ethan's persistence that Isaac not tell Hannah was enough evidence of his guilt.

"How is Lena doing? It frightens me how many people in our district have turned up with the cancer. And to make things worse, we're forced to spend extended time among the *Englisch* for treatment."

"Not all *Englisch* are bad, *Mamm*."

His mother gasped. "Isaac. I did not say they were bad. I'd just rather not have to spend so much time around them. And that cousin of theirs, Mary . . . well, she was a *gut* example why we need to stay separate from their kind." She turned to face him. "I shudder to think how you could have ended up with that *maedel*."

"It was never like that with me and Charlotte, *Mamm*. We were friends."

"There is always trouble when outsiders are allowed into our world. I don't think they should be able to convert to our ways. Ethan and Mary both brought trouble to our community. Ethan broke poor Hannah's heart, and Mary . . . *ach*, we know how that went."

By now, everyone knew that Charlotte had pretended her name was Mary, and they knew that Charlotte was Ethan's sister. What they didn't know was that Lena had agreed to stay with Charlotte in Houston during her chemotherapy sessions that would be starting in a few weeks.

Charlotte had just said good-night to Ryan when her cell phone chirped.

"Hannah?"

"*Wie bischt* . . . Charlotte." She paused for a long while. "I still can't get used to that."

"How is your mother?"

"That's why I'm calling."

Charlotte could hear the tremble in Hannah's voice, and she wondered if it was because she was nervous making the call or scared for her mother. "At first, *Daed* forbade *Mamm* to stay with you in Houston, but Jacob talked to him for a long time. I don't know what was said, but *Daed* has agreed. I'm worried that this will be too much trouble for you."

"No." Charlotte smiled as a heaviness lifted from her heart. "I am so happy to do this, Hannah. Like I said, I know I can't make up for what happened, but . . ."

"Were you able to read Ethan's book?"

Charlotte had hoped to avoid this conversation, and she'd prayed about it every day. She squeezed her eyes closed as she recalled translating the first few pages.

I am in love with a woman named Edna. I see her as often as I can. I feel awful for Hannah because I don't think I ever really loved her. I know I never deserved her love, but Edna is the only woman I want to be with.

From there, Ethan had gone on to detail his relationship with Edna, not Hannah. And forty-two pages later, it was quite clear to Charlotte that Ethan killed himself because he had a lot of emotional problems left over from when they were young—and because Edna would not leave John to be with Ethan. One page stood out in particular, and Charlotte had read it so many times, she practically had it memorized.

I've left eight voicemail messages for Edna this week. I can tell she has her cell phone turned off, and she won't call me back. Twice, when I caught up with her at the market, and another time at the bookstore, she tried to avoid me. I don't get it. She said she loved me. I'm starting to believe that love isn't real. It's a word people throw around to pull you in, only to throw you away later, like a piece of trash. But hey, who am I to talk? I did the same thing to Hannah, so maybe this is what I deserve. Whatever the situation, it's become abundantly clear to me that I'm never going to be happy. I thought I'd found God here in Lancaster County, but that's not panning out the way I'd hoped. He seems to have forsaken me, allowed me to creep into a sinful way of living, and then kicked me to the curb like everyone else I've ever known. Except maybe Charlotte. But my sister has her own issues, so I can't really go to her.

Charlotte was afraid that part would haunt her forever. She closed her eyes as she recalled the rest of the page.

So, here I am. Alone. The voices in my head are loud, and sometimes I want to just shut them up forever. Alma Jean pops into my head all the time. I can hear her saying, "Boy, get over here and drop your pants." I can feel the sting of the belt against my rear, so hard my skin would split and bleed, then she'd be mad because there was blood on the sheets. She was a mean foster-mother. But not the meanest.

I'm going to give Edna a week. I know she'll realize that I'm the one she wants to be with. She just needs some time.

Charlotte wondered how long Ethan had waited. She was still thinking about this when she heard Hannah's voice.

"Charlotte, are you there? Were you able to read Ethan's book?"

"What? Yes." She gave her head a quick shake to get her thoughts back in order. "It was in a fun little language we used to play around with when we were kids." She cleared her throat. "So, when is your mother coming for her treatments? I'm eager to see her. Thank you all for allowing me to do this. I miss you and—"

"What did his book say?"

Charlotte would have paid good money just to hear Hannah say that they'd all missed her, too, and to avoid this conversation altogether, especially by phone. But the moment was upon her. Was she going to lie to Hannah? Again? Or break her heart and tell her that Ethan loved Edna and gave up his life because he couldn't have her?

It was chilly in Charlotte's apartment, but beads of sweat gathered along her hairline. She'd promised God she would do everything in her power to be truthful, but at what expense? "Ethan had a lot of problems, Hannah. Emotional problems."

There was a long, brittle silence. "*Ya*. I know."

"Do you think that your mother will be on a special diet, or is there anything special that I can cook for her?" Charlotte squeezed her eyes tight again.

"It's true about Edna, isn't it?"

Charlotte took a deep breath. "Yes."

"I think I knew the moment I saw the picture. Despite Edna lying about it."

"Hannah, I'm so sorry."

"*Danki* for telling me."

Charlotte loved her brother, and she'd always miss him. But she was angry at him for hurting Hannah. "What about you and Isaac?"

"Things are very *gut*. *Danki* for asking."

Charlotte wasn't sure if Hannah's formality was because she was trying not to cry or if she was still just so angry with Charlotte that it was hard for her to share anything personal. "Are things getting serious?"

"*Ya*. I think so." She paused. "I don't know. Maybe."

Charlotte waited for Hannah to ask about her and Ryan, but she was quiet. "Well, that sounds good. I've been praying things work out for both of you."

"I'm not praying anymore," Hannah whispered. "It is hard for me to trust anyone." Charlotte had to pull the phone away from her ear as Hannah began to weep. "And it's not just your people that lie. Our own lie. And Edna and John will get married soon, and I don't understand why God let this happen. Charlotte, I don't feel God with me anymore. I'm scared of losing my mother. I can't seem to commit myself to a life with Isaac. I miss Mary. I miss my friend, my sister."

"It's still me, Hannah. I promise you. It's me." Charlotte grabbed a tissue as she broke out in sobs along with Hannah, who kept trying to say something, but Charlotte couldn't understand her.

Finally, after several attempts to speak clearly, Charlotte heard her say, "I feel lost. I'm thinking of leaving here. Leaving the Amish faith."

This could be Charlotte's shining moment in God's eyes, or she could fail miserably. But for whatever reason, everything that had happened up to now seemed to all come down to this moment for Charlotte, and even though she technically knew she didn't owe God anything, she wanted to do this right. There was purpose in it, and she could make a difference in a life. She curled her feet underneath her, forced herself to be calm and levelheaded, then silently prayed for God to give her the words, the understanding, and the wisdom to minister to one of His faithful followers who was in trouble. It was a role she couldn't have ever foreseen, but one she took on knowing that God's hand was on this.

"Hannah . . ." She closed her eyes, searching her mind for wisdom, for guidance. "God doesn't forsake us in our darkest hours. I know that now. Long before I knew Him personally, He was always with me."

Charlotte painfully recalled the time her foster-mother made her sit in the dark, in the closet . . . for hours . . . knowing that Charlotte was afraid of the dark. She'd never been introduced to God, but she remembered reaching out, begging for help, crying for someone to save her. She didn't understand it at the time, but a sense of calm came over her. She knew now that it was the Holy Spirit, and the following week, she was sent to another foster home. A better foster home.

"You're going to be okay, Hannah," she finally said after a few moments. "It's awful what Ethan did. And it's terrible that Edna lied about it. But that is her burden to carry. Now you know the truth. You've faced it, and I know it hurts. But I am going to help you get through this, the same way you helped me so many times without even realizing it. It's okay for your faith to falter. We all get weak and question God's plan for us." Charlotte paused, hearing the words come out of her mouth, but knowing God was responsible for them. "I think . . . I think it's when we are at our most broken that we are able to hear God the loudest, if we really listen. But so many times our fears and worries block out His voice or we turn away from Him. Stay on the path, Hannah. The one God chose specially for you."

They were quiet for a while, then Hannah said, "I know you're right."

Charlotte breathed a huge sigh of relief, still in awe of the way God was using her as His instrument. She spent the next two hours on the phone with Hannah, crying . . . and even laughing a few times—especially when they recalled the green hair incident. But by the end of the phone call, Charlotte knew that they were both going to be okay. And despite their very different backgrounds, a lifelong friendship had formed.

Charlotte looked forward to seeing what God had planned for the future. For both of them.

EPILOGUE

Dear Ethan,

It's been three months since I left Lancaster County, and for the first time since you left this world, I am starting to feel at peace. This is largely due to my new and wonderful relationship with God, but also because Hannah and her family have shown me love in a way I haven't known before. I wish you were still here with us, and I guess I will never fully understand why you felt like you had to leave instead of facing what was ahead of you.

Charlotte still struggled with the fact that Ethan felt like he couldn't go to her when he was at his lowest. But she prayed about it all the time.

I've learned to live with the fact that some things can't be fully understood, at least not until we get to

291

heaven. And now I know that God has a purpose for each and every one of us.

Lena has been traveling back and forth from Lancaster County to Houston. She stays with me when she's in town, and I go with her to her chemo treatments. Fortunately, she hasn't been as sick as some people get when they go through this. I introduced her to queso, and when she's feeling well enough, we stay up late munching on chips and dip and watching chick flicks. She said that watching television is a guilty pleasure that she thinks God would be okay with under the circumstances. She's truly the mother I never had, and I continue to learn from her.

As for Hannah . . . she's moving on, Ethan. She loved you, and I'll never understand what drove you into Edna's arms. But what's done is done. Hannah is finding happiness with Isaac, and I'm so happy for both of them. Edna married John Dienner. I didn't go to the wedding, even though Hannah asked me to attend with her. And maybe I should have gone, if for no other reason than to be there for Hannah since I know it was difficult for her to watch Edna and John take their vows. Hannah confronted Edna about a week after I came home. She told Edna that she knew about your relationship. Edna pleaded with Hannah not to tell anyone that the two of you'd had an affair. I don't know if I could have kept that information to myself, but then again . . . I'm not Hannah, and Hannah chose not to destroy Edna's life. What a wonderful sister-in-law Hannah would have been, but everything happens for a reason, according to God's plan, and Hannah and I are sisters in every sense of the word. She said I'm a Daughter of the Promise—someone who has sought and found new meaning to the words faith, hope, and love. Had things played out any differently, I might not have been introduced to God and taught how to trust Him with my life.

Charlotte took a deep breath, tucked her brown hair behind her ears, and thought about the Ethan she'd known. Edna had told Hannah that the affair with Ethan had been a mistake that she would regret and have to live with for the rest of her life. She said that Ethan became obsessed with her, following her around so much that it sounded like he was stalking the woman. Charlotte had to face the fact that no matter how much she'd loved her brother, deep down, she'd always known that Ethan's desire to be loved might someday get the best of him. The irony is that he betrayed someone who loved him deeply and unconditionally—Hannah. Charlotte watched him go in and out of depression their entire lives. She put pen to paper again.

I have trouble forgiving Edna. I know that by not forgiving her, I'm only hurting myself, so I'm working on that. It's also hard for me to forgive our parents, but I pray about that often. If I wanted to find Mom, I *could. And one day maybe I'll be ready to talk to her. But not yet.*

Lena will be back next week for another treatment. She dreads the chemo, but I always look forward to spending time with her. I haven't talked to Jacob or Amos since I left. Lena said Amos doesn't say much about me, but that he is grateful that I am taking care of her when she's in Houston. It's a privilege to do so. I sense that Amos still harbors some bitterness toward me, and I can't say I blame him. I told an awful lot of lies while I was there. But I will be going to Lancaster County next fall. Jacob is getting married! I think he's much too young. He'll be almost eighteen, and it's the Amish way to marry young, but he seems like a baby to me. I'm hopeful that by then maybe Isaac and Hannah will be getting married also.

She tapped the pencil against the yellow pad, then glanced at the framed picture on her nightstand. A photo of her and Ryan taken right before Christmas at the ice skating rink in the Galleria Mall. She'd almost toppled onto the ice when she'd captured the selfie of them. But as Ryan had done more than once over the past few months, he held her up and kept her from falling.

Ryan is wonderful, Ethan. I'm not sure if he is the one, but I care deeply about him, and our relationship is in a good place. I wish you were here to see for yourself.

I wish that we could have gotten you treatment for your depression. I wish that you'd never felt so alone and desperate that you felt the only way out was to take your own life. I wish . . . I wish . . . But God never wastes a hurt. So much has changed for me. For the better. I'd do anything to have you back, but I'm finally moving on with my life, putting each foot forward toward a brighter future.

So, until I see you again—and I do believe I will see you again—sleep with the angels, my dear brother.

Love,

Char

She pulled the drawer of her nightstand open and put the yellow pad and pen inside. She'd just closed it when the phone rang. Smiling, she glanced at the clock on her cell phone. *Right on time.*

"Hey, you."

Ryan called every night at ten thirty to tell her goodnight. Just the sound of his voice always made her smile. As she listened to him talk about his day, she closed her eyes and smiled again.

Thank you, God.

Discussion Questions

1. Charlotte arrives in Lancaster County as Mary, and she has an agenda—to find out what caused her brother to take his own life. But God has a much larger plan for Charlotte. What are some of the things that Charlotte learns about herself along the way?

2. Is it ever okay to intentionally lie? Or should it be avoided at all costs, no matter how much pain it might cost us or others? Is it okay to lie in an effort to spare feelings?

3. Do you believe that if a person kills himself or herself that he/she will go to heaven? And what if that person is mentally ill or dealing with severe depression; does that make a difference?

4. What would have happened if Ethan's journal had not been returned to Charlotte? Did you see signs

of her accepting God's plan, one way or another? Or would she be forever haunted by her need to know?

5. At what point in the story did you see Charlotte starting to change? And when did she start putting her faith in God? How did that ultimately change not only her thinking, but her actions?

6. Isaac has been putting his own life on hold to help take care of his parents. Who has the most influence over him, convincing him that it's time to live his own life?

7. At the end of the story, Charlotte is working on her relationship with God. Do you think that as her faith grows, she will ever seek out her mother? Or would doing that be a setback for Charlotte?

8. There are several things about Charlotte that irritate Hannah in the beginning. What are they, and when in the story did Hannah start to overlook these things? What were some of the things she grew to love about Charlotte?

9. Edna seems to walk away unscathed and goes on to marry John Dienner. Do you think that she should be held accountable for her role in Ethan's death? Is she partly responsible that Ethan chose to take his own life? Do you think that guilt will catch up with her, that she'll eventually confess to John?

10. Do you know what Pig Latin is? Did you ever play around with it as a child? Any fun stories to share?

11. What are your thoughts about the real-life ways that

the Amish are embracing more and more technology? Most of the Amish folks in Lancaster County use cell phones, for example.

12. At the end of the story, things are going well for Charlotte and Ryan. Do you think that Ryan began noticing the changes in Charlotte way before Charlotte did? Ryan tells Charlotte that the trip was never about Ethan, that it has always been about her. Do you agree? How might things have turned out differently if Charlotte had never gone to Lancaster County?

13. Jacob is fascinated with space, and Lena doesn't like his outside interest. Hannah even says that her mother is afraid Jacob's hobby will take him away from their community. But at the end of the book, Jacob is planning to marry Annie. Do you think he will continue his interest in space through books and by using his telescope, or will he feel stifled and feel the need to further his knowledge?

14. Charlotte takes a rope with her when she travels, to ensure that she won't be trapped by fire again. Is this going overboard or justified? Do you have a fear that you've faced but that still lingers in a way that influences your decisions and/or choices? For example, if you nearly drowned, do you avoid boats and water?

15. In the epilogue, Charlotte writes to Ethan that she will be returning in the fall to attend Jacob and

Annie's wedding. Do you think that Charlotte might consider converting to the Amish faith at some point?

16. What was your favorite part of the story?

ACKNOWLEDGMENTS

I 'm so incredibly thankful to God for this amazing journey I'm on, but there are always others to thank as well. It takes a giant team effort to get a book on the shelves, and I could never do it alone. I have a wonderful family, fantastic friends, a great agent, an amazing husband (love you, Patrick!), and an awesome publishing team. But there are always people behind the scenes who are helping in ways that they might not be aware of. Karen and Tommy Brasher are two of these people. Sometimes people do nice things for you, but they never really recognize the depth of their kindnesses.

Authors can be such weird people, and as such, we need the universe in near perfect order to be able to write creatively. At least, I do. So, it's an honor to dedicate this book to Karen and Tommy Brasher, with thanks and appreciation for helping to keep the planets in our world aligned and spinning. Happy husband equals happy wife, and combined, that means more books. ☺ We love you, Karen and Tommy.

To my editors, Becky Philpott and Natalie Hanemann, you ladies rock, and I love you both. A huge thanks for helping me mold my stories into a much better end result. And you always do it gently and with kindness, even if the project needs an overhaul, LOL. And thank you for having faith in me from rough draft to final product.

Natasha Kern, I've said it before, and I'll say it again—you are a woman with MANY hats, and you wear them all so well! I love and appreciate you.

Much gratitude to my wonderful assistant—Janet Murphy—although that title doesn't begin to cover her job description. XO

And a warm welcome to the newest member of our team, the fabulous Jamie Foley. So glad to have you on board, Jamie. ☺

To Renee' Bissmeyer, you've always cracked the whip when it came to me meeting my deadlines, in the early years, and even now when I need it. But you seem to have a little princess in training with her own mini whip—Diana Newcomer. LOL. Love you both! Thanks for keeping me in line when I'd rather be cleaning the baseboards or doing anything other than writing some days. XO

I'm blessed. ☺

DON'T MISS THIS NEW SERIES BY BETH WISEMAN!

(Available September 2019)

AVAILABLE IN PRINT AND E-BOOK

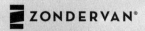

ABOUT THE AUTHOR

Photo by Emilie Hendryx

*B*eth Wiseman is the award-winning and bestselling author of the Daughters of the Promise, Land of Canaan, and Amish Secrets series, as well as novellas that have been included in many bestselling collections such as *An Amish Year* and *An Amish Garden*.

Visit her online at BethWiseman.com
Facebook: AuthorBethWiseman
Twitter: @BethWiseman